Payback is Bitter Vengeance

Book III of The Payback Trilogy

By

Douglas Ewan Cameron

W & B Publishers

USA

W & B Publishers

For information:
W & B Publishers
Post Office Box 193
Colfax, NC 27235
www.a-argusbooks.com

ISBN: 978-0-6923764-9-2
ISBN: 0-6923764-9-6

Book Cover designed by Dubya
Printed in the United States of America

Acknowledgments

This book would not have been possible without the help of long time friend and fraternity brother Bill McClellan. I don't own guns. He does and is very knowledgeable about them.

The French and Dutch in this book are translations provided by Microsoft Word for the Mac (Microsoft Office 2011). I trust that they are accurate.

As usual, I must thank my team of proofreaders and editors: David Buchthal, Bill McClellan, Mary von Zittwitz and, most especially, my wife Nancy Calhoun Cameron. And I welcome to my editing cadre Wolfgang Pelz, former colleague and good friend.

Finally, as I will do in all my published works, I must acknowledge two writers who have influenced me. First (and only chronologically) is Mary Higgins Clark whom I heard speak at a Book and Author Luncheon (or dinner) sponsored by *The Plain Dealer* of Cleveland, Ohio. She said that many of her works got their genesis with the words "What if?" That's how this trilogy got started.

The other writer is the late Philip R. Craig, author of the Martha's Vineyard based J.W. Jackson mysteries. My wife and I met him and his wife Shirley on a riverboat trip from Constanta, Romania to Amsterdam, Netherlands in 2005 and shared many a happy meal together including my wife's birthday dinner. He told me that in his writing, while he knew the story line, he often didn't know how it was going to come out and let the characters lead him. Often that is what I do, but this book required planning to make it come together properly.

To Bill McClellan, long time friend and fraternity brother, for his help and because he was the motivation.

And

To all victims of senseless violence

PART I
FIRE ONE
FIRE TWO

Chapter 1

"CAST off the stern line," Paul's order had come from his perch on the flying bridge of *Seventh Heaven*. The Dockhand had complied and Gjergj started pulling the line in, the stern swinging away from the dock just a little because of the pressure of the forward line and the incoming tide.

"Cast off the bow line," Paul called and he watched a second dockhand cast off the bowline and Henri pulling it in. Paul put the yacht into reverse and started pulling away from its dock. So began the first part of a planned two-year circumnavigation of the world.

Once clear of the dock, he turned the yacht around and started out of the Philipsburg, Sint Maarten[1] harbor toward the Caribbean. Hearing footsteps on the ladder, he turned and saw Henri's head appear at the top.

"Take the helm, Henri. I am going below to join Mrs. Peterson in a toast."

"Aye, aye, Captain Paul," Henri said.

---

[1] Sint Maarten (belonging to the Netherlands) and St. Martin (belonging to the French) share a Caribbean island approximately 190 miles northeast of Puerto Rico. There are no customs or border patrols between the two counties sharing the island.

Paul clambered down the ladder (actually a stairway but in ship's terminology all stairways are ladders) and walked through the main cabin to join his wife Harriet who was sitting at a glass-topped table looking at the receding town of Philipsburg. Next to her chair was a champagne bucket with a bottle of brut already chilled, towel wrapped around it, and two champagne flutes on the table. Gjergj had done his job well. Paul walked up behind his wife's left shoulder and put his hand on it. She turned her head and looked up at him.

"Hello, my darling," she said offering her face for a kiss which he obliged.

"And, so it starts, my love," Paul said picking up the champagne magnum and starting to work the cork loose. After a couple of expert pushes, the cork popped and the ever vigilante Harriet caught it.

"This one goes in our trophy case," she said.

"Isn't that rather full?" Paul said thinking of all the sports and scholarship trophies they and their children had earned during their 35 years of marriage.

"Not that one, silly. Our new one for our new life."

Paul poured the two champagne flutes full (to hell with the proper way to do it) and Harriet stood up and faced him, accepting a flute. They intertwined their right arms holding the flutes.

"To a brave new world," Paul said.

"To our *Seventh Heaven*," Harriet said.

They drank from their flutes, both emptying them, and then sat down to watch Philipsburg recede in the distance. Once out of the harbor's speed restrictions, Henri had opened the engines to a comfortable cruising speed on a beautifully flat, blue Caribbean. As they sipped from their second glass, Harriet mused, "I wonder what wonderful event will next earn its place on our trophy shelf."

"My guess is the Panama Canal," Paul said. "That's in a week. We'll have to stop somewhere before that to empty the holding tanks, take on water, etc. But we have no scheduled stops. We'll just play that by ear."

"The Panama Canal," breathed Harriet excitedly. "I don't recall. When are we scheduled to go through?"

"They have us in an 8:00 a.m. passage with several other small ships," Paul answered, being in charge of the navigation and Harriet the housekeeping, both with the help of Henri and Gjergj. "We have one day in Gatun Lake and will continue westward about 11:00 a.m. the next day. After that a leisurely voyage up the Mexican Coast and the Baja Peninsula to San Diego. The Smythes are joining us there and we will drop them in Oahu after spending a week visiting the other Hawaiian Islands."

"It will be so good to see them," Harriet said. "We'll be so brown and chubby by the time we get there, I am certain they will speed up their planned retirement."

"Brown I can live with," Paul said, "but not chubby."

He had always been a fitness buff and had maintained almost the same trim shape he had when graduating from medical school. His wife, "victim" of five pregnancies (only three of which were full term delivering healthy babies), was the chubby one. She had tried to lose weight and regain her pre-baby figure but been unsuccessful. Partially it was his fault, impregnating her incredibly easily but in truth, neither of them had minded. Lay the blame on the infants.

Facing retirement – make that planning retirement – in five years, they had chosen the Caribbean to be their playground. Anything was better than Minneapolis, especially in the heart of Minnesota's winters. They had spent vacations visiting various islands but always lurking in the back of their minds was travelling around the world, on their own and at their own pace. It was roughly two years before, when they were enjoying a quiet break on Sint Maarten, that they saw (or heard about, neither could remember which) an ad for a yacht for sale and they thought, *Our price – cheap.* They had a few reservations at the beginning.

"What are those blotches on that wall?" Harriet, ever the observant decorator, asked. The agent who was guiding the tour (the current owners were absent) had to look at some information.

"It says 'bullet holes'."

Bullet holes? Both Harriet and Paul mouthed. Nothing more was said and the tour continued. Harriet was the consummate house hunter (yacht hunter in this case) checking everything. The plastic dinnerware (plates, glasses, even cocktail glasses) would have to go. She didn't care if it made sense because of rough weather, china could be replaced. Some of the chintzier decorations (chintzy being in the eye of the beholder and hers was very well trained) would have to go. And, of course, the bullet holes would have to disappear completely and to her that meant replacing the wall with a pristine one.

Discussions between her and Paul went on for several days but in the end wisdom, frugality, and love for the future *Seventh Heaven* would prevail and an offer was made.

The salesman explained that the owners were indeed absent, not likely to return. They were in fact, on the opposite side of the world, location not specified. It might therefore, the salesman explained, take a while. And indeed it did. An entire twenty-five hours. Two days later, papers were signed and the yacht was theirs.

Restoration/remodeling then started immediately. Harriet insisted on being there to insure that it was done properly (the wall especially) and so Paul had returned alone to his practice in Minneapolis.

Chapter 2

Boats are constantly in and out of the Bobby's Marina in Philipsburg, so no one was really interested in the *Seventh Heaven*'s departure. Except for The Dockhand who had released the forward line. He had been around the marina off and on for almost a month, doing odd jobs for whatever tip a person would give him. As was usual, he was dressed in dirty khaki shorts held on his skinny but muscular body with a piece of rope tied in front with a square knot. You couldn't see the knot because of the equally dirty tee shirt that hung over his pants. It had a picture of a shark swimming toward you as you faced him. The shark's mouth was wide open and above the shark was the legend: *How about lunch?* The Dockhand's feet were thrust into a pair of ratty sneakers. He didn't wear socks. He had a scraggly black beard and was wearing reflective sunglasses. If he hadn't been wearing those glasses, you would have noticed that his left eye had a gray cast to it. In fact, he was virtually blind out of that eye. On his head, which was cleanly shaven, was a dirty beige baseball cap with crossed tennis rackets above the bill. As the *Seventh Heaven* had backed out of its docking place, he had followed it to the end of the dock, passing the other dockhand who, job done, was heading back to the office for his next assignment.

The Dockhand watched the *Seventh Heaven* make its turn and head out of port. He saw the man who had been piloting the yacht come down the ladder and join the woman on the stern deck. They seemed to talk for a minute, and then the man poured two glasses of champagne. The woman stood up accepting one. They linked arms and drank. *How touching,* The Dockhand thought. From his pants he pulled a black box about the size of a smart phone. Pressing a button, he watched the screen illuminate. There was a flashing white dot in the center of the screen and just above it and to the left was a big flashing red dot. As he watched it, the red dot seemed to move slowly toward the upper left corner of the screen. The Dockhand's lips twitched and he looked up toward the *Seventh Heaven* as it proceeded out of the harbor. "Have a safe voyage," he whispered to no one, "at least for a few days." Then he shut off the receiver and returned it to his pocket.

Turning he walked back down the dock, his right leg seemed to have a bit of a hitch and he started to limp. As he made his way past several moored yachts, he heard someone yelling, "Hey, you." He took no notice. Then he heard, "Hey! You! Gimp!" He stopped, his hands clenching. What he wouldn't have given for a Sig Sauer (his silenced pistol) at that moment. But keeping in character for the time being, he turned in the direction of the voice. A grossly obese man was standing on the stern deck of a small yacht, if one might call it that. From the rear deck, one had to go down a short ladder to get to the cabin. The man was wearing baggy blue jean shorts that were frayed at the bottom and an obscenely lime-green tank top. In his right hand he clenched a beer bottle. He had no hair and his face reminded The Dock-hand of a pig.

"You callin' to me, guv?" The Dockhand asked.

"Yes," replied Obese Man. "You work here, don't cha?"

"Yes, guv. Yes, I do. I do."

"Well, my toilet is stopped up."

"Your what, guv?"

"My toilet."

"What?"

Obese Man was exasperated.

"The toilet. Uh, uh, the loo."

"Oh, you mean the 'head'," The Dockhand said.

"Yes, the head. My head's stopped up."

Take a decongestant, The Dockhand wanted to say, having played this game along. But he didn't. "Okay, guv," he said moving toward the yacht, his limp exaggerated. As he neared the yacht appropriately named *Fat Chance*, he looked around to see if anyone was watching but saw no one. He climbed over the yacht's railing and stood facing Obese Man, who indicated the hatch to the yacht's lower area.

"It's down there."

"Sorry, guv, but marina rules state you have to show me and stay with me so I don't take nothin'."

"What, I never heard that!" Obese Man stammered.

"Okay, guv," The Dockhand said as he turned back to the railing.

"Oh, all right," Obese Man said. "I'll follow you."

"I'd prefer, if you don't mind, guv, that you precede me."

Obese Man glared at him and turned for the hatch. As The Dockhand had conjectured, Obese Man was going to have to squeeze through the hatchway so he decided to give him hand. It was a foot actually, well placed between Obese Man's shoulder blades that propelled him head first down the ladder. His head hit first rendering him instantly unconscious so he never felt his neck snap as his grossly overweight body followed his head to the deck. A horrific odor emanated from the man's shorts as his bowels relaxed and evacuated.

The Dockhand turned away and headed for the railing. "Guess you won't be needing me then, guv." He said as he climbed over the railing and headed for the gate, reminding himself to relax and not hurry. Halfway between the *Fat Chance* and the gate, he passed a portly woman wearing too-tight Capri pants and a bra top that she should never have worn. She had on a wide straw hat and was carrying what looked to be a heavy tote in her left hand and a mega-sized soft drink cup with a long straw in her right. Every couple of steps she would stop and take a drink. *Not coordinated enough to walk and drink,* thought The Dockhand. Outside the gate, The Dockhand unlocked the chain on his bicycle and was just getting on when he heard the scream. In his mind's eye, he imagined the mega-sized soft drink cup hitting the deck and spreading the remainder of its contents everywhere. He smiled and said softly, "C'est la vie."

***

Ten minutes later he was in his rented room. Stripping off his clothes, he thrust them and some other odds and ends into a duffel bag style carrier. After a quick shower, he dressed in a clean cotton yellow golf shirt, dark blue slacks, dark blue socks and brown deck shoes. Reaching under his mattress he retrieved a travel wallet and passport. He checked to be certain that he had left nothing behind – he didn't have much, at least not here. He went into the bathroom and got the hand towel and proceeded to wipe every surface of the small room that he could possibly have touched. This was a daily practice he followed whenever leaving the room for an extended period. Satisfied that he had made the room as sanitary as possible, he exited it, leaving the key in the door as arranged with the landlord. On the street, he walked to a corner and managed to flag a cab down.

In the cab, he said, "Airport," and settled back for the short ride. As he thought about what had transpired, his lips twitched into a sardonic smile.

Chapter 3

While Harriet's forte and responsibility was housekeeping/decorating, Paul's was in management. In their thirty-five years of marriage they had developed this simpatico arrangement and it worked well (and, more importantly, they were still madly in love). Paul knew that for short jaunts, island-to-island (nothing overnight) they could easily handle the yacht themselves. But to fulfill the purpose of the yacht – the reason they had bought it – they would have to have a crew. There was a crew space on the yacht, a private area with a head (bathroom in landlubber talk) and a set of bunk beds. There was a second bedroom (queen-sized bed) for guests so that needed to be kept free. They required a crew of two. Both agreed heterosexual males (although if two heterosexual females applied and could work together) would be the ideal crew. Paul started advertising in several newspapers and other sources around the islands announcing when they would return for interviews. They requested resumes (background information, i.e., previous experience was the manner in which he had phrased it) in advance and they would set up interviews. So on their next holiday, they held interviews: one day, fifteen minutes each person, three hours in the morning (five minute break in between so three per hour) and four hours in the afternoon. Callbacks were the next day. There were only two callbacks. Most of the applicants were druggies (background checks were run, costing Paul a small fortune, but he never regretted the money).

Henri was their first callback and the best candidate by far. Henri had been raised in the islands. Born on St. Nantes, son of a fisherman who moved the family to St. Barth's when Henri was five, he had grown up helping his father. He spoke perfect English and knew boats backwards and forwards. One of his maternal ancestors was Genivee Lacour, whose rebellious act against a pirate in 1728 resulted in the Village of St. Nantes (on the island of St. Nantes) being named Genivee.

In 1728 the Village of St. Nantes was a thriving fishing and commercial port of 1500 people centered around a beautiful wooden church named Notre Dame de Protection (Our Lady of Protection). John-Paul LaPre, a young privateer, anchored his ship in the bay and fired a ten-gun broadside at the town killing sixteen. His forces stormed ashore unhindered. Opportunely, five boats of the village's small fishing fleet returned home unseen by the pirates. With only fishing knives and gaffs as weapons, the ten fishermen stormed aboard the undefended privateer's ship and seized it and the captain who had remained aboard. With his own life hanging by a thread at that point, John-Paul had no choice but to have his men yield. They surrendered their weapons including the ship's cannons, which were unloaded on the future Guerre Isle. Then as beneficiaries of an act of Christian forgiveness, they were set free.

One year to the day later, John-Paul LaPre returned with a force twice as large on a bigger ship. He bombarded the town with broadside after broadside refusing to honor a white flag of surrender. With the town afire, he and his forces landed, gathered the families of the fishermen who had seized his ship, and locked them in the church. The last woman to enter the church was Genivee Lacour. She managed to get loose from her captor and, with a knife secreted in a pocket of her dress, attacked John-Paul LaPre. She was subdued once again but only after managing to put an ugly slice on his left cheek that left an equally ugly scar. Knocked senseless, she was thrust into the church, the doors of which were then locked, and the building set afire burning to death all the twenty-six people inside.

John-Paul set sail for further pickings at sea, but his luck failed him again within a week. As he was chasing an English merchant ship, an English man-of-war spotted him, approached his ship unawares and sank the ship with the loss of almost all hands. Seven of the pirates were rescued from the water. Aware of the atrocity that the pirates had committed on St. Nantes, the captives were returned to that port. In a short and extremely biased trial, all seven were sentenced to death. Having no gallows handy, the masts of the English man-of-war were used and in no time the seven were "swinging from the yardarms". To this day, the gallows of St. Nantes resembles a ship's mast and on St. Nantes, seven is considered to be an unlucky numb

The second callback was Gjergj. He was Greek by his father and Albanian by his mother. On the latter's side of the family there was darkness. But it was a darkness that he readily admitted and that honesty endeared him to Harriet. His maternal grandfather was in the Albanian mafia and was what Americans would call The Don, The Godfather. In Albanian a mafia group is a "fis" or "fare" and is run by the "Krye" or "Boss." But

Gjergj's mother eschewed her position and ran away at the age of eighteen. Fleeing to Greece she met Gjergj's father, fell in love and married. There was one brief confrontation two weeks after the marriage when her father found them. He was going to kill Gjergj's father, but she told him that she was pregnant and he would never see his grandchild. In truth she was but didn't know it at that time. Faced with the loss of his only possible grandchild, her father relented upon the condition that the child spend every summer with him from age eleven to eighteen. She and Gjergj's father reluctantly agreed. Gjergj was naturally trepidatious about the relationship having been told about his grandfather's position prior to his first summer. However, that first summer was spent hunting and fishing and sailing – for a young boy that was a fantastic experience. He willingly returned for the next six summers but not the seventh because his grandfather was killed by a rival shortly after Gjergj had returned to Greece from his seventh summer. For almost two years, Gjergj brooded about what might have come to fruition in his eighth. The summer after he turned eighteen, and accepted as a man by all, he left his home and vanished for six months. When he returned, he said nothing, but his mother knew that something was wrong. His brooding countenance had been replaced by one of peace and contentment. Through family contacts back in Albania, she learned that the current Krye, the one who had replaced Gjergj's grandfather, had been assassinated with a single rifle shot while hunting in the mountains. That explained the change in his moods. But there was blackness behind the good news because in the Albanian tradition, it was an eye for an eye and although the Albanian mafia brotherhood did not know who had killed their Krye, the bounty had been placed on the assassin's head and people were looking for him. Therefore it was time for Gjergj to leave Greece. It was easy to make an excuse because the Greek economy was in the dumps following their admission to the European Union. Many young people were leaving and moving to other countries in the federation, most notably Germany but that was not for Gjergj. Ostensibly that is where he was going, but in truth he headed for the Caribbean where he could be on the sea, his first love.

Chapter 4

With a crew in place, the Petersons could settle in to prepare for their retirement. They had met in college, The University of Wisconsin, during his senior and her sophomore year. When he had gone on to medical school at The Ohio State University, she had followed, completing her degree as a Buckeye. Upon her graduation they were married although they had been living together the entire time – although this was unknown by her parents, who at that time in the early seventies were still old fogies.

Their first child was born a year later and the race was on. It was tough during internship but they had weathered the storm with a little help from both sets of parents. He had joined an older man's family medicine practice in Minneapolis and Paul's bedside manner and forthrightness had made the practice a successful one.

Their oldest son John had joined the practice upon his completion of medical school just as the senior partner was ready to retire.

The second child and second son William wanted nothing to do with the medical practice and had become an attorney, taking up residence in Los Angeles in a successful firm favored by Hollywood's greats.

Their youngest child Sarah, a daughter, followed in her father and older brother's footsteps joining the practice the year before retirement. It was this move that motivated the retirement because the practice was perfectly established as far as facilities for two doctors, and the economy didn't dictate expanding at the time. So the path was set. Retirement and grandchildren, the latter not looking so good.

John, while dating several different women, showed no intention of settling down. His practice was his life and both seemed to thrive on the combination.

William followed in the footsteps of Hollywood's biggest stars, going through two wives in five years before settling in to be a voyeur of young wannabees. He looked to make partner in his law firm soon and his parents hoped that would settle him down.

Sarah, the apple of her father's eye, had declared herself asexual two years into college. "I really tried to like men," she had told them. "I've slept with a number of different men, but there was nothing. I figured I was a lesbian although women never turned me on. I tried that too – the lesbian thing, I mean – but that wasn't me either. I don't know what I am – asexual I guess. C'est la vie. Que sera sera."

***

And so as they set off on their circumnavigation of their "wonderful planet," their lives, while a bit non-fulfilling with respect to grandchildren, were settled and happy. But they didn't just go off – not without the proper farewells.

Paul and his three long-time golfing partners had to do it properly. They spent a week in the south, playing a series of courses and naturally finishing each day with cocktails followed by a lavish dinner. They wouldn't hear of Paul spending as much as a dime. "Your turn to treat will come," they said.

A similar thing happened with Harriet and her five closest friends who referred to themselves as "The Disparate Housewives," an obvious take off the show "The Desperate Housewives" that none of them watched (at least, none of them admitted watching).

Truthfully, the term was misleading because they were all very similar. Their husbands were well-to-do, as were also two of them who worked, one practiced law alongside her husband and the other ran a successful florist business.

Their big time celebration was a long weekend in New York seeing Broadway and Off Broadway plays and, with nothing said to their husbands, the Chippendales – twice.

Of course, Harriet and Paul were not to be outdone throwing a "neighborhood" cocktail party to end all parties. The term "neighborhood" was a misnomer as there were friends from all over the city as well as several out-of-town guests. It started at 1:00 p.m. and ended at 1:00 a.m. with transportation provided for those who felt they couldn't make it home. Of course with a party that long there was lots of food.

However, for Harriet and Paul, the best party was their farewell dinner with their children, William having flown in from the west coast. It was a low-key affair at the family's favorite local restaurant. There were gifts. John gave them both nautical caps – Paul's said "Captain" and Harriet's "Navigator," a reference to her always having to give Paul directions because of his lousy sense of direction. William gave them a DVD collection of 100 of Hollywood's best, including two that were yet to be released. They didn't ask how he had gotten them. Included were all the Bruce Willis movies that both of them loved. In fact, Paul's favorite Christmas movie was *Die Hard*. "It takes place Christmas Eve," he would tell people who questioned this.

But the favorite gift they both agreed were the two life rings from Sarah, one for each side of the yacht's stern deck. Beautifully inscribed on both was "Seventh Heaven."

Chapter 5

The fifth day of their trip, the *Seventh Heaven* was southeast of Jamaica heading west toward Kingston, actually a bit ahead of Paul's schedule. His plan had been to sail west from Sint Maarten south of Puerto Rico and the Dominican Republic, stopping to empty his holding tanks at Kingston unless problems necessitated an earlier stop. Then the *Seventh Heaven* would head southwest across the western Caribbean to the Panama Canal, giving the four their first taste of several days at sea out of sight of land. The weather had been gorgeous, just a rainsquall or two. Having been together for several short trips prior to this, the four of them had developed a simpatico relationship, although the distinction between owners and crew had been basically upheld. Both crew-members were decent cooks, having been trained by their mothers and in Gjergj's case also his grandmother during the summers he spent in Albania. Breakfast and lunch were basically self-serve and dinner was sit-down with three while at sea, one always at the helm as Paul distrusted the autopilot, and four while in port.

***

It was a warm afternoon, Paul was on the flying bridge, Harriet sitting on the rear deck reading her Nook, Gjergj was below busy with some housekeeping chores, and Henri was working in the galley beginning dinner preparations. Thus it was Paul who first noticed the small fishing boat coming toward them from forward on the starboard side on a course that, Paul calculated, would bring the small craft behind them. Rules of the sea didn't necessitate any action so he basically ignored the small boat.

Not so with The Fisherman. He was definitely observant of the larger boat. He was dressed in a khaki guide shirt hanging loosely over khaki cargo shorts. Both were immaculate for a man of his supposed trade. He had his bare feet stuck into a pair of deck shoes. His arms and legs were dark tan, some natural and some cosmetic to look more the part. He had a scraggly black beard tinged with gray. His thinning hair had been shaved and his pate had been carefully tanned but covered with a baseball cap emblazoned with crossed tennis rackets – that was unusual for a fisherman. Dark sunglasses hid his eyes. Had he not had them on and had the *Seventh Heaven* been close enough, that being right alongside, Paul would have noticed that The Fisherman's left eye had a gray cast. In fact, The Fisherman had virtually no vision in that eye. And if they had seen him walk, there was a definite hitch, almost a limp, in his left leg.

He had a small radar screen but, until acquiring visual contact, his eyes had been on a small handheld unit that he had mounted on the helm console using Velcro strips. The *Seventh Heaven* was a red blip on the screen; a signal sent from a small transponder he had managed to hide on the yacht several weeks before when the two crewmembers had been absent. His small fishing boat had two one hundred fifty horsepower Mercury four-stroke engines on the back and could really fly.

That was unusual for a fishing boat and, unless Paul had used binoculars (which he didn't), was unobservable until the fishing boat got close. If he had noticed, Paul probably wouldn't have thought anything about it. At this time the big engines were going their absolute minimum and he was dragging a sea anchor so his speed looked more like that of a trolling fisherman. The anchor had been put into the water as soon as he had acquired the signal from *Seventh Heaven.* The Fisherman had two rods out, again not unusual if fishing was his livelihood and it wasn't. In fact, the rods and all associated equipment were new, being used for the first and last time, their ultimate destination at the end of the day being on the sea's bottom. The rods were bent over, being held in place by downriggers and associated weights but that was as far as it went. There were no lures on the ends of the lines. The Fisherman wouldn't have known what to do if he caught a fish. But he wasn't after fish. What he had been hunting for three days was finally in sight. He was so anxious that he wanted to throw caution to the wind and gun his engines but that would draw undue attention and that could spoil the surprise. So over the course of half an hour, the two craft drew closer and closer until both helmsmen knew with certainty, added by the adroit skills of The Fisherman, the fishing boat would pass about a hundred yards behind the *Seventh Heaven.*

As the distance closed Paul waved but the salutation was not returned. Paul thought the man was too intent upon his fishing. Intent, yes, but not with fishing. None of the other three aboard the *Seventh Heaven* noticed the fishing boat, two being inside and Harriet too involved in her novel that was nearing its climax, as was her life.

As the fishing boat passed the stern of the yacht, two things happened almost simultaneously. The Fisherman put the engines in neutral and picked up a tubular object that had been lying on the right by his feet. From the left he picked up another shorter tubular object although this one had a bulbous end with short fins about a third of the way from the end. He inserted the smaller end (without the fins) into the tube, locked it in place, and removed the priming tape from the end. Quickly sighting on the open doors to the main lounge of the yacht, The Fisherman pressed the trigger and the RPG-7 rocket leapt out of the tube making a beeline for its target. As he watched it, he picked up a second RPG-7 from his left and inserted it into the tube but did not remove the priming tape. The Fisherman was ready with a second if it was needed, but it wasn't.

The rocket roared by Harriet who had hardly any time to react before it smashed into a forward bulkhead. The resulting explosion knocked Henri sternward, as he was on his way there at the moment – the rocket narrowly missing him on its brief passage – his lifeless body landing just outside the doors. Harriet was knocked overboard after being pelleted by glass fragments from the sliding doors. The exploding missile also detonated explosives The Fisherman had planted at the same time he had planted the tracker. Gjergj was killed instantly by the explosion as the interior bulkheads and decks imploded. His body trapped below decks where predatory sea life would find it in due course. Paul was blown upward and outward still sitting in the captain's chair, his body riddled with many particles large and small, but he was beyond caring or feeling.

***

It was ten minutes before The Fisherman put the engines into gear and began a systematic search of the flotsam left by the explosion. In that time he had pulled the rods and committed them to the deep and cut the rope holding the sea anchor letting it follow the rods. He had flattened himself on the deck as soon as the yacht exploded, but the small boat suffered no damage. The second RPG and the launcher were assigned to the deep and he picked up his 9mm P226 Sig Sauer with laser sight. An AK-47 lay on the deck. It wouldn't be used and would also be deep sixed (closer to deep six hundreded). The majority of the pieces of *Seventh Heaven* had sunk by that time and basically only three things remained afloat. Harriet, who was still alive, Henri's body floating lifelessly, and a life ring bearing the inscription "Seventh Heaven."

Using a boat hook, The Fisherman picked up the life ring and with a black marker, crossed out the name of the yacht and wrote another before returning the life ring to the sea. He brought the fishing boat alongside Henri's body that was floating face down. The Fisherman knew without a doubt that Henri was dead but used his Sig Sauer to put a bullet in Henri's head anyway. *Can't be too careful,* The Fisherman thought as he watched the corpse start to sink below the waves on its journey to Davy Jones's Locker.

Harriet was still alive although her injuries wouldn't keep her that way for very long. She had heard and seen the shot and knew what was in store for her as

The Fisherman brought his boat alongside. She saw the pistol pointed at her and before The Fisherman could pull the trigger, she managed to ask a simple question, "Why?"

That caused The Fisherman to pause. Then as a sardonic grin bared his teeth, he shrugged and said, "You bought the wrong yacht."

Then he mercifully ended her life with a double-tap to her head.

Chapter 6

Something had gone wrong. I could sense it. *Something had gone terribly wrong.* The shock of that thought ringing in my head brought me bolt upright in bed. It was as though something was wrong with the baby. But I knew that wasn't it. Beside me, Tres was sleeping peacefully. But the thought persisted. *Something had gone wrong.*

I knew that I wasn't going back to sleep, so I got up and went to my child's room. The baby was sleeping peacefully, little arm around the teddy bear. Breathing a sigh of relief, I went into the computer room. Outside it was still dark. Through the stained glass window, I could see the lights of the towns across the fjord and on either side of me. I opened the stained glass window simply to see better because the window opening was still protected (to some extent) by bulletproof glass outside. I knew that nothing was perfectly safe, but I took every precaution I could. The lights on the security system were all green – there had been no breaches. Let me rephrase that – there had been no breaches that I could see. I would take a walk around later; if I had not been so certain about the system I would have gone immediately.

Waking up the computer, I ran through all the outside cameras, but there was nothing to see. No life revealed by the infrared system either. I know – or have been told or read – that you can defeat such a system. I logged into the email account that Joaquin and I had agreed to use. There were no messages in the inbox – hopefully there never would be. A couple of expected ones in spam. Even though the account had never been used to send or receive, you always get spam. I checked the drafts folder – nothing. The agreement was that if he ever needed me and could reach me no other way, he was to leave a message in drafts. I would do the same. Read this somewhere, one of the many crime, mystery and suspense novels that we read. We had just had an iChat the previous day. He had great news. They were expecting their second in five months. His daughter needed a little brother – or sister. They were old fashioned and didn't want to know.

Check one off the list – at least temporarily.

I checked the mercenary bulletin board that Beecher McFalls and I had agreed to use in case of an emergency. There was no message for A. J. Billings. I put a post up for C. E. Dowd to contact P. T. Burnham. If there were a reply, I would know he was all right. We both had alerts set in case we were contacted by the other. Mine had not gone off.

Check another off the list – again at least temporarily.

Alan? I logged into his computer and checked the account that he had been instructed to use. All deposits and withdrawals ended in an even number, dollars or cents, made no difference. There were no odd numbers at the end. All was cool.

Check another off the list – at least temporarily.

My agreement with Quentin Baston was that he or his wife would call if there were a problem and he hadn't.

One more to check. I logged into the Kindle account that Pieter Devenpeck had set up. The balance was the same. Nothing was amiss.

Check another off the list – at least temporarily.

I should have been peaceful. At rest. But that nagging was still there: *Something had gone wrong – terribly wrong.*

I got up and went to check the interior perimeter, first closing the stained glass window. Then I started that search. At the top of the stairs to the main floor, I paused, and put on the infrared goggles. The pattern of beams on the stairs was just as they should have been. I completed the circuit of the upper level and then turned the beams off on the stairway using the 30-second button. Ten seconds later I was at the bottom of the stairs and waited until the flash of light on the security panel at the top of the stairs told me that the stairway system was on again. I went around the perimeter of our great room – formerly the nave of the church where we made our home. All was well. The reinforced front doors were still tightly bolted. The motion sensors were on. In the kitchen (formerly the sanctuary) I got myself a glass of water and sat on a stool at the counter where we ate breakfast and lunch.

What the hell was wrong? "Something had disturbed the Force" as Star Wars fans would say, but what? My brain had been running at warp speed ever since I had been so rudely awoken. What was it?

Chapter 7

Times were good for Andrews Investment Management. Alan Murphy had been able to hire two new people bringing his staff to twelve, and the money was rolling in. Well, at least compared to what it had been when he assumed control.

David Jones, recent graduate of The Ohio State University, had been the first. He graduated second in his class in the School of Business and had amassed a personal portfolio of slightly over $100,000 during his five years at OSU. Five years because he had been there on a track scholarship. He ran the 400 meters and anchored the 1600-meter relay team.

He had started with a small portfolio of $10,000 when his grandmother died with a wealth of nearly two million. That had been divided in five parts among her heirs: $400,000 to each of her children (two boys and two girls, David's father being one of the boys); $10,000 to each of her ten grandchildren; and the remainder divided in some fashion between ten charities that she had favored. The fact that David had been able to increase it tenfold in five years was indeed remarkable. Unknown to Alan, it had been greatly helped with laundered money from a successful 'pot' business David had run.

Upon graduation, he had sold the lucrative business for $100,000 ($20,000 in hard cash, the rest in installments.) As he had explained to the sophomore to whom he sold it, "I know where you live." Rumors of what happened to people not paying their debts to David insured that the remainder would be forthcoming. The rumors, except for the one where he had broken the arm of a freshman who had stiffed him for a mere nickel bag, were all fiction but they guaranteed payment.

He had grown up in Green Township on the southeast side of Akron, Ohio. His father worked for Firestone, now Bridgestone, and his mother had been fortunate enough to be a homemaker until the three children were out of the house, David being the last. Now she sold real estate and was beginning to make a name for herself in a very tough market although things were beginning to soften. It was too soon to tell but Alan felt that David Jones would make a big impact in his team and that meant more money for him.

***

The other hire was Felicity Dawn Morgan, graduate of Western Kentucky and working on a M.B.A. from Capella University. The courses were online and her first course was 8004 Strategic Thinking and Innovation. Her teacher was Dr. James Morgan (no relation). She had just started that program, but her 4.0 G.P.A. told Alan that she would be successful. He had contacted Dr. Morgan, and he had concurred. The stock market and bonds were new to her, but she had taken to it like a duck to water and, although she had no clients of her own yet, she was gaining ground.

Felicity was black, Negro, colored, African-American – take your choice of the term you feel to be most politically correct, but stay away from the derogatory "N" word. That was a strictly verboten term – definitely not to be used by members of his firm either publicly or privately lest news of such a faux pas get back to Alan. His relationship with Stuart Andrews, the now deceased co-founder of the firm, made that a strict rule in his persona.

There was a picture of Stuart hanging in the waiting room. It was an oil painting done from memory by one of the staff, who dabbled but was really quite good given time. She had done it without saying anything to anyone until she had brought it to the office six months before. Alan had been considering a change in the name of the group to bring it more in line with him as the main hog, but the appreciation showed by the staff that remained after Stuart's untimely demise on a Caribbean cruise changed his mind. *Best to keep the troops happy*, Alan had thought and so he did.

Some of the staff knew but kept secret the fact that Alan had left the business after three years because he was just not into it. He had gone to work for a big firm, learned the trade and done well and when Stuart's death put the firm into receivership he had stepped forward and made the purchase.

Felicity had grown up in a small Kentucky town, only daughter of a poor couple who struggled to survive in a semi-hospitable environment. Her childhood had been happy and she had thrived in school, savoring mathematics, English and history. It was in school that she had learned the truth about her parents. At first she heard people describing them as functionally illiterate. She knew that their reading skills were small if non-existent. Later she heard the term "retarded" which was changed to the more politically correct "intellectually challenged." That label was also applied to her and when she first started school she had been environmentally retarded because it is difficult for two such parents to properly raise a daughter. However all that changed in school – well, after some initial problems.

First, she had to deal with a white girl who taunted her every chance she got. " 'Tard, 'tard," she'd hear, "dumb old 'tard." That went on for about a week until she walked up to the girl, stared her in the face until the girl had started to speak and then hit her with a right cross. After a crying bout by the girl and Felicity reprimanded with a note sent home to her parents (they couldn't read and she couldn't read yet), they became best friends.

The second confrontation was with a boy, also white, who tried to get her to show him her privates and when she wouldn't do that, he tried to get her to play with his. Finally when she stoutly refused, he shoved her and started to walk away. He had progressed about two feet after turning away when she blindsided him and was sitting on his chest, her knees holding his arms down, whaling his face with lefts and rights before being pulled off by a teacher. She was sent home (again with a note saying she couldn't come back to school for a week but this time verbally explained to her). To avoid embarrassing her parents, she had feigned illness for the rest of the week. The boy never bothered her again and became, albeit unknown to her, her silent champion.

She was never bothered again because by the end of first grade she was outshining the rest of her class and everyone one knew that she was definitely not a " 'tard."

She was third in her class in a large county high school and had earned a full ride to Western Kentucky, the only way she could have gone to school. She devoted herself to studies, dating intermittently and no one more than twice. She was on a mission to make a name for herself and a million dollars before she was thirty and nothing could get in her way. This effort showed in her drive since joining the firm.

Alan was happy with his choices, certain that they would be valuable additions to his team. The team was a good group; they were sociable and seemingly enjoyed each other's company, most always willing to help out and to accept help. He couldn't believe his good fortune. Things were certainly on the upswing. Life was good.

Chapter 8

Charles Godot is a weird duck, Alan thought. He had been coming around seeing different members of the team for two weeks, and then had not been seen for the next five weeks. The first day he had shown up he had stated that he wanted to invest but needed help. Admittedly he had qualms and wanted to be certain that whosoever handled his money had to be compatible with his personality and investment philosophy. Could he possibly "interview" each of the members of his team? It wasn't that strange, but people usually didn't interview everyone, just selected one or two. Godot was French or so he said. He had made his money the "hard way" – more than that he wouldn't say. He stood about five foot ten, had an athlete's body, lean and muscular, no fat. He was tan but not overly so. He dressed impeccably wearing oxblood wingtips with his dark suits, white shirts and somber ties. He had a scraggly but well kept black beard tinged with gray but the rest of his head was cleanly shaven as many people with male pattern baldness did in this day and age. His eye color was difficult to discern as his glasses had lenses tinted a dark gray as though to serve as sunglasses also. His hands were uncalloused, judging by the feel when he had shaken his hand on several different occasions so Alan was unable to decide what the "hard way" meant. It most certainly wasn't by manual labor. Then there was that slight hitch in his walk, not a limp exactly, almost the way a person might walk with an artificial leg. But other than that there was no sign of any impediment.

He spent several hours doing his interviews, one each morning and each afternoon during the two weeks except for the last two days. Then he had spent two hours with six of his people, three a day in a second interview process, two in the morning and one in the afternoon. Alan was pleased to see that David Jones and Felicity Morgan were among the six he had chosen. At the end of the second day he had spent half an hour with Alan, explaining that he wanted to take a few days to think about things and then he would return to announce his choice. He would not give any idea as to a leading candidate or candidates just simply that he would deliberate and make his choice. He had explained his weeding out to Alan in a private session.

"First out, Paul Marlow (nicknamed Philip by a couple of his colleagues) has been in the investment business forty-two years and with your firm from the beginning. He's at retirement age and has slowed down. I don't think he has the drive he once did nor do I feel that he has kept up with certain market trends. Second out, Mildred Pearce. Understandably a spinster. Mousy woman, quiet spoken. Understands the market as far as I can determine but doesn't have, in my opinion, the killer instinct. Wants me to buy sure things. I can't make money that way.

"Third out, Dawn McGuire. Married – no, divorced. Two kids, one in high school and one in middle school. I don't understand the term." When Alan started to explain, Godot held up a hand. "Don't need to understand the term. She's adequate, has many clients. Would be better if she didn't spend so much time painting." He said, waving his hand in the direction of Stuart Andrew's portrait. "Fourth out, Robert Dunlap. Three wives, none at the moment. Don't like a man who can't keep a woman." He leaned toward Alan in a confidential manner even though no one could hear. "He told me that all his wives had filed for divorce, and he doesn't understand why. I did after five minutes with him. Terrible body odor. Don't know why they married him in the first place. Oh, yes I do. Money. He makes money.

"Fifth out, John Miller. Ten years in the business. But doesn't understand it. I think you should give him a closer look when you get a chance.

"Sixth out, Stephen Smith. Has nothing to do with the fact he's gay." Alan was stunned. He hadn't realized that. "He's quick, knows the market, will go places but ... just not my style. There was no oomph."

So here he was again, on a Monday morning after an absence of five weeks, showing up at ten o'clock as scheduled with Alan's secretary the previous week. He seemed relaxed and confident as he strode into Alan's office and offered his hand.

"Welcome again, Mr. Godot," Alan said. "You seem especially cheery this morning."

"Yes, I guess I am," Godot said as he seated himself in one of the wingback chairs Alan had for his clients. "I had some business to conduct last week, the preparations were lengthy which is the reason I was gone for so long, and it went off like clockwork."

"You did well, then?" Alan asked trying to get some information and a further idea about what this man did.

Godot smiled and quipped, "You could say that I made a killing."

"Excellent. So have you made a decision?"

"Yes," Godot said. "Ms. Felicity Dawn Morgan."

For his purposes, there hadn't been any question from the beginning when he had been introduced to the team. She was the only person of color there.

"But let me explain my reasoning on the others. You may not agree, but then all people are different and that's what makes the world go round.

"So, seventh out – David Jones. I learned something in the second interview that, had I known from the first, would have excluded him. He's into drugs."

"What!" Alan said. "Not David."

"Yes, I recommend you do a surprise drug test. Simple urinalysis. Doesn't cost much and might make your life simpler in the future.

"Continuing, eighth out, Robert Morris. Married, six children, ages two to sixteen. Loves them all, the mother especially. I mean, that's obvious, six enfants." Godot couldn't resist a smile. "And therein lies the problem, at least for me. His hours are put in here and then it's family, soccer, baseball, basketball swimming, choir, and church every morning before work. The pope should give him a medal. But he has no time other than he puts in here and that won't do for my money.

"Ninth out, Michael Connors. Good man, sharp as a tack. Has a good feel for things and will go far. Works hard. Newlywed – and that's the problem. His wife is pregnant. He's worried. Had no brothers or sisters. Doesn't know a thing about babies – except how to make them." And he learned forward and whispered, "But I am not so certain about that." Then he said back, winked and laughed. "When the kid comes, he'll be a wreck and so might my investments."

Alan had been taking notes and nodded.

"Now to the last three. This was tough." Easy to say although it wasn't.

"Tenth out. Janet Thornbush-Higgins. What a mouthful." He wasn't talking about her name but her breasts of which she enjoyed showing glimpses.

"Knows where she is, where she wants to go, knows what to do. But ... she's either a tease or an insatiable nymph. Not good for my money." He had kept her in the final mix in hopes he could convince her to go out and then to bed but she wouldn't. Hence the tease indication.

"Eleventh out, Mary Ann Mervin. Married, mother of two who are out of the house. She and her husband want to work ten more years or so and retire. That's fine but I get the feeling she is more into making their own future bright and not so much mine. Whomever I get, has to be interested in me – my funds, I mean – more than themselves and their own.

"That's it. They don't know how I have characterized them, and you shouldn't tell them, but you have some things to go on."

Felicity was brought in, and the three of them spent half an hour discussing things and then she and Godot had gone to her cubical and set up the legal apparatus for transfer of money to and from a stock account that she established. There would never be any transfer; his account was fictitious just in case, by some long shot, anyone would ever find any record of his being there. Things completed, Godot took his leave telling her that he would transfer money when he got home in a day or so. For several minutes Felicity had sat in her cubicle soaking in her success and reveling in her future now that things were starting to come together. She got up and headed for Alan's office as he had requested and noticed that David was looking at her with a stare that said, "You don't deserve it." She felt that if he vocalized his feelings, that "N" word would have been used. Maybe even the "R" word.

"Congratulations, Ms. Morgan," Alan said. "That's fantastic. Mr. Godot made a good choice."

"Thank you," Felicity responded, a slight blush coloring her face, although admittedly difficult to see she could feel it. It was at that moment as she looked down, she noticed a black portfolio leaning against the chair in which Godot had been sitting. She reached down and picked it up. "Is this yours, Mr. Murphy?" she asked, being incredibly formal.

"No, I remember Godot having one like that. Maybe it is his."

"I'll try to catch him," Felicity said, and headed toward the doors. Knowing that the building's lone elevator was slow and there only three floors, she raced down the stairway, across the lobby after a brief stop to ascertain that Godot was not there and then out on the street. There were a number of pedestrians, but Godot was nowhere to be seen. At this point in time he was in his car and paying his parking fee at the entrance to the parking deck a block away. Felicity shrugged and turned back. She took the elevator to the third floor and stepped out, holding the door for a young pregnant woman who was heading down. The two smiled at each other and the doors to the elevator closed. Turning around, Felicity crossed the hallway and reached for the handle on one of the double glass doors each bearing the etched words "Andrews Investment Management".

At this point in time, Godot was sitting at a stop-light a block away facing the direction of the building. In his right hand, was a transmitter, its black face containing two buttons and two lights. One button had already been pressed turning on the transmitter. A red light had briefly flickered and then turned to green. A sardonic smile bared his teeth as he pressed the other button and said, "Goodbye all." Almost simultaneously small explosive packages he had surreptitiously placed under the desk of each of the team members exploded ripping the desks apart and sending metal, plastic and glass shards everywhere. The force of the combined explosions ripped outward breaking windows and sending pieces of glass showering down on the street. The glass wall front of Alan's office collapsed, the top of his glass desk lifted upward and street-ward pushing him with it through the windows to land in the middle of the street below, but he was dead by the time he hit the window. The front doors to the office complex were shoved outward spewing glass particles everywhere, many into the remains of Felicity Dawn Morgan, who was already dead from an explosive sheet in Godot's portfolio. That had been intended for Alan since he had been unable to plant anything because of the nature of Alan's glass topped desk. The combined explosive forces blew the elevator doors into the shaft where they dropped on top of the descending elevator bearing the young pregnant wife of Michael Connors. Other than being thrown to the floor and having to wait thirty minutes to be rescued from the stopped elevator, she was fine.

Chapter 9

I sat bolt upright in bed. I was sweating. I was chilled. I was scared. It was happening again. Something was wrong. Terribly wrong. Beside me Tres was sleeping peacefully. Knowing that I wasn't going back to sleep, I got up and dressed in a tee shirt, sweatpants, socks, sneakers. I left the bedroom and looked in on our youngster – sleeping peacefully. At the top of the stairs the security board was all green. Stair system lit. On the computer, I checked the outside cameras. Nothing. It was silly. I was having a nightmare – but I didn't remember it. Back at the top of the stairs, I turned off the beams and walked down, my Sig Sauer at the ready.

Once the beams were back on, I searched the perimeter, but all was quiet. It was later than the other time. Three in the morning. But that meant nothing. Did it? I started some coffee and went to the front doors. On the right was a heavy door, locked, that used to lead to the crypt under the church. When the church had been desanctified, the bodies had been removed leaving a big empty room running the length of the nave. Must have been natural, at least most of it, or it would have taken ages to hew out of the granite using antique tools. Even today it wouldn't have been easy. I unlocked the door using the keypad that accepted only my and Tres' thumbprints. No little toddler was going to get downstairs.

When I opened the door, the stone stairway was illuminated and would stay so until ten seconds after my feet broke the beam on the final step. Starting up the stairs would turn on the lights again. The room I entered didn't look like a crypt because it had been completely redone. It was this room that had been the motivating factor in choosing this particular church from among the many that had been left vacant with the advent of Communism in the region. With that hold gone, religion was coming back but slowly. Many of the adults of the time were dead and it would take a while for the need for religion to grow amongst the young.

Once a quiet place for bodies, this room had been cleared out to make a narrow room, 30 feet by 150 feet. We had it completely soundproofed and it was our shooting gallery. Yes, still paranoid. Initially I spent about an hour a day down here. Now an hour only a few days a week. I clipped a target on the line and ran it to the end and then put on shooter's earmuffs and donned shooter's yellow tinted eye protection. Standing with my head down, looking at the ground in front of me, I took a deep breath, raised my head and Sig simultaneously and emptied the magazine. I picked up the brass as I ran the target back to me. Eight of ten in the black. I had improved greatly during the past year. Almost on a par with Tres, but she was still better with the rifles. I didn't plan on being a sniper so it didn't bother me. I affixed a new target and ran it back while I ejected the empty magazine and inserted a new one. I turned my back to the target, whirled going into a crouch, pistol coming up into both hands and emptied the magazine. This time, nine of ten. I felt good. I hung the ear protector on the rack, put the protective glasses back in their case and placed the target with the other so Tres could see. Just a friendly competition. I compared my groupings with her last two – mine were a little tighter in the black I thought, but she was nine of ten in both. The brass went into a bowl – almost full. I would have to reload soon. We reloaded our shells because we didn't want anyone to know about the gallery. The workmen had no idea as we had finished it ourselves after the soundproofing had been put in. I took a few minutes to field strip and clean the Sig before reassembling and filling the magazines. Then I mounted the steps.

Outside the sun was beginning to show over the mountains and I welcomed the new day. Taking a cup of coffee, I turned off the stairway beams and went up to the computer room and started checking email. There was one from Beecher: subject: ?

I clicked on it. There was a link to a news site in the Caribbean.

WHAT DOES IT MEAN?

An oil tanker on the way to the Panama Canal spotted a life preserver floating in the water south of Jamaica today. The preserver was originally labeled "Seventh Heaven" but this had been crossed out with a black marker. On the other side was written "R.I.P. Zàkpa." A search of records has shown that there was a yacht named *Zàkpa* originally registered to a Jośef Viljoen, a South African. The yacht was sold to Joaquin and Jovelyn Gagalac and renamed *Banyuhay*. Two years ago the yacht was sold and registered in the name of Paul Peterson of Minneapolis, Minnesota in the United States. The yacht was renamed *Seventh Heaven*. We were unable to contact Mr. Peterson although sources do report that the yacht left St. Maarten a week ago starting a two-year circumnavigation of the world. The yacht is scheduled to go through the Panama Canal tomorrow.

A chill ran through my body. Deep inside I knew where the *Zàkpa* was – the bottom of the Caribbean somewhere. I felt sorry for the family of Mr. Peterson, but there was no time for that. I started through my checks of statuses. I knew that Beecher was okay or at least had been. Joaquin and Quentin were okay, at least on the surface. Something could have happened and no one could have been able to send the code. Alan's bank account was good – all even numbers. I decided to check his computer. There was nothing – I couldn't get in. Strange. I checked the Miami Herald.

MYSTERIOUS BLAST DESTROYS BUILDING

An explosion of unexplained origins destroyed the third floor of the Andrews Financial Building in suburban Miami this morning about 10:00 a.m. Witnesses report what seemed to be a series of explosions occurring almost simultaneously. Reports differ from 1 to 10 in the number of explosions. The blasts radiated outward and the roof collapsed but the lower two floors were left basically intact. Occupants of these floors suffered some minor injuries, mostly auditory. A pregnant woman whose husband worked for Andrews Investment Management was trapped in the building's elevator for forty-five minutes but was otherwise unhurt. The blasts started fires, which were brought under control fairly quickly. Emergency teams are combing through debris searching for bodies. The body of Alan Murphy, owner of Andrews Investment Management, was discovered in the middle of the street in front of the building. Alan was co-founder of the firm with Stuart Andrews, whose death three years ago highlighted a trial on St. Nantes. Andrews' wife Elise and brother-in-law Howard Blake were convicted of drowning Stuart Andrews with the help of Keith Mitchell. The latter committed suicide in Los Angeles and left a letter telling of the conspiracy.

I sat there stunned. First the life preserver and then this blast, the origin of which was no longer mysterious – at least to me. The two events could mean only one thing no matter how incredulous it seemed: **Michel Villar was alive**.

Chapter 10

Three years before, Michel Villar had been the preeminent jurist on St. Nantes, if not the entire Caribbean. A case of murder by drowning had been brought to him by Huard Jubert, the prosecuting attorney for St. Nantes. An American named Stuart Andrews had been drowned on a fishing excursion while his cruise ship was anchored in the port. Two men, Howard Blake and Keith Mitchell, were accused of the murder. Also included was Elise Blake Andrews, wife of Stuart Andrews and sister of Howard Blake. The evidence in the case at that time was mainly a deathbed confession by Keith Mitchell who, after writing it, had apparently committed suicide. That fact that Stuart Andrews had gone missing at sea was not disputed. His wife claimed that the four of them had reboarded their cruise ship *Caribbean Isle* after the fishing excursion. Stuart had then become reclusive and belligerent because of the downturn in the stock market. He was in the stock market business, owning Andrews Investment Management based in Miami. Prior to the revelation of Keith Mitchell's confession, Quentin Baston, St. Nantes fisherman who had taken the three men fishing, had disappeared when his boat exploded some weeks after the fishing expedition. As the investigation had progressed, an eyewitness came forward – Quentin Baston. His story was that his death had been staged with the help of a friend because he feared for the safety of himself and his family. He furnished physical evidence: a packet of $10,000 – blood money given to him by Howard Blake to gain his silence – and a camera which contained a digital picture of Howard Blake moving toward Stuart with an upraised Heineken beer bottle. Quentin said that Howard had knocked Stuart out and removed all personal effects from his body. Then he and Keith Mitchell had hung Stuart over the side to drown him before letting his body slip into the Caribbean.

What had intrigued Michel Villar about the case was that he knew Stuart Andrews. He had hired Stuart to launder funds for him, funds from a group in the Netherlands. He knew more about Stuart than any other person besides Stuart himself. He knew that Stuart had a second identity of Dawoh Mbayo of Sierra Leone. This identity was completely valid because Stuart had a right to citizenship through his mother who had been born in Sierra Leone. He was also an American by birth through his father and, of course, having been born in the United States. Stuart had at least one more identity – that of a South African named Jośef Viljoen although that identity, originally acquired through the Netherlands group for which Michel Villar fronted, had expired.

Michel Villar began checking and discovered that Dawoh Mbayo had flown from St. Martin to Amsterdam less than a week after he was supposed to have been drowned off St. Nantes or three days after he was supposed to have committed suicide by jumping off the *Caribbean Isle*. He had been in Amsterdam about a week and then flown to Paris with a connecting flight to Sierra Leone. A connection he never made. However, Jośef Viljoen had appeared out of nowhere and flown to

Bermuda. Imagine Michel Villar's surprise when Dawoh Mbayo had appeared in his courtroom during the trial, supposedly reporting for a Sierra Leone newspaper.

After the trial, in which Elise Andrews and Howard Blake were found guilty and sentenced to death, Michel Villar had boldly gone to the yacht owned by Jośef Viljoen. The yacht was named the *Zàkpa*. Boarding the yacht he had confronted Stuart Andrews with his knowledge but with the inferred promise that the information would never be used. He had left Stuart with a picture found in the possession of Keith Mitchell. Stuart had mailed the picture to Mitchell and Mitchell had, according to postmark, received it the day he killed himself. The picture, given to Michel Villar by the Los Angeles police lieutenant who had found it while investigating the scene, was never used in the trial. Whether it might have made a difference was questionable in his mind and it was his decision not to use it. The picture was of the St. Nantes harbor and had the inscription on the back:

> *Four went out. Three came back.*
> *We know what happened.*[2]

Stuart had come back to St. Nantes, buying the house in which he found refuge after his ordeal at sea. When word had come to Michel Villar that there was a contract on his head, he had sought out Stuart (then going by the name of Dawoh Mbayo or Daws). He had basically blackmailed Stuart into helping him by telling him that he and his crewman, a Pilipino named Joaquin

---

[2] This part of the story is the first book of the trilogy: *Payback is a Bitch.* What follows is the second book: *Payback: Time to die … again.*

Gagalac, could be tried for the murders of Elise and Howard because he had concealed the fact that he was alive and had orchestrated evidence in the trial. The evidence was factual but some of it would have been difficult to uncover.

Stuart had conceived of the idea of an automobile accident that would put Michel Villar in the hospital with minor injuries giving the hired assassin Fredek Gavrilovich Kondrashin, d.b.a. the Facilitator, a chance to kill him. Michel Villar had foolishly offered The Facilitator money to fake his death but that plan backfired when the assassin got more money from the man who offered the contract. The Facilitator had forced Michel Villar's car violently off the road, and Michel Villar was rushed to the hospital with possible life-threatening injuries. Fortunately the medical apparatus fashioned by Stuart's girlfriend Treshauna (Tres) Jones had worked and Michel Villar survived The Facilitator's attempt in the hospital. Michel Villar had been secretly taken away and conveyed to the *Zàkpa* then owned by Joaquin Gagalac and his wife Jovelyn and renamed the *Banyuhay*.

While he was recovering, a group of hired mercenaries headed by Jacques St. George had invaded Stuart's house in an attempt to gain access to Stuart's considerable funds. With the help of Beecher McFalls, former C.I.A. agent, Stuart had managed to lure most of the mercenaries into his house that was then destroyed by hidden explosives taking most of the mercenaries with it. Escaping from the safe room in the bottom of the house, Stuart had managed to terminate the remaining mercenaries. Then he, Tres, and Michel Villar had gone after The Facilitator. Evidently shocked by the fact that

Michel Villar lived, The Facilitator suffered a fatal heart attack but not before revealing who had hired him, although by riddle. Tres solved the riddle and the trio knew that the culprit was one of the two lawyers who had defended Elise and Howard. Chyrise Callahan, Howard's lawyer was ruled out, and Phil Dombrey, Elise's lawyer, identified. When faced with the possibility of a trial, Phil Dombrey had chosen to commit suicide. Michel Villar had then disappeared. Stuart had been led to believe that a French cartel called Cercle des Frères (Circle of Brothers) was the group for which Michel Villar fronted and that had come after his money. A chance encounter in a cafe on St. Maarten convinced him otherwise. Whoever the group was, it was located in Amsterdam. Stuart tracked down Pieter Devenpeck, the man he assumed to be the leader of the group, and learned the truth from him. With Pieter Devenpeck's help, he had gone on a hunt to find Michel Villar who was hiding in Caracas. Stuart had put a super poison in Michel Villar's drink. It was first to paralyze and then to stop the heart of the victim. It was then that Stuart had made the same mistake his brother-in-law had made. He had thought that his victim was dead and had left.

Part II
Don Giovanni

Chapter 11

SIXTEEN MONTHS EARLIER

She opened the door and stepped inside. Light came from a nearby room. There was no sound, but the alarm was a silent one. She turned to the keypad and saw the flashing red light that meant the alarm was set, so she entered her code. Then she turned the light on to hang up her raincoat, now dripping on the floor. His was hung up already but still dripping water every so often. That meant he been here awhile. Turning the light off in the foyer, she headed for the lighted room. Entering the living room, she saw him sitting in a wingback chair, not moving. A crystal tumbler lay on the rug, wet spots all around. Something was wrong! Quickly she moved to him and crouched down to look at his face. The eyes were open but unmoving. She waved her hand in front of his face. No reaction. She put one hand over his left eye and counted to ten. When she removed the hand the pupil hadn't changed. She raced to the kitchen and opened the refrigerator, grabbing at a carton, which professed to hold a processed cheese food. She tore off the lid and grabbed the fabric case inside, dropping the carton's bottom and turning back toward the living room. Back by his side, she dropped to her knees in front of him and ripped his shirt open, baring his chest. Then she

opened the fabric case on his lap exposing six hypoder-
mics. She took the one labeled "fixed – dilated" and removed the sheath. Turning the needle upward she
flicked the syringe body with her finger and pressed the
plunger slightly expelling a little air and a small amount
of liquid. Placing her hand over his heart, she felt for a
space between the ribs and then plunged the needle in
until it could go no further. She pressed the plunger fully
in and then pulled the needle out, flinging the hypoder-
mic away. She then repeated the process with the hypo
labeled "Adrenaline." For a few moments she sat back
on her heels and watched his face. There was no reaction. Folding up the syringe packet, she stood up and
started back toward the kitchen, having no idea what she
was going to do. A cough and low moan startled her and
she turned around, heedlessly dropping the syringe
packet at her feet. His head was drooping and his left
arm hung at his side. The thought *He's alive* flitted
through her mind, but she knew that those movements
could also mean that he was dead. Too shocked to move,
she stood there until she saw his left hand twitch and she
raced to him.

Raising his head, she saw that his eyes were
closed. She raised one lid and saw that the pupil was re-
actant. He was alive! Retrieving a sofa pillow she raised
his feet and placed it under his legs against the legs of
the chair. Then she stood and moved in front grabbing
his feet and pulling. He wasn't a big man but was bigger
than she. However, she was amped. He slid off the front
of the chair and his buttocks landed on the cushion. He
fell over to the right. Continuing to pull his feet she got
him off the cushion and flat on his back on the floor.
She removed his shoes and socks, undid his belt, fly and

zipper and removed his trousers. His shirt was loose and didn't matter. Felt his pulse – weak and ragged. She listened to his heart – weak but beating. From the bedroom she got a quilt and pillow, as well as a battery-powered blood pressure monitor and stethoscope. He was the most prepared non-medical person she had ever met.

She fitted the pressure cuff on his left arm and ran the machine. 90/60. Weak but acceptable. She slid stethoscope's chestpiece up under his shirt and listened to the heartbeat. Weak but regular. She sat back on her heels. *Now what?* Feeling that he was probably suffering from shock, she put the sofa cushion under his feet and covered him with the quilt. Trying to get liquid in him probably wouldn't work and could cause him to gag, ruining all her efforts.

Now what? This time that question had no answer so she sat on the floor and waited.

Her eyes flitted open and then shut again as she felt something touch her. She opened her eyes and discovered she was lying on the floor on her side. She had fallen asleep. Again she felt something touch her, move against her, and she sat up. His left arm was extended toward her and the hand, at least the fingers, was moving. She looked toward him and saw his head turned in her direction eyes wide open. They blinked.

She smiled. "Hello," she said.

There was a faint reply.

"What?" she asked.

Again he said something she couldn't understand.

She moved to him and leaned down, her ear by his mouth.

"Eau (Water)," came raspingly from his lips.

She jumped up and raced to the kitchen grabbing a glass and filling it with water. Then with a second thought, she grabbed a dishtowel, threw it on the counter and added a handful of ice cubes from the refrigerator's freezer. She folded the dishtowel over them and used the heft of a kitchen knife to crush them. Grabbing the towel and the glass she raced back to him and knelt beside him. He hadn't moved but turned his head so he could look up at her.

"Ice first," she said. "So you won't gag."

He blinked and she slid a sliver of ice between his lips. She could see his cheeks move as he sucked on the ice using his tongue. A smile of contentment flitted across his lips and he said, "Plus (More)."

Happily she fed him ice for the next several minutes and then he seemed to go to sleep. She felt his pulse just to be certain and watched the slow and rhythmic rise and fall of his chest. Then she took his blood pressure again: 115/72. The pulse was 75.

He's going to live.

Chapter 12

ONE YEAR AGO

Recovery had been slow. He had lain on the living room floor until mid-afternoon the next day. She was a dutiful nurse and had kept him clean and warm. After sleeping eight hours, he had been able to take water and four hours later he could sit up. Another two hours and he wanted to get into bed. He had crawled to the couch and used it for support. With her help, he had managed to stand. An arm over her shoulder and a cane remaining from his broken leg, they had managed a twenty-minute walk the thirty odd feet to his bed. He had fallen into it and she had helped him get settled and then covered him with the quilt retrieved from the living room. He had quickly fallen asleep. She didn't want to leave him but there were things that they needed (bed pan, etc.) because it was going to be a while before he could get out of bed. She left a note and then went out.

Her first stop was at the local newspaper where she left them an obituary he had prepared months before and given her instructions to have it published in just such an event as this.

Maurice Vitor left this temporal existence following a heart attack. He was born in Bourbon, France, January 1, 1954, and was educated in Paris. He worked independently as an accountant for thirty years before moving to Caracas where he spent the final years of his life. He had no family and there will be no services. His ashes will be spread at sea. Tennis was his great love and friends should make memorial contributions to the Caracas Indoor Tennis Club. His hope is that he will be more successful in his next life.

She had found this to be a strange in that he was not dead, but then in some respects he was a strange man. Again at his request, she used the back door to come and go for the next few days until he was strong enough to be moved. When he could be moved, they had taken a very few belongings and left by the back door, using her car to get to her place on the other side of the city. It was three months before he could start neighbor-hood walks for which he used his cane because of a leg problem that he associated with a prior injury but had somehow been aggravated by whatever had happened to him. He never talked about that and she had understood. There was a darkness in his past and some of that had come forward to hurt him. Another problem was his left eye had developed a gray cast. He had gone to an oph-thalmologist as soon as he was well enough to get out. The best that the doctor could determine was some kind of damage to the optical nerve that had left him 20/800 vision and there wasn't much that could be done to im-prove that. He had therefore adopted eyeglasses with a dark gray tint to hide that malady. He had grown his beard to about half an inch in length but continued to shave his pate.

Once he had his strength back, he had started to jog and spend days in the sun. His jogging increased to five miles a day and he bought a gym membership and spent several hours a day at first under the tutelage of a personal trainer and then on his own. One of the things that he worked on was his legs and most of the time he could walk easily and showed no sign of a problem. There were days however when a problem was readily apparent. He spent hours on the computer doing she knew not what but she was happy that he was alive and busy. Something was driving him and she was certain that it had to do with whatever had happened to him. She knew it wasn't physical – someone had given him something. Once she had asked him about it, specifically about the syringe marked "fixed – dilated." He had only said, "that $100,000 investment saved my life." After that he refused to discuss it. When they had started sharing each other's life, keys were shared but separate apartments kept, he had instructed her in the use of each of the syringes. She knew something about injections already having started nurses' training but had given up because of the stress – stress that had driven her to "experimenting" with drugs. The experiment had come to be a habit but she had gone into rehab and kicked it. There were occasional moments when she missed the peace it gave her, but the other parts of it she could live without. When they had started their semi-communal living, she had quit working and let him support her. He asked nothing of her but companionship and strict allegiance. She didn't ask and he didn't ask. They had that idyllic life, but since the incident – she didn't know what else to call it – things had changed. He had changed – not that anyone wouldn't have changed after a near death experience. But it was more than that. Outwardly their relationship was the same but inwardly things were different. He had never gone back to his place. He had her go and collect his meager belongings, mostly clothes. Everything else was sold – even the condo. Now he seemed unsettled, almost ready to move on. He had told her early in their relationship that there might be a day when he would have to leave. When that happened she wouldn't have any worries. Her condo was paid for; she would have a monthly allowance. The only change would be that he wouldn't be there any longer. She felt that day wouldn't be far off. And she wasn't wrong.

He was as ready as he could be and the longer he stayed the more likely that someone would come to find out what had happened to him – up close and personal – and would start digging. Someone good at ferreting out those in hiding would find out that he wasn't dead. He had his ticket, early flight out, and so was up at 3:00 a.m. using his mental alarm. He dressed quietly and quickly. His clothing was minimal. Most of it had been given away because of his change in size. He had actually bulked up one size because of his current fitness regimen. Intentionally all he had at this time was one carry-on bag and a computer bag – this was the important thing because it held all the secrets that he needed. Ready to go but there was one last thing.

He stood by the bed looking at her. The woman who had saved his life. It could have been any woman – he would have had his pick – but he had chosen her because of her background in nursing and it had paid off.

Big time it had paid off. And now was time to say good-bye – him to Caracas and her to existence. He picked up a pillow off the king-sized bed and then put it back. Too tell tale. Obviously murder. True, because people knew he was there, they might say "Murder" but there was the other possibility.

He went to where she kept her emergency stash. Even though she said she was clean, he knew that she had dabbled. He used stuff he had purchased off the street but the rest of it, all the apparatus, was all hers. He fixed a needle – too big – it would look like a mistake. He put a band around her arm, found a vein, inserted the needle and pushed the plunger, then released the band permitting the free flow of death. He stripped off the latex gloves he had been wearing, put them into his pocket and walked to the front door. He picked up his carry-on and computer bag, set the alarm, opened the door and left, closing it behind him. He never looked back and never thought of her again.

Chapter 13

When he left Caracas he had gone to Cartagena in search of an education. Not what one might commonly think of as an education because this was an education in death. He knew about guns, at least how to aim, shoot and reload, but beyond that he was clueless. In his prior life, which he left behind him in Caracas, his credo was "Make love, not war." Now it was to become "Make love to war." There was nothing else until he had rid the world of two kinds of people: those who had wronged him and those who knew anything about his past. Both lists were short because he had been a private person. Some of those people were already dead. In order to do what he needed to do, he needed to know how to kill in as many ways as possible. Therefore, in Cartagena he went looking for someone to become his teacher. But the dapper Italian playboy who arrived at the Rafael Núñez International Airport was not the person who left the airport. After passport control and customs, the dapper Italian playboy went into a stall in the men's room and remained there for thirty minutes. Most of that time was spent patiently waiting trying to be certain that there was no one there when he exited the stall that was there when he went in. The man who came out was similar but different. Clothes-wise the only change was that the black guide shirt was gone, tucked into his carry-on. He was still wearing beige Dockers and the white polo shirt but his shiny brown shoes had been replaced by dirty cross trainers. He now wore a baseball cap with crossed-tennis rackets – the one part of his past he couldn't leave behind. The patch, which he would use later, was replaced by reflective sunglasses. He had reservations in a hotel, but he didn't go there immediately. First he had a meeting.

The taxi had dropped him in the middle of a business street in a poorer part of Cartagena. He looked around and saw nothing that appeared to be a proper meeting place with Don Giovanni. *Strange name*, he had thought, *for a drug lord in a Spanish country, but strange are the ways of the lords.* That brought a chuckle even from him. He was still looking around when his phone rang indicating a text message. Pulling the phone out, what he saw were numbers. He plugged those into the GPS app and pressed GOTO. An arrow appeared indicating "to the right." Picking up his computer bag, he put the strap over his head, the bag resting under his left arm, his left hand holding the GPS. Then with his duffel carry-on in his right hand, he followed the GPS. Right turn into an alley, unsavory but he had no choice. Besides, this was an unsavory business. At the end of the alley a left turn, then right crossing the street into another alley, this one no better than the first. At the end a right turn, ten steps and he was at his destination: Corzo de Cantina. A tattered brown wooden door set in the middle of a stained stucco fifty-foot stretch with no windows. Of course, there had been no windows in the alley either. It was early even for the Columbians, he doubted that it was open, but he tried the door and entered the cantina. Inside he was greeted with gloom. Shutting the door, he stood still letting his eyes adjust to the dim light provided by two bare bulbs hanging above the bar area. Then he saw the man standing in front of him. Big, ugly, wearing dirty white baggy pants, and an equally dirty long-sleeved baggy white shirt. The man's main feature was the automatic pistol that was pointed at him. No way to get by should he feel like trying, which he didn't, so he said, "Amigo del Diablo," as he had been instructed. The Beast said nothing but indicated that he should leave his bags on the floor and he complied. Then he indicated Michel's wrist and the nearby table. Michel put his watch on the table. The Beast used his free hand to mime a phone. His cell phone went on the table. When his pockets were empty, the Beast pointed toward a door in the back right of the cantina. Threading his way between tables, Michel opened the door and was momentarily blinded by the light that streamed out.

To the right, just beyond the door, was a dirty urinal with rust stains in the bowl. Beyond that was what he judged to be a stall and across from the stall a sink, at least judging by the faucets, but now it was more of a table. Ah, a briefcase made the table. He couldn't make out more because blocking part of the view was a man. This one dressed in a beige suit, light shirt, tie, incongruous in this setting.

"Come in and close the door," the man said in perfect English. There was nothing to do but comply.

"Take your clothes off and throw them into the stall," the man said indicating the aforementioned facility.

Chapter 14

"What?" Michel Villar stammered.

The man repeated his instructions.

"Why?"

"Call it a physical examination, if you wish," the man answered, shrugging indifferently.

Michel's instructions had been clear. "If you want to see Don Giovanni, do as you're told."

His option was to turn around and leave. But there was The Beast out there – an ugly beast with an uglier pistol. He doubted that he would just be allowed to walk away.

Michel pulled the polo shirt off and tossed it over the top of the stall wall. A hand reached up and caught it so fast that Michel couldn't determine whether it belonged to a man or woman. He stepped out of his shoes and bent to pick them up.

"Slide those, don't throw," the man said and Michel complied, kicking one and then the other under the stall wall. The polo shirt appeared, hanging over the top of the stall. Undoing his belt, Michel dropped his Dockers, stepped out of them, picked them up and threw them over the wall. He looked at the man.

"Everything."

"Even my shorts?"

"Everything."

"Isn't there at least a gown for some perfunctory decency?"

The man smiled. "I am not a pervert. I am a doctor, but this isn't my office. No gown."

Michel dropped his shorts, stepping out of them one leg at a time, lifting each leg to remove the sock both of which went over the stall wall, followed by his shorts. Just as his Dockers they were slung to hang on the wall.

"Good," The Doctor said opening the briefcase, picking up a bottle of hand sanitizer, and squeezing some out on his hands. After cleaning them, he picked up an otoscope from the briefcase.

"Spread your legs out and lift your arms," The Doctor instructed and Michel complied with a vertical spread eagle. Stepping in front of Michel, he looked in his nose and both ears, never changing the specula. Stepping back to the sink, he put the otoscope down and put on a pair of latex gloves. Back in front of Michel, he said, "Open wide," and proceeded to make a finger inspection of Michel's mouth. Then he ran his hands down and up Michel's arms, torso, front and back. As Michel shivered from the touch, The Doctor stopped. "Aphephobia?" and Michel nodded. This fear of being touched had developed during his last five years on St. Nantes.

"I understand and will be as quick as I can." He finished the body scan, even running his hands down Michel's penis and lifting the scrotum.

"Face the urinal, bend forward and put your hands on it."

"Is this really necessary?"

The Doctor looked at him, shrugged. "Your decision."

Michel complied, tensing as The Doctor started to spread his buttocks. "Relax, it will be over quickly. Faster and more comfortable than a prostate examination." And it was but no less invasive.

The Doctor stripped off his gloves, which he threw into the stall from which issued a cry of surprise. He picked up a bottle from the briefcase and handed it to Michel who raised an eyebrow.

"You followed directions about the water, didn't you?" The Doctor asked. Michel nodded that he had, drinking a sixteen-ounce bottle of water on the way from the airport. "Then fill the bottle." Michel complied, glad that he could because his bladder was full. The Doctor looked at the bottle when Michel handed him as he stepped back from the urinal having completed the emptying of his bladder. The Doctor looked at the bottle closely and then poured the contents into the urinal. The bottle then followed the gloves into the stall where it seemed to rattle around.

"He's clean," The Doctor said, apparently to the person in the stall. There was an acknowledging grunt from within.

"What if I hadn't drunk the water?" Michel asked.

The Doctor walked to his brief case and picked up a narrow glass tube. "I assure you it wouldn't be pleasant."

Michel grimaced and then asked, "What were you looking for?"

"Recording devices, microphones."

Michel looked down at his penis.

"I like to think I am endowed but...."

"Miniaturization is all the rage. Now put your nose in the corner made by the stall and urinal walls, close your eyes, don't even try to look. Count to one hundred, then get dressed and come out."

Michel complied, heard the briefcase opened and then closed and two sets of footsteps, one heavy (The Doctor) and one light making sex determination difficult. When the door closed, Michel went into the stall discovering that the toilet was simply an oblong tile in the floor. He was glad that who was in there had caught his clothes – at least he hoped that he or she had. Fortunately a roll of toilet paper rested on the floor against the wall and he cleaned himself from the rectal examination and got dressed. Upon opening the door of the toilet, he found himself face to face with The Beast.

Chapter 15

For a moment neither moved. Maybe because The Beast's brain was so slow, but Michel because he was so scared of The Beast's ugly pistol pointed at the middle of his chest. Maybe he was expecting an assault – Michel busting out the door with non-existent guns ablazing – but with his reaction time ... Oh, well, that wasn't happening. The Beast finally came to life, stepped to the right side, gun held in his left still pointing at Michel, with his right hand pointed at the far corner made by the alley and street walls. Michel once again threaded his way through the gloom pausing at one table. On it sat his carry-on – open and obviously tossed – and his computer bag, laptop out and opened, login page visible, cursor blinking. Moving on toward the corner he was suddenly blinded by four fairly high-power spotlights, two each on poles set either side of a grungy – no, absolutely filthy – wooden table. He stopped, hands up in front of his eyes.

"Sit," directed a voice from behind him and, discerning the outline of a chair, he pulled it out and sat, trying to block the lights.

"So, whatever chur real name is, what chu want from Don Giovanni?"

The voice, coming from the corner across the table between the lights, was one of those nondescript types – difficult to tell whether it was male or female.

"You are Don Giovanni?" Michel asked trying to fight through the lights to see who was asking?

"Does it matter?" the voice said. "I am the one chu talking at."

Getting up and walking out was not an option and, after the humiliation he had been through, he was at least going to do what he had come for.

"I want to learn to kill people."

The laugh from Don Giovanni was almost maniacal. Something metallic landed on the table in front of Michel and then something else. Michel reached out his right hand and picked up a pistol, type indiscernible because of the lights. His left hand found first the blade and then the haft of a big knife.

"There, chur prayers are answered."

"No, that's not what I meant," Michel was shaken. "I know how to kill people. I want to learn about the weapons that kill people. I want to know about pistols and rifles and rockets and grenades and ... explosives."

"Oh, so chu want to go to school with me?" It was almost a snicker. "Chu going to carry my books?"

"No, I know that you have an armed force to protect ... your holdings." *That being marijuana and heroin in addition to yourself,* Michel could have added. "I've been told that you train your soldiers and they are quite formidable."

"Chu told you this?"

Michel could sense Don Giovanni sitting straight up now, forearms probably on the table, leaning forward toward him. Regardless, Michel could still not see other than an extremely dim form.

"Uh, people."

"What people?"

"Friends."

"Chu have friends who know Don Giovanni?"

The manner in which it was said was such that Don Giovanni seemed surprised that Michel had friends at all.

"Not 'know you personally' but know about chu."

That last word had slipped out inadvertently and at once Michel was sorry.

"Chu making fun of Don Giovanni?" Somewhere behind him a pistol was cocked.

"No, no, no," stammered Michel, hands in the air as in surrender. "I would not make fun of you. I need ... I want your help. I admire you."

"Chu admire me?" The voice a little more relaxed. "Chu don't even know me."

"True," Michel relaxed a bit and lowered his arms. "I know about you. I know your reputation. You are a powerful figure in Columbia. Hell, in Central America ... and in South America."

There was a moment of silence.

"Where are these friends of churs?" Don Giovanni's vanity and curiosity rising to the fore.

How much did Michel want to divulge? He needed to know about weapons. He had many people to kill. He felt he had covered his tracks well. Don Giovanni would not be able to track him back beyond Panama City.

"Caracas."

"Really? Venezuela?"

"Yes."

"Chu in Venezuela knows Don Giovanni?"

In for a dime... "Juan Carlos."

"Chu know Juan Carlos?" The voice evoked definite interest.

"Not personally, but a friend does." That was true; his paramour had mentioned him once in passing.

"So, okay." Don Giovanni seemed to be impressed. "So you go to my school for a month?"

"No." He didn't have time. "I can learn what I need in two weeks."

"But that is not enough time. You have to spend half the time with entrenamiento físico."

"No, I don't want physical training," the similarity in Spanish and French words made this understandable. "I will do that as needed. I have a bad leg so my physical abilities are limited. Running is difficult, for example. What I need is to know about guns and explosives. Maybe some invasive techniques."

"Invasive techniques. That is entrenamiento físico, is it not?"

"No, yes ... maybe. I can explain to a trainer ... instructor ... what I think I want."

"Chokay. And if I do this for chu, what chu do for me?"

Now we're at the nitty gritty, Michel thought.

"I can pay."

Don Giovanni laughed. "Pay. I don't need chur money. I haf money."

"Then what do you want in exchange?"

Don Giovanni was silent for a minute.

"Where are this people chu want to kill?"

"All over the world. The Caribbean, the United States, the ..."

"The Chu-nited States?"

"Yes."

"Then here is what I want chu to do to learn."

Chapter 16

He opened his eyes. It was dark. He felt groggy. Sick to his stomach. Where was he? He tried to pull together his memories. He and Don Giovanni had talked about ways he could help – be willing to help – because he couldn't risk being caught by any type of law enforcement. Then Don Giovanni had told him it was time to go to the camp.

Michel Villar had stood up and walked to the table where his carry-on and laptop were. "Chu won't need those," Don Giovanni had said from his or her dark corner.

He had started to protest when an arm had grabbed him and forcibly led him out the cantina's door. Outside was a black sedan and he had been roughly pushed into the rear seat. The Doctor was there, holding something in his hand. As he tried to focus on it, the world had turned black – something had been thrust over his head. Then someone grabbed his arm; there was pain as something – a needle – was thrust into his arm. Then he had awoken.

He tried to sit up, finally made it. Suddenly he was blinded as a light above him went on. Not overly bright but enough to dazzle him. He shut his eyes and then slowly opened them.

A young woman dressed in a dark green tee shirt, her breasts barely disturbing the fall of the material, and matching fatigue pants was standing at the flap of a tent – he was in a tent. She was holding a small tray on which he could make out a bottle of water.

"Chu be 'ungry," she said, handing him the tray.

"Where are we?" Michel asked taking the tray and resting it on his legs. It had the bottle of water, a plate with some type of bread, potatoes and some greasy meat in a red sauce with lumps.

"Here," was her answer.

"Where's here?" Michel asked, picking up the water bottle and, twisting the cap, relieved that it hadn't been opened.

The woman shrugged, turned to go.

"What time is it?" Michel asked.

"Midnight," the woman said as she disappeared through the tent's flap.

Michel realized he was hungry and devoured the food. Whatever it was, it certainly was tasty. He was sopping up the last of the red – and spicy, he had discovered – sauce when he heard noise at the tent flap. It was the woman again, this time holding a plastic bag. She said nothing, just watched as he shoved that last of the bread into his mouth and wiped his hands on a paper towel. It had been a messy meal because there were no eating utensils.

The woman thrust the bag at him and picked up the tray. Turning she started toward the tent flap.

"Wait," he said, careful not to use his knowledge of Spanish.

She stopped and turned to look at him.

"What do I do now?" he asked.

"Sleep," she said and disappeared out the tent's flap.

In the plastic bag were his watch and wallet. He put on his watch and stood up and surveyed the tent. The only furniture in the small tent other than the cot was a footlocker. Opening it he discovered clothes -– two dark green tee shirts, two pairs of white boxers, two pairs of green socks, a pair of green fatigue pants, a fatigue jacket, a green ball cap, a belt and a pair of boots. He removed his clothes, which he folded and put into the footlocker. Then he got dressed in a set of his new clothes, obviously the uniform of wherever he was. Then he moved to the tent flap and stepped out and almost ran into a smaller version of the Beast and similarly armed.

"¿Qué?" Small Beast said, holding up a hand indicating he should stop.

"Baño," Michel said realizing he needed to use one.

The Small Beast pointed to a building about ten feet in front of the tent and followed Michel, but waited outside. No one was in the latrine, which was exactly that, a series of eight holes in a board set on two concrete blocks at either end over a ditch of indeterminable depth. There was no sink or hand cleanser but thankfully there was toilet paper. When he exited the baño, he tried to look around but Small Beast herded him back to his tent.

"Sueño (Dream)," Small Beast instructed. Michel knew he had no choice but to comply.

His day began at six, although the rest of the camp was active at five thirty. There was no reveille; his alarm clock was his guard, who varied every eight hours during the first week. After dressing, having chosen to sleep in his shorts, he was permitted a trip to the baño and then breakfast was delivered by the young woman. She delivered all meals to his tent for the two weeks he was there. He was quite impressed with her because despite all his efforts, all his charm, even using the modicum of Spanish he had "picked up" while doing "his time" as he came to think of it, she divulged nothing. Not even her name.

After his morning meal he was taken to a weapons demonstration, always by the same instructor, possibly because he was one of the few who spoke English – no one spoke French. He was always alone with his instructor; every other person in the camp was elsewhere, although in the afternoon he could hear gunfire so he knew that the range was active. He learned about a great variety of weapons: pistols (Glocks, Berettas, Heckler & Kochs, Sig Sauers, Rugers, Walthers), assault rifles (AC-556, AK-100s, AK-47, SC-70/90, Heckler & Koch G36), sniper rifles (M24, M21, L42 Enfield, PSG1, Dragunov SVD, Armalite AR50), and rocket propelled explosives (RPGs, especially the RPG7). Everything had to be committed to memory as he was not permitted to take notes. It was one weapon or one manufacturer a day. First instructions on shooting and then he would have an hour or so shooting although he never got to fire an RPG or a LAWS because they didn't have any. After target practice – and by the end of the two weeks he was a decent shot – he had to field strip and clean the weapon, clean until his instructor was satisfied. Then it was back to his tent where he might have a wait, never long, for his noon meal.

Afterward, he was taken to another venue where he either learned about explosives or he worked with an instructor learning about climbing walls, getting down a cliff which was just the wall he learned to climb with ropes and grappling hooks. He wanted to know about picking locks but that was something for which Don Giovanni's men had no use.

He worked all afternoon, even when the rest of the camp, except him and his instructor, took siesta. Often his instructor was not overly happy with that arrangement.

Back in his tent, he had an hour or so to kill before dinner and then he would fall exhausted onto his cot.

Chapter 17

Maybe because he had toed the line so well, never trying to wander off, after one week he went through his daily ritual without a guard, but there was always one there in the evening when he returned before dinner and a guard remained there all night. The first day of this regimen was one he would not forget. After lunch he was on his way to his explosives class as he thought of it and passed a group of men outside the mess hall. He had passed them before, but always with his guard and nothing had ever been said although the men always watched him. That day, one of them stepped in front of him, bringing him up short. He tried to move around but the man blocked him. He wasn't a tall man, actually more Michel's size but heavier. He had a paunch despite doing all the physical stuff that Michel knew went on with the trainees for Don Giovanni's personal force.

"Excuse me," Michel said in English.

"¿Cuál es tu problema, gringo? (What's your problem, gringo?)" the Paunch asked. "¿Eres demasiado bueno para comer y trabajar con nosotros? (Are you too good to eat and work with us?)"

Although he understood every word, he persisted with the illusion that he spoke little Spanish. "I don't know what you want, but I have some place to go," and he tried to shoulder by The Paunch who shoved him back.

"¿No eres muy sociable, estás? (You are not very sociable, are you?)" The Paunch continued. "Tal vez usted no tiene el gahones a hacer lo que hacemos. (Maybe you do not have the balls to do what we do.)"

Michel just stared at him.

"Déjalo ir, Jośe. (Let him go, Jośe.) No vale la pena. (He is not worth it.)" One of his friends shouted.

Jośe waved his hand to indicate he understood and stepped back his extending his right arm in the direction of Michel's travel as though indicating he could proceed. And he did, at least one step, and then Jośe brought that right fist smashing into Michel's gut in a roundhouse swing. Caught by surprise, the blow knocked the wind out of Michel and he dropped to the ground on all fours.

"Creo que no tiene el cahones. (I guess he doesn't have the balls)," Jośe said and his friend laughed.

Gasping, Michel got air back into his lungs. He had landed right next to Jośe who stood legs apart in a bit of a swagger stance. Gathering himself, Michel pushed himself upward twisting his left side toward Jośe and bringing his left fist between Jośe's legs connecting solidly with his balls. Michel grinned at the sound of the impact and the simultaneous gasp from Jośe. Continuing his upward trajectory as Jośe's torso bent forward from the pain, Michel's head connected with Jośe's chin. Jośe head went flying backward carrying the rest of his body with it and he landed flat on the dirt path, too stunned to move.

Michel dusted his pants off and then bent over Jośe so that only he could hear what he said. "¿Cómo es eso de cahones, Jośe? (How is that for cahones, Jośe?)"

Then he continued his walk to his class. For the rest of his stay he had no trouble with anyone else, and he never saw Jośe again. But that was not the end of it. In the middle of the night, he was awakened by someone entering his tent. He started to sit up, but a small hand covered his mouth. "Stay there," said a voice he recognized as his waitress's. There was the sound of clothes rustling and then he felt her climbing onto the cot. He reached for her, but she pushed his hands away. "No," she said. "Don't touch." Then she reached for his penis that was already growing hard. She bent and took it into her mouth, her tongue licking it as it reached its full rigidity. Then she adjusted her position and he felt her lowering herself and felt himself entering her. She gasped at the first deep penetration, her arms stiff, hands on his chest. He ached to reach for her but knew that would break the spell so he just settled in to enjoy it. After a minute she began to move slowly up and down and then, as though she was listening to Ravel's Bolero in her head, her tempo increased, faster and faster and then she gasped and the movement stopped. He could feel her body quivering as her orgasm peeked and then ebbed. *Don't stop*, he wanted to say and thankfully she didn't. She realized that he hadn't ejaculated yet and so she started her movements again and when he came, she did so again although not as strong. She sat still on him for a moment feeling his erection softening. "Muchas gracias," she said. Then she got off him, obviously adjusting or putting on her clothes before he heard her exit through the tent flap.

There were no repeat performances the rest of his stay, and she never gave an indication that anything had happened between them. His graduation from the camp came just after lunch of the fourteenth day. He had spent the morning field stripping and reassembling all the weapons to which he had been introduced. He had finished his lunch and set the small tray on the table when The Beast and The Doctor entered his tent, the Doctor holding what Michel knew to be a black bag that would serve as a hood.

"Look," Michel said standing and facing the two men. "I can live with the hood. I understand you don't want me to know where we are, but I don't want the needle again."

"We don't have a needle with us," the Doctor said.

"Good," Michel said.

"Now get dressed in your clothes," the Doctor instructed and Michel complied. The Doctor stepped forward and put the bag over Michel's head and then took an arm and started guiding him toward the tent's flap just as Michel started to feel warm all over.

"What," he stammered, "you said..."

"It wasn't a needle," the Doctor said, "It was in the food."

***

When Michel woke up, he didn't move a few minutes, trying to determine where he was. He was sitting in a chair, his upper torso, head and arms on a flat surface. A table, a wooden table by the feel of things. He opened his eyes and saw blackness, and then gradually the blackness grew lighter although not by much. Then he knew where he was: the Corzo de Cantina. Slowly he sat up and saw two men standing, backs leaning against the bar and facing him: The Beast and The Doctor. The latter came to him.

"How do you feel?"

"Better than the last time."

"Good, you didn't have as much."

Looking at his watch, Michel knew he had been out for just over three hours.

"How long have I been here," he asked.

The Doctor smiled. "A while."

Something was put on the table in front of him and something else on the floor beside him. The first was his computer bag and the second his carry-on. From outside, a car horn blew three short blasts.

"Your taxi's here," The Doctor said.

"Taxi?"

"Yes, it will take you to the hotel."

Michel stood up, wavered a bit and then steadied. He picked up the computer bag and his carry-on. As he turned toward the door, The Doctor opened it and held it for him. Outside was a dirty yellow taxi, back door open.

"The fare has been paid as has the hotel for two nights. You will get instructions tomorrow," The Doctor said and Michel stepped through the door. It shut behind him and he heard a bolt being slammed. Looking around he saw that the street was basically deserted, just as it had been when he had arrived two weeks before.

"¿Vienes, señor? (Are you coming, sir?)" the taxi driver asked. Michel slid the carry-on on the seat, got in holding the computer bag and the taxi started moving before he had the door closed.

Chapter 18

The Phantom Mirage Air Hawk F-20 Assault Jet screamed across the Caribbean virtually just inches above the crests of the waves. The stealth jet was so new that very few knew about it. It was so new, so advanced, that the pilot just had to sit there and watch the displays in case something happened. Michel Villar had managed to sneak onto the top security French base on St. Martin and stun the French pilot who was preparing for a re-connaissance flight. Dressed in the pilot's all encompassing gear no one could tell who he was, and he had gotten into the aircraft and entered the coordinates of the target. As the jet reached the coastline, its nose raised so that it could clear the sand dunes. Then the target came into sight – a big hanger type building on property surrounded by twelve-foot chain link fences topped with razor wire, electrified and watched with security cameras.

Michel Villar could see five men standing in a row in the open doorway of the building. Numbers 1,2,4 and 5 were dressed in black from head to foot and wore sophisticated helmets with a multitude of modern electronics gear attached. They had bulletproof vests and formidable looking assault rifles held in their hands. The man in the center (number 3) was dressed all in white to match his sun-bleached white hair. A head shorter than any of the other four, he was smoking a stogie so large it looked like he had trouble holding it in his mouth. Michel Villar had only a fleeting second to make this observation before he felt the jet shudder twice as two air-to-ground missiles were released. No sooner had that happened than the jet tilted left and started climbing. Michel watched as suddenly the quintet of watchers realized what was happening as the two missiles streaked toward them, but it was too late. Just as they started to scatter the missiles struck the hanger wall, one on either side of the door and exploded, completely obliterating the barn. Michel Villar began to laugh maniacally: *Michel Villar 15, Stuart Andrews 0.* He was laughing so hard that the plane was shaking.

Suddenly he realized that the plane was not shaking from his laughter, but because it had been hit either by shrapnel particles from the building or from a ground-to-air defense missile that Beecher McFalls had installed. Lights were flashing on the console, bells were ringing, and smoke was filling the cockpit. Suddenly the canopy was blown off and one second later a second explosion lifted him and his encompassing seat out of the aircraft. A hundred feet above the jet at the apex of his trajectory, he was forcefully separated from the seat and a few seconds later his parachute opened. He knew that he wasn't very far from the ground and looked down to see that he was going to land in the middle of the burning inferno that had been the hanger.

He was startled to see that in the middle of that inferno, still dressed in impeccably clean white, holding the biggest assault rifle that Michel Villar had ever seen and still smoking the immense stogie was Beecher McFalls. His landing was rough and he found himself on his back. Struggling to rise, he was forcefully thrust back to the ground by the shining white boot of Beecher McFalls. Michel Villar found himself staring down the muzzle of the assault rifle behind which was the smiling face of Beecher McFalls. Yellow teeth clenching the stogie, McFalls snarled at him. "Wrong, asshole. The score is McFalls 1, Villar 0. Game over." And in ultra slow motion Michel Villar saw the expulsion of explosive air starting the bullet's flight and watched it proceed down the rifle's barrel toward the middle of his forehead. He heard someone screaming but didn't know who it was.

***

Then he realized it was he, sitting up in his bed, sweat dripping from his face, his boxer shorts drenched as were the bed's sheets. When he had been on St. Martin looking for the Bastons, he had spent several fruitless days surveying the stronghold of Beecher McFalls before deciding that an incursion by him alone would not work. It was too well defended. It would take Seal Team Six or an air strike. Obviously the latter became the foundation for his nightmare.

Chapter 19

"Good morning, Father," the passport control agent at Miami International Airport said, looking up as a passport and customs declaration card became visible in front of him.

The person holding the articles was wearing the stiff white collar, dark vest and a coat one associates with a Roman Catholic priest. Even the black brimmed hat perched atop a bald pate testified to the accuracy of his statement. That face belied that association though with several weeks' growth of beard and a gauze pad taped over the man's left eye.

"Good morning to you, sir," the man said, "But 'Father' is not an appropriate title. I am an Anglican minister. That's Church of England if you are not familiar with the term."

"I am," the agent said, opening the passport to the picture page. "Ralph Fletcher" was the name, and under title was "Rev." "Reverend Fletcher."

"Yes."

The agent pointed at the eye.

"What happened? Look through the wrong keyhole," the agent said smiling.

"Would have been better. I've been helping to build a church in a small Columbian village and some

... uhh ... inconsiderate person hit me in the eye with a two-by-four."

"Ouch," the agent said.

"Definitely," The Reverend said.

"Traveling through?"

"Yes, a brief stay in New York to visit my brother and an ophthalmologist and then home to York."

The agent ran the picture page through a bar code reader and compared the picture that appeared on the screen with the visage in front of him. Then he inked a rubber stamp, flipped through the passport to a page where there was space and left an imprint.

"Enjoy your stay, Reverend," the agent said handing the passport and customs declaration back to him.

"I will," the man said taking the passport.

***

When Michel Villar had reached the hotel in Cartagena two days before, he had been given an envelope by the clerk. Once in his room he shed his clothes and headed for the shower, standing and soaking for a long time trying to wash off two weeks of dirt, grime and perspiration. While at the camp he had not bathed or shaved and had not been provided with deodorant. *I smell like a pig,* he thought as he had stepped into the shower. After toweling off, he put on the complimentary bathrobe and went to get his razor out of his carry-on. As he unzipped the bag, he saw the envelope he had been given. He had dropped it on the bed as he headed for his cleansing ritual in the bathroom. There was his name – or at least the one he had been using – and under it "<u>IMPORTANTE</u>". He turned to go back to the bathroom and then stopped, returned to the bed and picked up the envelope. Ripping it open he read, "DO NOT SHAVE. You need the beard to help to match the picture on the passport you will be using. Be ready to leave the hotel at 8:00 a.m. the morning after tomorrow."

***

At 5:00 p.m. the next day, a box was delivered to his room. In it were the clothes he was wearing at Miami International Airport. When he left the hotel shortly before 8:00 a.m. the next morning, he was met by The Doctor who gave him last minute instructions on the way to the airport in a taxi.

Michel Villar followed the signs to baggage claim and waited with others for his bag to show. Soon two almost identical aluminum suitcases came on the belt. Michel looked at each one carefully, finally choosing the one that had an orange sticker on the handle. He picked it up and headed in the direction of the arrow indicating "Customs/Exit." After several steps his passport slipped from his hand and he stopped to pick it up, at the same time removing the orange tag from the suitcase handle. That went into the next waste can. As he neared the customs queue at the second kiosk, there was a disturbance two or three queues away – shouting and a dog barking. The border patrol canine handler who was having his dog sniff bags for contraband immediately turned and went toward the disturbance. Because the customs kiosk line was for people having nothing to declare, it went quickly and Michel was through and gone by the time the dog and his handler came back.

Once into the public area, Michel saw a Latino dressed in chauffeur's livery holding a sign that said, "R. Fletcher." The man took Michel's suitcase and led him outside into a parking lot where a black sedan was parked. Instead of putting the suitcase in the trunk, he put it on the back seat. As the sedan pulled away from the airport, Michel took off his clothes, opened a Dopp Kit on the seat and pulled out a white cloth that he put around his neck. Using a battery powered beard trimmer and mirror from the Dopp Kit, he trimmed his beard as short as he could, then used a battery-powered electric razor to complete his shave, leaving a goatee and mustache. After brushing all the loose hair he could onto the cloth, he removed and folded it, placing it into the Dopp Kit. Selecting a plastic zip lock bag from the Dopp Kit, he opened it and took out a wet washcloth he used to wipe his face, removing the last of the errant hair. The washcloth went back into plastic bag and that back into the Dopp Kit. Then he dressed in his own clothes from the carry-on. Once changed, he turned the suitcase so that the combination lock was on the bottom, and turned the combination to 432. Opening the suitcase, female clothing spilled out. "Obviously the wrong suitcase," Michel muttered. Then he pulled one of the straps that should have held clothes in place and the inside to the lid came up revealing stacks of American currency – over five hundred thousand dollars he had been told. He knew that on the other half of the suitcase, cutting the "lining" would have revealed several kilos of pure Columbian heroin. The disturbance at customs had been staged so that the canine could not get a whiff of the drugs although Michel had been promised that it couldn't. If he had been stopped and asked to open the suitcase, his combination of 586 wouldn't have worked. If it had been forced open, Michel could honestly claim, "That's not mine! I'm not a cross dresser. I must have grabbed the wrong suitcase." He hadn't but the one he had checked was the one that was still revolving on the carousel and would until some airport employee removed it. Had he had to do so, the combination of 586 would have opened that one and clothes in his size would have backed up his assertion about the wrong suitcase.

However, that one wouldn't be claimed and would end up in lost and found. He would have just hoped that his disguise would hold up under the closer scrutiny that would have come with the discovery of the contraband.

The passport he had used would be returned to its owner who was in fact helping to build a church in a rural Columbian village and had no idea that his passport left Columbia without him.

***

After stowing the money in his carry-on, he put the clothing, both female and ecclesiastical, into the suitcase along with the passport and the Dopp Kit, closed the lid and set the combination to 666 as agreed. Then he told the driver he was ready. The suitcase would be taken to its final destination by the driver after dropping him off.

In fifteen minutes he was let out in front of a hotel in downtown Ft. Lauderdale, far away from Miami International where he had arrived. He would meet his contact, pass him the money and be done with Don Giovanni. Or at least he hoped so. Then he could get to work on his own projects: first the *Zàkpa* and then Stuart's former business.

PART III
DIVE, DIVE

Chapter 20

"It was stupid. I should have checked."

"You did check," Beecher McFalls countered. "We both read the obituary. His place was sold immediately."

"But a friend, someone close, could have come in just after I left."

"You said his pupils were fixed and dilated, didn't you?"

"Yes," I replied.

"Then it was over," Beecher McFalls said. "I've used it once or twice and at that point just minutes remained."

"Maybe it was faulty."

"No way."

"No antidote?"

"Not that I know of."

"Still if someone had come in …"

"Daws, quit browbeating yourself and second guessing. How long had you been conducting surveillance?"

"Two weeks."

"Any friends, the sleepover kind?"

"No, but …"

"Any visitors?"

"No, he was solitary. Dined alone. Did everything alone … except for his language lesson."

"You asked?"

"Twice, in different restaurants. I asked if that could be an old friend of mine's husband. I was told that he had been dining alone. Never a companion."

"Well, there you have it."

"Still ... I think it is best not to take chances."

"It's your call ... your dollar."

"Yes, take Quentin and his family to a safe house for a few weeks until I can run a thorough check. He'll object. Want to stay but pull him out. Tell him Josef insists. After all, I am godfather to his son."

"Will do."

"And don't tell me where they are."

"Of course."

"And watch your back."

"Always do. If you're correct, you're the one in danger."

"I will be, but not immediately."

"Why do you say that?"

"Look at the first two hits. Things associated with me or with Michel in a negative way. The yacht was mine. That was indeed intended as a message to me. R.I.P. Zàkpa. That was a message for me."

"Yeah, could be but it was so iffy."

"True but eventually the yacht would be missing. It would make the press and the connection would be made. Either by me or with a little help."

"And the explosions?"

"The lawyer who was after Villar defended the wife of the man who founded that firm, Stuart Andrews. Michel Villar was the judge and that is why he was a target."

"But not why you went after Villar?"

"No."

Beecher McFalls had never questioned my motivation. He knew that somehow Villar and I were both mixed up in something involving Pieter Devenpeck.

"Villar tried to steal money from Devenpeck." *Successfully,* I added to myself. "But he wasn't satisfied and came after my money. That's why I had to stop him."

True in part but he also knew who I truly am and would reveal that in order to further his own ends.

I am Stuart Andrews. I didn't die in the drowning that was the reason for that trial, and I didn't commit suicide like my wife Elise and her brother Howard tried to convince people. I survived the drowning attempt after sixteen hours in the Caribbean and found refuge in The House at the End of the Road, which I later bought and then had to destroy when invaded by the "Circle of Brothers." Then I, using funds and an identity unknown to either of the two conspirators (I don't count Keith Mitchell, the guy Howard got to help him with the lure of money), I exacted my vengeance. Michel Villar knew about me through his association with Juliet Mills, a Los Angeles police lieutenant who was in charge of the investigation into the suicide of Keith Mitchell. It was an actual suicide aided by my veiled threat of public death by guillotine on St. Nantes. Lt. Juliet Mills was a witness in the trial and gave Michel Villar a picture that I had inadvertently left at the suicide scene. It was of the dock area in Genivee from which we had left on that fishing excursion and on the back I had written:

Four went out. Three came back.
We know what happened.

I had mailed it to Keith Mitchell and neglected to retrieve it when I left. Michel Villar had given it to me after the trial when he came to the Zàkpa. With it he imparted the knowledge that he knew who I was. That was the threat he hung over my head when he came seeking my help to escape assassination by a group he called *Cercle des Frères*, Circle of Brothers. Supposedly it was a secret French mafia for whom he was the monetary front. In fact, he was handling funds for Pieter Devenpeck's nameless Dutch group and had hired me to launder money for him. When he came for help, he told me that I could be tried for murder because I had been the reason that Elise and Howard were hung. I wasn't dead and I hadn't stepped forward. In fact, I had attended every day of the trial in the guise of a reporter for a Sierra Leone newspaper. When I learned of Michel Villar's role in everything, I had no choice but to silence him because he would do the same to me. So I had tried and apparently failed and now he was after me and everything that I hold dear. I am going to do my best to stop him and this time, I'll make certain that he is dead.

Chapter 21

The most difficult part of what lay ahead – or, at least the most immediate difficult part – was going to be parting with Tres. Actually getting her to accept parting. I knew she would resist because it was the only sensible thing to do. There was our child to think of.

Lost in my musing, I almost missed that almost imperceptible sound behind me. Trying not to show that I had heard, I started moving my right hand toward the Sig Sauer I had placed on the desk. Almost instantaneously I felt arms going around my neck. I knew those arms. I knew the feel and I relaxed.

"What is so interesting that you have to get up in the middle of the night?" Tres whispered sexily into my ear. Treshauna Lee Jones had come into my life shortly after my return to St. Nantes. I had injured an ankle in a jogging accident and gone to the emergency room in case it was more than sprained. She had been one of the nurses who were involved in my treatment and, I thought stupidly at the time, I had made a pass at her. She must have accepted the pass because she basically followed me home and took me to bed – I didn't protest too much.

I didn't say anything and sensed she was reading the article about the explosion that was on the screen.

"What happened?" she asked.

I paged back to the article about the *Seventh Heaven.*

"Oh, no!" she said standing up, her arms leaving my neck. "But you killed him."

I swiveled around in my chair to face her. She had put on a tee shirt to cover herself although there was no need. She had a hand to her mouth.

"I thought he was dead. But obviously not. Either that or someone is exacting revenge on his behalf."

"But..." I sensed her mind racing. "The only person it could be is Guillaume Martineau and he's dead. Isn't he?"

I had wondered that same thing. The last time I saw Guillaume Martineau, he was racing away from me in his small yacht, more a small cabin cruiser, after I, with the help of Beecher McFalls, had rescued Quentin's son (my godson) Pay-Koo from his clutches. I had exploded a bomb affixed to the hull of Guillaume Martineau's boat by Beecher McFalls. By all rights he should be dead. I had already discounted him in my thoughts.

"Yes, of that I am certain." I noticed her staring at me. I knew she wanted to say, "You said that Michel Villar was dead also."

"I saw the boat blow up. I could see him at the wheel. My eyes never left him."

"I know. It's just..."

"WHAT?" I found myself screaming. "IT'S MY FAULT THAT AT LEAST SEVENTEEN INNOCENT PEOPLE ARE DEAD!" I partially regained control of myself. "I should have stayed there to be certain he was dead."

Tres stepped forward putting her arms around my neck, her breasts pressed against my naked chest. I could feel the heat through the thin material of the tee shirt.

"And what would you have done if someone had walked in?"

I didn't say anything.

"Would you have killed them?"

"I don't..."

"Well, you couldn't have said, 'As soon as I know he's dead, I'll leave.' They would have seen you. They would call the police and the manhunt would be on – again."

I shook my head. "I don't know. I'm not a murderer."

Tres looked at me questioningly.

"I killed in self-defense. Those men who invaded our house. That was self-defense."

She continued looking at me.

"I didn't kill Richard Barton. He fell overboard and the sharks got him." Richard Barton had kidnapped Tres because she had turned him into the medical board for raping her and ended his medical career. He was going to throw her to the very sharks that ate him.

Tres still looked at me.

"The Facilitator died of a heart attack. You were there." He had been a hit man whom Michel Villar claimed to have used in his capacity within the non-existent cartel he called "Cercle des Frères" or Circle of Brothers. His real name was Fredek Gavrilovich Kondrashin and he had accepted a contract to kill Michel Villar. That is what brought Michel to me in The House at The End of the Road on St. Nantes and had led Tres and I to where we were now, although it had not been an easy road.

Tres hadn't said a word.

"Phil Dombrey killed himself. Yes, he was coerced into it by Guillaume Martineau on behalf of Michel Villar. And yes, that was the same way in which Keith Mitchell's life ended, but I did the coercing. And before you say another word, I know that Michel Villar, speaking as a lawyer and a judge, said that I was guilty of killing Elise and Howard. Okay, if that's true it was murder. But, damn it, I would do it all again."

Tres grabbed me and held me tight as I did her and we stood there for a few minutes. Then she leaned her head back and I looked down at her smiling face, tears streaming down her cheeks.

"I would too," she said and hand-in-hand we walked up to our bedroom. It was mid-morning when a taxi came and collected her and our child. She knew where she was going – I didn't. When I felt the need or felt that it was safe, I would use our prearranged drop box and let her know. Until then there was to be no contact.

Two hours later, carrying a small bag and a computer case, I left our home, the security system on high alert and woe to the miscreant who entered without both codes.

Chapter 22

"Good morning, Madame Baston." The two men at the door were big. Broad shoulders, close cropped haircuts, muscular arms showing from the tight sleeves of black tee shirts tight across muscular chests. They wore black pants with many pockets and shiny black boots. She suspected that there was a weapon in at least one pocket.

"Who are you?" she asked, suddenly fearful.

"We're friends. Beecher McFalls sent us."

"How do I know that?"

The First Man handed her a smart phone. "Press call."

She did and heard a friendly voice. "Jośef?"

"Yes, hello, Celesse. Are you with Beecher's men?"

"They say they are, but how do I know."

"Ask them for the password. They should say 'Alpine chalet'."

She looked at the man and motioned to the other, who was further away and would have had less chance to hear. He stepped forward and the other stepped back looking from side to side.

"What is the password?" she asked.

"Alpine chalet," The Second Man answered.

"Okay. Just a minute." Then into the phone, "Yes, it's them. What's the problem?"

"Precaution – at least for right now. Just do what they say. Don't ask any questions."

"We thought this was over. You said it was."

"Yes, I did. And I am sorry. As I said, this is just a precaution. You will be taken care of. You and Quentin and the children need to get away for a few days."

"A few days?"

"I hope so. I'm sorry to uproot your family like this, but it is important."

"If you say so," Celesse responded not sounding very convinced.

"Celesse, have I ever lied to you?"

"No. But ..."

"Remember when I had to take Quentin away for safety?"

"Yes."

"It's like that again. Please, do what the men want. Do not argue. Time could be of the essence."

"Very well, Jośef."

"Thank you. We will talk in a few days."

Celesse gave the phone back to First Man who had stepped forward. Second Man had stepped back, looking, watching.

"Where is Quentin?" First Man asked.

"He's got a client. They're fishing."

"One client?"

"Yes."

"Where are the children?"

"In school, except for little Quentin. He has a cold."

"Let's get him now."

First Man followed her into the house where the child was playing.

"There is no time to waste. Get him and come with me."

"But clothes, …"

"Everything will be provided. Please hurry."

Celesse picked little Quentin up.

"Qui est l'homme, maman? (Who is the man, mommy?)" the boy asked.

"Un ami. Nous allons en voyage." (A friend. We are going on a trip.)

They hustled out the front door and First Man closed it behind them. There was a van sitting at the street and the two men got her and little Quentin inside and then Second Man got in back with her and First Man in front. There was a Third Man driving. There was a car seat for little Quentin and Celesse buckled him in.

"The school." The First Man said.

He turned so that he could see Celesse.

"Do you know anything about this client?"

"No. I think he's been with Quentin before but I don't know."

"Where were they going?"

"Deep sea fishing – I don't know where exactly. He didn't say."

"Is there any other fisherman – a friend – you know who isn't fishing today?"

"Patrick Laplace. His motor needs work. Quentin helped him with it yesterday."

The man used his iPhone.

"Get Patrick Laplace." was all he said.

At the children's school, Celesse went in and went to see the schoolmistress.

"We have a family emergency. I need Marie and Pierre," she told her. Together they walked to the classroom where Marie was and the schoolmistress went in. She talked to the teacher and then returned with Marie.

"What's wrong, mommy. Is daddy okay?"

"Yes, he's fine but we have to go away for a few days," Celesse explained as they walked towards Pierre's classroom. The schoolmistress looked at her rather strangely hearing this explanation, when "grandmother is really ill" or something similar was expected. After Pierre was brought out of the classroom, the three of them hurried to the van where Second Man helped them inside. The schoolmistress watched them get in the van and drive off. *Strange men in black,* she thought. *That's suspicious. Maybe I should call the gendarmes.* But just then another teacher called to her and, in a few moments, the thought was forgotten.

***

The van bearing the Bastons drove to the airport where a helicopter waited. There was another man in black standing outside looking very guard-like. When the van pulled up, the fourth man got into the helicopter pilot's seat.

The four of them were helped into the helicopter. Second Man brought the car seat for little Quentin. She was surprised to see Patrick Laplace seated inside.

"What is the problem?" Patrick asked in French. "They say that Quentin is in trouble. Again?"

"No, not trouble, Patrick. Danger," Celesse replied in French.

"Danger. Am I also? I don't..."

"No," interrupted the First Man also in French. "You are in no danger. We need to get Quentin off his boat and away from St. Nantes. We need you to take care of the boat and the client."

"But how would I …"

"Ever been lowered from a helicopter in a sling?"

"No. This is my first time in a helicopter. I have never been in a plane before."

"Well, there are going to be a lot of firsts today then."

The engines of the helicopter started and the noise grew loud. The First Man gave earphones to Celesse and Patrick Laplace.

"We will contact your husband by radio when we are close," First Man explained. "He knows a code we will use so he will know we are coming and he can tell us if he is in danger."

"What if he is in danger?" Celesse asked.

First Man pointed toward Second Man who had gotten into a harness with a strap fastened to the side of the helicopter. He was holding an M24 (Sniper Weapon System or SWS).

"He won't be for long," First Man said.

The helicopter lifted off.

"Monsieur Laplace."

"Yes."

"Where would Quentin be today?"

"He told me he was going north."

"Good."

As soon as Patrick had said that, the helicopter turned as it rose and the whine of the rotors increased as the helicopter headed north. In a few minutes, Celesse and Patrick Laplace heard, "Signal acquired. Distance fifteen miles."

In the cockpit, the pilot made a call on the helicopter's radio. Both Patrick and Celesse could hear the conversation.

"*Renaissance, Renaissance*. This is St. Nantes Weather."

He waited.

"*Renaissance, Renaissance*. This is St. Nantes Weather."

"*Renaissance* here."

"Possible wind gusts of 45 knots from the northeast corridor."

"Yes, that was predicted," came Quentin's answer after a slight pause.

"That's good," First Man said as he cut off the rest of the conversation to talk to Celesse and Patrick. "If he felt he was in trouble he would have said, 'That's not good.' Everything will be fine. We'll be there in ten minutes."

Celesse shook her head. So many things Quentin knew that he didn't tell her. But then, she admitted, if she had known there was a code like that, she would have worried.

Aboard the *Renaissance*, Quentin put down the microphone. His client Gustav Schmidt asked, "Is there bad weather? Are we in danger?"

"No, all eez well but there eez some difficulty. I am zorry for the inconvenience but I have to leave."

"Leave? Here in the middle of the Caribbean?"

"Yez," and Quentin tried to explain. "There eez a helicopter coming. A man will come down. I will go up. Another fisherman, Patrick Laplace. He eez my friend.

He eez a good fisherman. He will come down and finish the fishing with you. There eez no charge. You will catch fish just like with me."

In fact, they had already caught two Mahi Mahi.

Soon they heard the helicopter and could see it coming from the south. The sea was a little rough so Quentin had to keep the boat moving. The helicopter took position above the *Renaissance* and Quentin put the boat on autopilot. Looking up, Gustav Schmidt could see a man in black leaning out of the door. The man stepped out and was hanging from a cable suspended from a metal rod that extended from the door. The man was lowered down and as he neared the deck, both Quentin and Gustav grabbed him. First Man slipped out of the sling and put it over Quentin's head. Quentin thrust his arms through and the sling settled under his armpits, the cable rising up in front of him.

"Ever done this before?" First Man asked.

"Non," Quentin replied.

"Just hang on tight," First Man said.

He made a circular motion with his hand and Quentin started toward the helicopter. When he was hanging just below the winch arm, a man's arm reached out and grabbed the sling and pulled Quentin into the helicopter's door.

"Zat was fun!" Quentin said. Turning to Patrick Laplace he said, "Thank you, Patrick. I am sorry I cannot help you fix your motor."

"C'est la vie," Patrick said as the sling was put over his head.

"Just relax," Second Man said.

"I don't like high places," Patrick Laplace said.

"Close your eyes. Don't look down."

Patrick felt himself being dragged toward the door but didn't fight. At the doorway, Second Man grabbed the sling and said, "Just step out. Don't look down."

Patrick closed his eyes and stepped out. There was a slight jerk as his body settled into the sling. He opened his eyes and saw Second Man in the helicopter. He was pointing his thumb down indicating he was going to start lowering him, and Patrick looked down instinctively. Below were the *Renaissance* and two men, First Man and Gustav Schmidt. He was happy to discover that he did not have a sense of height and looked back to tell Second Man he was ready only to discover that he had already been lowered ten feet.

He looked down at the *Renaissance* and soon was in the grasp of Gustav Schmidt and First Man.

"I want to try that," Gustav Schmidt said.

"Not today," First Man said, removing the sling from Patrick Laplace.

"This is Patrick Laplace," First Man said to Gustav Schmidt as he slipped the sling over his own head and under his arms. "He'll be finishing the fishing today. Taut lines." And he disappeared into the air. Soon he was dangling below the helicopter as it made a wide turn and headed west toward St. Martin. First Man quickly disappeared into the helicopter.

"Wow," Gustav Schmidt. "That was something. Wait 'til ..."

"Fish on," Patrick Laplace yelled and grabbed a rod.

Chapter 23

During the forty-minute flight to St. Martin, the children were all atwitter, enjoying the ride, wanting to know where they were going – why they were going was not important. It was a vacation. A break from school. They liked school, but like most children they were always happy to get a break. Just like a snow day for children in North America.

Like their children, Celesse and Quentin wanted to know where they were going, but First Man couldn't tell them because he didn't know. All he knew was that they were to retrieve this family from St. Nantes and take them to St. Martin. Even if he had known he wouldn't have told them because they couldn't know until they got there. Once in the helicopter they had given him everything in their pockets. They were virtually being reborn.

The children watched the helicopter land at the airport on St. Martin chattering with excitement. Quentin, being only three and not feeling well, had fallen asleep and was being held by Celesse. When the rotors had stopped turning, First Man and Second Man helped them out of the helicopter. Second Man carried little Quentin in the car seat. No sooner were they on the tarmac than a minibus drove up with Beecher McFalls at the wheel.

"Welcome to St. Martin," he said as they were helped in by First Man and Second Man who transferred the car seat bearing Little Quentin. "Your stay will be brief. That plane is ready to take off."

"Plane?" said Celesse and Quentin, while the two children clapped in excitement. It was a short run to where a private jet sat waiting.

"This is the plane?" Celesse asked.

"Yes," Beecher said. "Your personal home for the next few hours."

"But we can't afford this."

"You don't have to," Beecher explained. "Your friend has taken care of everything."

The two children ran up the steps of the plane followed by Second Man bearing the car seat with Little Quentin. They were welcomed by a young black man wearing a short-sleeved white shirt with a navy blue tie and trousers.

"Sit wherever you want," he told them indicating ten seats, all luxurious. They both selected window seats.

Celesse was next on the plane and she looked at the luxurious interior and shook her head in wonder. When Quentin saw it he just laughed.

"Ah, zat Joṡef. He eez a man of miracles."

"He is a man with money," Celesse said.

"My name is Guillaume," the young black man said. "I am your host for your flight. Please take a seat and buckle up, we are ready to depart."

"For where?" Quentin asked.

"I don't know," Guillaume said. "We will all find out together."

After takeoff, Guillaume consulted with Celesse and Quentin as to clothes sizes for everyone and then went to the cockpit. During the flight there were movies to be watched on individual screens in each seat and video games that could be played. Guillaume was around serving drinks, snacks and meals.

Time passed quickly and comfortably and day turned into late afternoon. When the pilot announced that they would be landing soon, Guillaume arrived with passports.

"These are French passports. They are only a formality. Where you are going, you will be alone – in a guarded facility – so you won't need to use the names on the passports."

"Are we prisoners?" Celesse asked.

"No," Guillaume said. "You can leave the facility at any time if you so wish but you will be accompanied by a guard if you do. Everything will be supplied at the facility."

"How long will we be there?" Quentin asked.

"I don't have an answer to that," Guillaume said. "Maybe someone at the facility does. I also have been instructed to tell you not to say anything to anyone until you get to the facility. Someone there will answer all your questions."

When the plane landed, it taxied to a private hanger. An official came on board, stamped the passports and wished them a good stay. They deplaned with Guillaume carrying the car seat with Quentin in it to a waiting van that all got in. Guillaume waved good-bye as the van departed and then returned to the plane, which soon took off heading back to St. Martin. The Bastons were driven for an hour, finally arriving at a walled compound with an iron gate attended by an armed man in a little hut. The driver stopped at the gate, the guard looked into the van and then opened the gate and the van drove through and up to a ranch house.

A short fat dark-skinned woman dressed in a white dress with a navy blue jacket and a tall light-skinned man wearing white slacks and shirt topped with a navy blue jacket came out to greet them. A man dressed in navy blue shirt and pants with a holstered pistol stood by the door.

"Welcome to Hacienda del Costa," the woman said. "Oh, what beautiful children. Oh, and the little one is so cute. Please, we know you are tired. You probably want to go to bed. Here it is early but for you it is late. Please let me show you to your rooms."

"Where are we?" Celesse asked.

"Why? Didn't I say," said the woman. "The Hacienda del Costa."

"Yes, yes, I know that," Celesse said a bit perturbed. "But in what country?"

The woman looked at the man who nodded.

"Why, Costa Rica! Didn't you know?"

Chapter 24

Life at their "private resort" was good for the Bastons. They were the only "guests" there and pretty much had the run of the place. There was the main house where they took their meals. In the house, in addition to housing for the staff, were a game room, library, and indoor pool. The last was welcome on rainy days, but there hadn't been many. Meals were quite enjoyable in their "private" dining room. Breakfast and lunch were buffet style and within a day or two entirely directed to their wants. At breakfast Celesse and Quentin were presented with menus for the sit-down evening meal and they made their choices then.

There were six bungalows between the main house and the beach, three on each side of a grassy area where the kids could play. In back of the bungalows was about fifty feet of low landscaped lawn area before a twelve-foot adobe wall topped with three strands of razor wire. But the wire was more than that: each strand was attached to a sensor so that when disturbed, an alarm would sound and lights would illuminate the entire compound and fifteen to twenty feet of clear ground outside the walls. The walls ran to the beach where a chain link fence replaced the adobe and ran to the water's edge. Beyond that the Bastons didn't know what was there, but they knew something was other than the line of buoys that marked the designated swimming area.

Their bungalow was the middle one on the right-hand side as you exited the main house heading for the water. It was therefore isolated and quiet. The kids spent most of the day on the beach or in the game room. There was no web connection, no phones, and no cell phones (for the guests). In that respect, they were isolated. If they needed something, it would be provided. They were not permitted to leave the premises although they had been told differently before they arrived. The children didn't mind. It was a wonderful vacation. But both Celesse and Quentin were getting antsy by the middle of the second week. Quentin had taken to surf fishing, but he really longed to be out on the water. He had requested a boat so he could go fishing and was told that would be considered, but there had been no response.

The security detail was virtually invisible. When they were on the beach there was a man on either side at the end of the wall but they didn't intrude. They just watched. At dusk lights came on inside the compound lighting the area between the rows of bungalows and armed guards walked the interior perimeter.

Ordinarily the Bastons stayed in the main house after dinner with the kids all playing video games on the computers, Celesse reading and Quentin watching television, usually a fishing show, but occasionally the two of them watched a movie. There was a large collection of DVDs from which to choose and to either watch there or take to their bungalow. It was usually dark and the lights were on when they made their way back to the bungalow. Then the children were put to bed and their parents enjoyed a little quiet time before they also went to bed.

It was near the end of the second week when things changed, but nobody within the compound noticed. It was an hour before dawn when a figure dressed in camouflage clothing and carrying a small backpack made his way through the woods outside the compound on the left side as one faced the water. The man had scouted both sides the previous two nights and had selected this side because of the one tree that could provide him a fairly comfortable vantage point from which to see into the compound. He scaled the tree careful not to leave any scuff marks and settled himself into his chosen bower. He secured himself to the trunk with a safety harness such as a hunter in a tree stand might use.

From the backpack he took camouflage netting that he draped over himself even though he felt that in his leafy bower he was virtually undetectable. *Can't be too safe*, he reasoned. Then he pulled a pair of high power digital binoculars and a small dish receiver from the backpack. The latter he secured to a branch, pointed it at the rear of the main house and placed a Bluetooth ear bud into his right ear. Then he settled himself back to wait and watch. He dozed off and was awakened by a buzzing that he quickly realized was the laughter of children. *How annoying,* he thought but quickly realized that was exactly what he was going to hear most of the day. The children were running from one of the bungalows on the far side of the compound. He could see a woman behind them. Using the binoculars, he ascertained that it was Celesse Baston. Hearing a door close, he moved the binoculars and spotted Quentin leaving the middle bungalow. Now he knew where they were stay-

ing and just had to watch to learn their routine and decide how he would take them out.

***

It was a long and boring day, with frequent cat-
naps as he learned the routine of the Bastons. He had
some energy bars in the backpack for sustenance and
several bottles of water. He was using a catheter bottle
for his urine and, just in case, wearing an adult diaper
although the thought of eliminating in that was not at all
pleasant. He was extremely careful not to drop any debris on the ground. He had already learned that the outside of the compound was not patrolled during the day
but he didn't know about nighttime and didn't want to
take a chance. He knew that he would have one shot at
them and had to make it good and guarantee a clean get-
away. There were other targets waiting for him somewhere. He would find them but after taking the first two
out so quickly and easily, he knew that the rest would be
more difficult. Most probably as the hunt went on, the
quarry would be more elusive and more prepared. That
made the game fun. The thought of this brought a sardonic smile to Michel Villar's lips. *Let the game begin –
oops*, he thought, *make that let the game continue.* The
score was Michel Villar 3, Stuart Andrews 0.

Chapter 25

Just eight days before Michel Villar brought his vendetta to St. Nantes the day after the Bastons had fled. Deciding to be bold and get the lay of the land quickly, he parked his rental car on the street in front of the Bastons. He had knocked on the door a second time when he heard a voice calling him, "Monsieur, monsieur. (Sir, sir.)" He turned and saw a fragile old crone standing on her stoop next door. She was wearing some kind of ragged wrinkled housedress. Her thin gray hair was pulled back into a bun. She obviously had osteoporosis and had both hands on a cane for support.

"Oui (yes)," Michel Villar responded.

"Ils ne sont pas domicile, (They are not home,)" the old crone said.

"Je peux le voir, (I can see that,)" said Michel Villar, and added silently *you old crone.*

"Non, non, (No, no,)" the old crone said shaking her head. "Je veux dire qu'ils sont partis loin (I mean they are gone away.)"

"Quelle? (When?)" Michel Villar asked.

"Hier, bien sûr. (Yesterday, of course.)"

Why "of course?" thought Michel Villar.

"Ils avaient été enlever! (They could have been abducted!)" the old crone said.

This tidbit of information sparked Michel Villar's interest and he walked to the old crone's house.

"Enlevé? (Abducted?)" he said.

"Oui, deux homes. Trois en fait. Un est resté dans le van. (Yes, two men. Actually three. One stayed in the van.)"

"Une van? (A van?)"

"Oui, les blancs, mais les hommes étaient noirs. (Yes, white but the men were black.)"

"Negros?"

"Non, Non. Ils étaient habillés en noir. Comme James Bond. (No, no. They were dressed in black. Like James Bond.) Ils sont venus et elle est allée avec eux prenant (They came and she went with them taking Pay-Koo.)"

Beecher McFalls, Michel Villar thought. "Pay-Koo?"

"Le petit garçon. (The little boy.) Quentin. Ils l'appellent Petit Quentin parce que son père est Quentin. (They call him Petit Quentin because his father is Quentin.) Pay- Koo (P.Q.) est son surnom. (Pay-Koo is his nickname.)"

"Qu'en est-il de Pierre et Marie (What about Pierre and Marie?)"

"Je suppose qu'ils sont allés trop. (I guess they're gone too.) Ils allaient à l'école, mais n'est pas venu domicile. (They went to school but didn't come home.)"

Spirited away by Beecher McFalls. That means Stuart knows.

"Qu'en est-il de Quentin? (What about Quentin?)"

"Je vous ai dit, que Celesse l'a emmené avec elle. (I told you, Celesse took him with her.)"

"Non, pas la (No, not the) ...," *brat* he wanted to say. "Pay-Koo. Son père (His father.)"

"Je ne sais pas. (I don't know.) Je pense qu'il est sorti au début mais n'est pas venu maison. (I think he went out early but didn't come home.)"

Michel Villar was livid. It was difficult to control his rage. He wanted to strangle the old crone with his bare hands but managed to control himself. He should have come here directly after bombing, but he was too weak. The drug that Stuart had used to try to kill him affected his stamina in addition to blinding him in one eye and affecting his leg, the one he broke when The Facilitator tried to kill him. He had needed to rest for a day – the day that the Bastons were saved. No other word would suffice.

"Je vous remercie, Madame. (Thank you, Madame,)" Michel Villar managed through clenched teeth. He turned and walked to his car. Settling himself behind the wheel, he closed his eyes and took several deep breaths. Feeling calm, he started the car and, sensing he was being watched, turned and saw the old crone watching him. He wanted to give her the finger, shout obscenities. But didn't. Instead he waved at her and drove away.

He decided that he might learn something from the marina where Quentin kept his boat and so he drove there. Quentin's boat was tied up and there were tarps covering some of the equipment. There was another fishing boat next to it. A man was standing on the dock and another on the boat and he could hear them talking.

"...Puis ils ont mis la sangle autor de moi et m'a balancé sur. (Then they put the sling around me and swung me out.)"

"Avez-vous été effrayé, Patrick? (Were you scared, Patrick?) Vous n'aimez pas les endroits élevés. (You don't like high places.)"

"Non, ... eh bien, oui. (No, ... well, yes.) Mais quand j'ai regardé vers le bas, j'ai découvert que je n'étais pas. (But when I looked down, I discovered I wasn't.) Donc ils m'abaissé jusqu'à la *Renaissance.* (So they lowered me down to the *Renaissance.*) Il y avait cet homme de l'hélicoptère il et l'homme Quentin avait prises de pêche. (There was this fellow from the helicopter there and the man Quentin had taken fishing.) Ils m'ont aidé dans l'écharpe et les collègues de l'hélicoptère remonta dans l'écharpe. (They helped me out of the sling and the fellow from the helicopter went back up in the sling.) Il n'était pas encore dans l'hélicoptère lorsqu'il a commencé à voler loin. (He wasn't even in the helicopter when it started flying away.)"

Intrigued, Michel Villar walked to the boat.

"Is that Quentin Baston you are talking about?" he asked the fisherman on the boat, speaking in English so that they would think he was a foreigner.

Patrick Laplace looked at him quizzically.

"And what business do you have with Quentin, monsieur?"

"He is supposed to take me fishing tomorrow," Michel Villar replied.

"Do not think that will be so," Patrick said. "He and his family have flown away."

"So I heard. In a helicopter you said?"

"Yes, a big helicopter. Like the military," Patrick said with a big smile on his face. "I got to fly in it. First time in a helicopter."

"Were there soldiers?"

"No, just men in black. But they had guns. One had a sniper gun."

"How did you know?" Michel Villar asked, trying to keep the conversation going and getting as much information as possible.

"It had a telescope on it," Patrick said as though his veracity had been questioned.

"Was his family with him?"

"Bien sûr! (Of course!) What man would fly away and leave his family behind?" Patrick said indignantly.

"I meant no offense. Just trying to determine if he will be here tomorrow for fishing."

"I don't think so. He didn't say but I got the impression that they were going to be gone for a while," Patrick said. "I can't take you tomorrow. My boat is still not running well." He turned to the other man. "Et toi, Louis? (What about you, Louis?)"

"Oui, I could," the other man said eagerly.

Michel Villar knew that he had to keep up appearances.

"Good. What time?"

"Is 9:00 bonne?

"Perfect," Michel Villar said. "Meet you here?"

"Yes, zat would be good."

They shook hands and Michel Villar walked away never looking back and having no intention of going fishing tomorrow or any other day. He was hunting, not fishing.

Chapter 26

After walking away from the two fishermen, Michel Villar was despondent. His quarry had escaped and by now were miles away in a safe house somewhere. It would be difficult to find out where. But he had time and money with which to buy information. But first he would need to find someone who had that information. Still that wouldn't relieve the sorrow he was feeling. Something was unfulfilled. He had come here to kill the Bastons. He had a good plan. He would go to the house and kill Celesse and the children unless he was fortunate enough to find Quentin at home. His plan was to get Quentin to write a note saying that he had become depressed after the time in the limelight of the trial and he would end it all. The note would have been left in the house. He would have taken Quentin out in Quentin's boat and killed him. Then he would have inflated a life raft and rowed back to the island. Now that plan was gone as far away as the quarry. Unless ... there was an alternative victim, one he had considered early in his planning and discarded as inconsequential, but now would suit his purposes to a T.

***

It was late when Huard Jubert arrived home. Francine would be upset because it was a special night – the 70th month anniversary of their meeting. Still the romance was there and he was glad. Despite his tardiness, he was certain that the evening would be a success. Dinner might be cold so to speak, but what was inside the box in his pocket would certainly set fires burning. He had thought long and hard about marriage and had finally decided that it was the correct thing to do. They had tried to have children, but had learned that it was not possible for Francine to conceive and the thought of adopting was not acceptable. He smiled to himself at the evening's prospects as he inserted his key into the lock but discovered upon turning it that the door was unlocked. Quite unusual because Francine was a security freak. Lock the car doors, lock the house, you can't be too safe despite the fact that crime on St. Nantes was virtually nonexistent.

Opening the door he stepped inside and called, "Francine, ma chérie, je suis domicile (Francine, my dear, I am home.)"

There was no answer. Strange. She had told him to be punctual that she had a big surprise planned. Maybe she was on the deck with wine – champagne – with which to start their celebration. All the better. He put his barrister's bag – a gift from Francine on their first year anniversary – on the table and headed for the deck. But then he noticed a light in the dining area and went there.

The light that he had seen was four candles – *A romantic candlelight dinner,* Huard thought. *Leave it to Francine.* Entering the room, he saw Francine was sitting in her normal seat facing the kitchen.

"Vous n'a pas répondu, mon amour. Ce qui... (You didn't answer, my love. What ...)

The look on her face, the fixed stare of her eyes made him look at the other end of the table. A stranger sat there. The man had a black beard and was wearing grey tinted glasses. His head was shaven. He had a half full champagne flute in his left hand and in his right was a pistol that was pointed at him.

"Good evening, Huard," the man said in English. "Please join us."

Francine looked at him, eyes wide open. She was terrified. It was then he noticed that her hands were taped together with duct tape.

"Who are you?" Huard stammered. "What do you want?"

"Right now, I want you to sit down," the man said, motioning with his pistol to a chair on the other side of the table. Huard moved sideways around the table never turning his back on the stranger. As he passed behind Francine he laid what he hoped was a reassuring hand on her shoulder, yet she seemed to shudder at his touch. As he moved he saw that the pistol never moved away from him. He looked to see where he was going and saw that there was a pair of flexi-cuffs sitting on the plate. He pulled the chair out and sat down.

"Now please, Huard. Be a good boy and put the flexi-cuffs on." This from the stranger. Huard looked at the man and saw that he was smiling. Despite the beard, it was a smile that he recognized.

"Sacre bleu. It can't be. You're dead!"

"Despite a few too many close brushes with death, I am very much alive."

"But why?"

In a calm voice, Michel Villar said, "Be a good boy and put the cuffs on, Huard."

Huard just looked at him. The pistol's aim had changed and was then pointing at Francine. For the first time Huard noticed the red dot, now in the middle of her forehead.

"PUT THE CUFFS ON NOW," Michel Villar practically screamed.

Huard complied, his face contorted in a combination of disdain and horror.

"Now tighten them," Michel Villar said.

"How?"

"With your teeth!"

Huard found the proper piece on one cuff, bit on it and pulled. Then he did the other one.

"What do you want?" Huard asked.

Michel Villar sat quietly for a moment composing himself and possibly thinking of what to say. The gun never wavered from its aim on Francine.

"What I want is to finish this excellent glass of champagne. Must be some kind of celebration," he said. "Then we are going to take a walk down to your boat and take a little ride."

He paused and took a sip of the champagne.

"When we are out far enough, you and your lovely paramour are going for a midnight swim. Sort of a marathon swim, from the boat to land."

"But that's suicide. We'll never survive."

Michel Villar smiled. "Stuart Andrews did."

Chapter 27

Huard looked at him with a look of incredibility.

"But Stuart Andrews is dead."

"Not unless he died in the last, oh, twenty-four hours or so."

Huard was stunned.

"Did you know that during the trial?"

Michel Villar smiled at him and nodded.

"But why? You let innocent people die!"

"THEY WERE NOT INNOCENT," Michel Villar screamed and then sat silently trying to compose himself. "They plotted and tried to kill Stuart Andrews. They were guilty of attempted murder and numerous other things with lesser penalties. But, as you well know, Monsieur Prosecuting Attorney, on St. Nantes attempted murder of that nature is punishable by death."

"Yes, that is one of the penalties, but there are lesser penalties depending upon the circumstances."

"Well, if they had been tried for attempted murder, they would have been found guilty, and I would have imposed the death sentence. They deserved it."

Michel Villar lifted his champagne flute in mock toast and drank, finishing it.

He put the flute down on the table and wiped his lips with the linen napkin, which he then folded and put on the table. Then, thinking better of it, he stuck it in his pocket. *A little trophy of the evening*, he thought.

"And now," he said rising and picking up the empty champagne flute, "it is time for our boat ride."

He motioned them both to rise and Huard did, a look of unmitigated hatred on his face. Francine, however, remained immobile.

"Get her up," Michel Villar said. "Carry her if you have to."

"Won't that raise the neighbors' suspicions?" Huard said.

"It might if anyone sees us. But I think that the lady can walk."

Huard went to Francine's chair and knelt down. She wouldn't look at him so he turned her face so that she was looking at him. "Je t'aime (I love you,)" he said and tears came streaming out of her eyes. He helped her to her feet and they walked to the glass door leading to the deck.

"It is very gallant of you to let the lady go first, but I would prefer that you preceded her," Michel Villar said. "Just remember that my pistol will go off at the slightest attempt by either of you to escape." With this statement, Michel Villar took a swig from the champagne bottle he had picked up from the table, holding it by the neck with the base of the flute against it. *No sense wasting a good vintage* had been his thought.

With Huard leading and Francine shuffling behind still weeping, the three started down the steep walkway to the dock. There were several boats belonging to nearby residents docked along with Huard's boat *Je suis la Mer* (*I am the Sea*). Michel Villar was extremely watchful of the two, trying to anticipate a break by Huard because he felt that Francine was too weepy. But in fact, neither of them did anything but it was

Michel Villar who, so intent on watching his hostages, didn't watch the path. So when his right foot was placed awry, his bad leg collapsed and he pitched forward into Francine virtually catapulting her into Huard.

If they had been alert, this would have been their chance to attempt an escape but Francine was too depressed to think rationally and Huard was blinded by his hatred for Michel Villar and his concern for the love of his life. Thus his first thought was of her, and he turned to her, helping her up. By then Michel Villar was up and the pistol once again aimed at Francine. His disappointment with the fall was not the fact that his leg had unexpectedly given out, but that he had dropped the champagne bottle and it had bounced and rolled off the path and now lay somewhere in the darkness, the neck of the bottle pointing downhill and permitting the effervescent vintage to pour onto the ground. He knew this because he could hear the gurgling. The flute had broken but fortunately he hadn't been cut.

"Nice try, you two," Michel Villar said surprised at his own jocularity. "Let's keep moving."

They made it to the dock and to Huard's boat before Huard remembered that he hadn't brought the keys. For a brief moment there was a faint glimmer of hope. Michel Villar seemed to recognize the cause of the slight hitch in his walk.

"Not to worry, Huard, I have the keys."

Hopes dashed, Huard helped Francine on the boat and they sat in the rear as indicated by Michel Villar. He then deftly wrapped their ankles in duct tape. Certain that they wouldn't get away, he started the engine, climbed up on the dock and undid the two lines and nimbly leapt back onto the *Je suis la Mer*. He landed solidly on his left leg first and then his right silently congratulating himself on his success. Skillfully maneuvering the boat away from the dock, he headed seaward showing no wake until he was far enough from land. Then he opened the engine full bore, enjoying the warm evening air as the breeze caused by the boat's motion whistled about his head. He ran for about half an hour going around the island then far seaward. There it would be unlikely that anyone would search for them, especially because the boat would be found in the water just off the dock.

When he was satisfied with the distance, he turned on one of the boat's spotlights illuminating the stern deck. Taking a small box cutter from his pocket, he cut the tape from Francine's ankles and hands, removing and pocketing it. Then he put the box cutter at Huard's feet and stepped back to the helm, pistol on him.

"Get the cutter and cut the tape on his ankles."

Francine crawled to the box cutter and sawed at the tape until it parted.

"Now throw the knife over board."

There was a small splash as she complied. Next he slid a pair of diagonal cutters over to her.

"Cut the flexi-cuffs and throw the cutters over the side." Again a small splash showed her compliance.

"Get the tape and the plastic and give them to me." He reached out his left hand, the pistol in his right pointed at her head. He put the tape and plastic cuffs into a pants pocket.

"Now it's time for your swim."

Silently the two got to their feet, relying on each other for support.

"Can we have just a moment?" Huard asked pleadingly.

"All right," Michel Villar said.

Huard reached into his pants pocket as he sank to one knee. He brought forth a box and opened it, showing her its contents. "Francine, veux-tu m'épouser (will you marry me?)"

Chapter 28

For the first time that evening, a smile broke forth on her face and for a fleeting instant she forgot the dilemma they were in. "Oui, oh oui," she said as he slipped the ring onto the ring finger of her right hand. They then embraced for a long kiss until Michel Villar had his fill.

"Assez. Into the water."

Huard looked at Michel Villar with total disgust written on his face. Turning to face the stern of the boat, he took Francine's hand and they stepped first onto the transom and then into empty air. There was one big splash and Michel Villar stepped to the rear of the boat.

"Which way is land?" Huard said as water streamed down his face.

Michel Villar indicated a direction.

"By the way," he said, "you have one advantage that Stuart Andrews didn't have."

"What's that?" Huard asked.

"He was unconscious when he was dumped into the sea. But then again, you have one disadvantage that Stuart didn't have."

"What?"

"He was alive." And he double-tapped them in their heads, Francine first because, after all, he was a gentleman. From near the helm he retrieved a pail filled with fish offal he had gotten from the waterfront fish market that afternoon, putting it into the boat before he had gone to the house and surprised Francine. Throwing the contents in the area where the two bodies were beginning to sink, he wondered how long it would take for sharks to arrive. He threw the bucket into the water, put several bullet holes in it, and watched it start to sink. Turning to the helm, he turned off the spotlight, made certain that the running lights were on because he didn't want to get in trouble and started back to St. Nantes. On the way he dropped the pistol in the Caribbean just before he crossed back into the waters belonging to St. Nantes. He had no intention of swinging from the yard-arm.

When he got to the other side of the island he went in to about a quarter of a mile offshore and stopped the boat with its lights off. He disrobed and put everything, except the latex gloves he had been wearing since arriving at Huard's house, into a waterproof bag and sealed it. The bag had two cords and he put it on like a backpack. Then he pulled a kickboard out of a locker where he had put it earlier. He started the boat's engine so that it barely moved and turned it out to sea. Getting up on the transom with a firm grip on the kickboard, he jumped out from the stern so that he didn't have to worry about being hit by the prop. He was able to get into shallow water in about twenty minutes. Walking up on the beach near a hotel, he removed his clothes from the bag and dressed. Throwing the kickboard as far as he could down the beach, he removed the latex gloves and put them, the duct tape remnants, and the flexi-cuffs into the waterproof bag. With the bag over one shoulder he headed for the place where he had parked his car before walking to Huard's house. Once at the car he drove to the hotel where he had secured a room. In the morning he caught the first plane out of St. Nantes to St. Martin. He knew that was where the Bastons had been taken and he would continue his search there.

***

His plan of operation was simple on St. Martin and had one rule: he wouldn't ask questions. This was Beecher McFalls territory, and he had to keep it low key. No doubt by now both Beecher and Stuart knew that something was afoot. They might even have an idea who was coming for them. That meant they would be prepared. And they would be watchful – extremely watchful. He planned to circulate through the bars and cafes. Listening to casual conversations. Never staying too long at any one place but returning every other day or so to catch a change in clientele. He was hoping he would encounter someone for whom the old maxim "Loose Lips Sink Ships" didn't apply. It took almost a week, but it worked. He was in one of several bars near the airport that he frequented more than any others because the Bastons had come in by air and most likely they would have left by air. They wouldn't be on St. Martin or on St. Maarten, the Dutch side of the island, because that was too close. They would be far away.

He had just entered and was looking for a place to sit wandering through the place looking for a seat when he heard, "Strangest thing. They didn't have any luggage." This was from a man. Michel Villar stopped and appeared to search the crowd as though he was looking for someone but he was all ears. "And they went all the way to Costa Rica? Three kids and their parents and no luggage?" From the woman with him. "Yes, they arrived at the plane in a van. Don't know where they came from before that. In Costa Rica, they were picked up in a big off-road vehicle. I thought I saw guns but I'm not certain." "So, this one was to Costa Rica. Where else have you flown?" "Well, I just got back from …," Michel Villar moved on so not to be noticed. He had his information.

***

In Costa Rica he once again was discreet but did question about guarded compounds as discreetly as possible. He was given a couple of suggestions. He said he was a travel agent and was looking for secure areas for high-level clients. There were several public places, well known and recommended, but there were rumors of a couple of private ones with few people in and out. Those he checked out. It was the third one where he had struck pay dirt.

Chapter 29

As the day had waned, the Bastons had showered or bathed, he knew not which, dressed in clean clothes and gone to the main house. For dinner, Michel Villar assumed. They were there a long time; it was dark when they had finally come out and started back for their bungalow. With darkness he had felt that he could safely remove and stow his camouflage netting. He could have taken out one or two of them with a rifle at any time, but he wanted them all. Especially Quentin and his namesake, Petit Quentin or P. (pay) Q. (koo) as he was called. Quentin, of course, because of the role he played in the trial and subsequent events following his "death." He could be forgiven for the trial but not the rest. True he had not been directly involved in the death of Guillaume Martineau, who had been Michel's best friend and confidant in recent years. Not about the money, of course, Michel Villar had been extremely tight lipped about that because of his position in the courts. He figured that it was money that had driven Guillaume to kidnap Pay-Koo and that had led to his death.

Guillaume had demanded a ransom from the man he knew only as Jośef, who in reality was Stuart Andrews (who was "officially" dead) or Dawoh (Daws) Mbayo (who was also "officially" dead) depending on the time frame. Stuart/Daws/Jośef had delivered the money (well, he had delivered something his sources reported) and Guillaume and his boat had disappeared. That Stuart could not have done without help, and the best source of help would have been Beecher McFalls. He knew that Beecher had also helped Stuart in setting up security for Stuart's house. *What did he call that? Something stupid! Oh, yes, The House at the End of the Road.* Also, from what he had been able to ascertain, although reports were sketchy, Beecher McFalls had a hand in rescuing Stuart and the lovely Treshauna (Tres) Jones when members of the Cercle des Frères had besieged the house, or so Stuart had believed at the time. Michel Villar had concocted the idea of Cercle des Frères in order to get Stuart to help him fake his death. He had told Stuart that it was the organization for which he had been the monetary front when he had gotten Stuart to launder the money for him. In truth the money had been from a nameless organization in the Netherlands. Michel Villar had claimed to have a new laundering source and had been given a tidy sum of money that he wanted to steal. So he needed to disappear permanently.

At about the same time he had learned that there was a contract out on his head – the holder of the contract was one Fredek Gavrilovich Kondrashin, former K.G.B. agent who free-lanced as a hit man. Michel Villar had nicknamed him "The Facilitator". The plan to fake Michel Villar's death had gone awry for two reasons: first, he had revealed the plan to The Facilitator and tried to bribe him with a large sum of money to go along with it. Second, The Facilitator had told the issuer of the contract that he had a better offer. That person was Phil Dombrey, who had been the lawyer for Stuart's wife Elise during her trial for Stuart's "murder by drowning." Phil Dombrey had offered The Facilitator even more money, an offer that he couldn't refuse. So The Facilitator had tried to kill Michel Villar twice: first by forcing his car violently through a guardrail and second, by fatal injection in the hospital following the accident. The latter had been cleverly (and thankfully) thwarted by Treshauna Jones and Stuart. The car wreck had resulted in a broken left arm and right leg and the loss of his spleen as well as damage to other internal organs, which had healed over time.

Michel Villar was roused from his thoughts by the laughter of the Baston children as they exited the main house followed by their parents walking hand in hand. *There must be some kind of entertainment in the house to keep them there so long*, Michel Villar thought. He wondered if it was a nightly thing or just a freak. If it was a nightly thing, then he could wait until dark to climb the tree instead of sitting in it all day. But to ascertain that, he would have to spend another day in the tree anyway. Best thing to do was to get the armament he would need and sit in the tree for a day. He had to make certain that the entire Baston family was in the bungalow when he destroyed it. But first he needed to learn what went on at night – security wise.

Because of his daydreaming (or evening-dreaming) about the past he had missed the start of evening patrols. He put on his night vision glasses from the backpack and started observing. There were lights down the center of the area between the bungalows, low level lighting but enough to find one's way easily. He couldn't detect any kind of laser beams on the near side of the wall. The wiring at the top was deemed sufficient then. Didn't matter, he was not going to attempt to get over the wall, not with his leg. Damn Stuart anyway. His leg had been much better until that drug that Stuart had used to try to kill him. Now his leg was extremely troublesome not to mention the loss of vision in his left eye. *But then*, he constantly reminded himself, *save for his paramour he could be dead. Should have been dead.*

There were three guards patrolling. One on each side between the bungalows and the walls and one in the center. The paths followed were seemingly random. The man in the middle would wander a bit and then, for example, go between the two of the bungalows on the near side. The Near-Wall-Man would become the Middleman. He then might wander and become the Far-Wall-Man or the Near-Wall-Man. Michel watched for five hours, unable to ascertain a pattern except the men were replaced every three hours. Not all at once, but one at a time: the first man after one hour; the second after two; and the third after three. Each no more than three hours on patrol. This was the only pattern that Michel Villar could determine. Interesting if one wanted to invade the compound. You could get the pattern and then plan the time to invade. Probably just after a relief. That is, if you wanted to invade which he didn't.

Chapter 30

Satisfied that he had what he needed (except for the weapon), Michel gathered his belongings in preparation for leaving his leafy bower. He was ready to start his descent when he remembered one important piece of information that would be required. He took off his small backpack and removed from it a laser range finder like many golfers use to find out how far away the pin is. He carefully measured the distance from his tree to the front of the Bastons' bungalow. "Bang, you're dead," he whispered. Then with the range finder in the backpack and that secured on his shoulders, he began the arduous climb down the tree. Arduous because his right leg was tired even though he had been sitting all day. It ached and throbbed. It wouldn't do to have it suddenly collapse on him as it had on the way to Huard's boat. He would land noisily on the ground and possibly be hurt. Thus, as he climbed down, in the same manner as he had climbed up – he made certain that his handholds were secure and he went down one leg at a time. Actually it was easier going down because the left leg carried all the weight. Coming up he had to put weight on the right leg, using the left leg to move up a branch and then lift him up. Even so, he was exhausted when he reached the bottom of the tree. He realized then that he would have to have a quicker and less demanding way down after he attacked.

It took him thirty minutes to find his way back to his vehicle. That would have to be faster also. He had tried it without wearing his night vision goggles, but now knew they would be required. After putting his backpack into his jeep, he removed the catheter and took his first real piss of the day. He removed his (thankfully) unused diaper and put it in a bag to be disposed of later. Back in his room he dropped his backpack on the floor and fell onto his bed, asleep before his head hit the pillow.

The sun streaming into the room awakened him enough for him to get out of his clothes and then crawl under the covers.

***

It was 1:00 p.m. when he awoke the second time. He showered and changed clothes, putting his gear away in a locked suitcase, away from prying eyes. In a small cafe he got a couple of cups of strong Costa Rican coffee and a sandwich and he was on his way.

"Welcome, my friend," Pedro said when he was admitted to the backroom of the shop. "Did everything work out?"

Pedro, if that was his name, was a short fat Spanish type with a thin mustache, thinning hair and big ears – big hairy ears. His shirt was dirty and looked like the one he had on the first time Michel Villar had visited him except that now it was, if possible, even dirtier.

"Excellent," Michel Villar said. "I have just one more need."

"Well, if Pedro don't have it, it can't be got," the Costa Rican said.

"I need to destroy a house from," and Michel Villar consulted his notes, "Eighty-two yards away."

Pedro looked at him a little astonished. "You want to destroy a house? From so far? Can't you be close?"

"Impossible. Eighty-two yards. To be precise, eighty-two point one three seven yards."

"That would take a missile, no?"

"As long as it is easy to carry."

"Si, si. I have a LAWS. You know, Light Anti-Armor Weapon System. It is light, contract, porable."

"You mean 'light, compact, portable'," Michel Villar corrected.

"Si, Si, comtact and portble," the Costa Rican stumbled.

"How much?"

"For you, $65,000 U.S."

Michel Villar didn't quibble. It was cheap at the price. Cheaper than the RPG he had purchased to destroy the *Seventh Heaven* (nee *Zàkpa*.) But here he was playing dumb. He didn't want the spic to know how much he knew about guns. He counted out the money and handed it to Pedro who also counted it – twice – and then put it in a safe. He shouted at someone who brought in a plastic suitcase and put it in front of Pedro. Pedro nodded and the man opened the case. In it was a greenish-brown tube nestled in Styrofoam.

"So, señor, you now possess a LAWS."

"How does it work?"

"Show him," Pedro said to the man.

The man explained that the tube was extended from the rear. Then all one had to do was sight it in and pull the trigger. This was done mostly by pantomime.

He put the launcher over his shoulder, sighted and said, "Booms." Then he put the tube on the table and indicated that Michel should pick it up. Michel Villar picked up the launcher and started to put it into the suitcase.

"Oh," said Pedro. "You want the case too? You didn't say."

Michel Villar knew he couldn't walk out of the store with a LAWS slung over his shoulder. He sighed, "How much?"

"Only $15,000 U.S."

Highway robbery, Michel Villar thought but counted out the money.

"Anything else, señor?" Pedro asked.

Only another one to blow your ass to bits, thought Michel Villars.

"No, don't think so. Oh, wait, do you have a hundred feet of nylon rope."

"Señor, I sell guns not rope."

Michel Villar turned to go.

"Good hunting, señor," the Costa Rican said.

***

Outside, Michel Villar put the case in the back of his jeep and then drove to a nearby shopping area. He quickly found a store where he bought a hundred feet of nylon rope and in another replenished his supply of energy bars and bottled water. Back in his room he put the food and water into his backpack and put the LAWS into a nylon bag. He would attach that to the rope and when he got into his leafy bower, he would pull it up. The rope was also going to be his fast way down. That thought made him realize that he would want some leather gloves so that sliding down the rope wouldn't burn his hands. He put his gear away and went out again. It was a fairly simply task to find gloves and then he went to a nearby cantina and had a big meal. Then it was back to his room and back to bed, the alarm set for 1:00 a.m., the start of the last day the Bastons would have on this planet.

Chapter 31

Michel Villar was up at 12:59 a.m. and shut off the alarm. He felt refreshed and vitalized. He showered and dressed once again in his camouflage fatigues and rubber soled shoes. After sanitizing the room to remove any fingerprints, he gathered his equipment and a small suitcase from under the bed. He left the room and locked it even though he wasn't coming back. He was at the base of the tree at 3:00 a.m., earlier than he needed to be, but he was excited. On the way he had thought about climbing up in the tree and blowing them away in their sleep. But no, that is not what he had in mind. He wanted to watch them as they carefreely went through their last day on Earth.

Removing the length of rope from his pack, he attached one end to the cords that held closed the bag with the LAWS. After feeding out about fifty feet of rope in neat coil on the ground, he put his right arm through the remaining coil and then slipped it over his head. Looking up the tree, he picked the path as he remembered it and commenced his climb. He went slowly, resting his right leg on each limb up even though it was his left leg doing the work. It took him half an hour, but he had plenty of time. Settling himself on his perch, he fastened his safety belt and made certain that the pack was secure. Then he started pulling the rope. At first it went easily because of the extra rope he had laid out and he carefully wound the rope around his head and under his shoulder as he pulled it up. Soon he felt the resistance of the weight of the bag and its contents. He grasped the rope more firmly and started pulling it up. It was easy for about two times around the coil and then the bag stuck somewhere below. He let the rope out about one coil and then tried again. Once more it stuck. Cursing under his breath, he let the rope out and then held his right arm out. Letting the rope slide through a loosely clenched right fist, he pulled up with his left hand. The bag came up about six feet, his left arm fully extending in the opposite direction from the right. He clenched his right fist tightly and let the rope go with his left. Moving his left hand to his right, he grabbed the rope again and started pulling, releasing the tight grip of his right hand. The bag caught again, but higher up and it took a couple of tries to free it but he did.

Once he had the bag up he tied it around a limb and let it hang along the tree trunk where he felt it was invisible. Then he put on the camouflage netting, mounted his listening system, draped binoculars around his neck and settled in to wait. On the drive over he had again debated whether or not to just kill them in the predawn darkness but had decided that wasn't wise. He had a plane out the first thing tomorrow morning and didn't want to hang around playing fox to the hounds that he knew would be out. The faster he could get away the better. He had chosen an inland airport requiring a drive but knew that security would be more intense on airports close to his location. Thus he kept to his plan.

The day seemed to drag even more so than the previous one had. The Bastons were up and ate breakfast, changed into beachwear (evidently beachwear was not proper in the dining room, because they had to change for lunch also). Then they hit the beach but there was one difference today. Nothing important but lunch was delivered picnic style to the beach by one of the guards as he came to relieve another. Other than that, life was pretty static.

As the day started to wane, the Bastons left the beach and the shelter of their little cabaña and headed back to their bungalow. From the time they were in there the previous day, Michel Villar had determined that they showered or bathed before dressing for dinner. That had been confirmed because when they had returned after the lengthy dinner/recreation evening the lights in the front of the house went off quickly and if anyone had stayed up it was in a room with blinds drawn so that no light revealed any tempting targets. But his target was a big one – hit the front door. Boom – case closed. Court adjourned.

As darkness deepened he started his prepara-tions. First he took the nylon rope and, holding the two ends, he carefully threaded the rope through his left hand dropping one end on either side of the branch until he reached the middle of rope. Then he put away the lis-tening apparatus, the binoculars and then the netting. He put on his night vision goggles he would need for sight-ing the LAWS and finding his way through the jungle to his jeep. He put on the left leather glove he would need for his rapid descent and put the right one in his pocket. Then he untied the bag containing the LAWS and took it out. He extended it as he had been taught and put the case back into the bag, which he planned on leaving be-hind. He couldn't be bothered with anything extra – it being discovered after the fact didn't matter. He knew they would pinpoint his leafy bower quickly. He put the LAWS across his lap, holding it with both hands and waited. This wait, which became interminable, gave him time to go over the final seconds in his leafy bower. Once he had fired the LAWS, he would drop the tube and put on the right leather glove. Then he would swing his left leg up and over the branch so he was sitting sidesaddle. He would then pull up the two pieces of rope and grasp it in both hands about three feet below the branch. He would roll over on the branch on his stomach and, using his right arm for leverage, push himself back off the branch feet first. He knew there would be a jerk but that would start the slide down. He would control the speed of descent with his hands. When he reached the ground he would pull the rope down but leave it lying on the ground. Then he would run. Over and over again he mentally rehearsed his descent.

Finally he heard the laughter of the children and could see them exiting the main house and running through the center of the yard despite their cries to be careful. Celesse and Quentin walked behind them, hand in hand. By the time they reached the bungalow the children were already inside. Michel Villar's hands were sweaty with anticipation. He held the LAWS across his body like a rifle at port rest. He had decided he would wait until the door closed; he would extend the tube, aim and fire. As the parents reached the door, they stopped and appeared to be having some earnest conversation. Quentin opened the door and Celesse went in. Quentin turned and started back to the main house.

Chapter 32

Michel Villar was livid. What was that freaking asshole Quentin doing going back to the main house? He was supposed to be dead by now, body mangled, torn and bleeding. All of them were supposed to be dead. He was so angry that he wanted to fire the LAWS at the main house and take out all those protective assholes along with Quentin. It took all his inner strength – the part that knew that he had to wait – to force himself to calm down. He was still shaking when Quentin came out of the main house ten minutes later and strolled leisurely down the path toward his house. The entire way, Michel Villar was telling himself that he needed to calm down. He couldn't shoot accurately unless he had control of himself. But it was slow in coming.

Quentin reached the bungalow, entered and the entrance light went off. It was time. Michel reached for the LAWS tube, which he had placed on the branch in front of him as he waited, but it slipped and fell – but only two feet because his left hand still held the strap. For a moment he almost lost it again but then he gathered himself, closed his eyes, took a deep breath and counted un, deux, ... dix. Then he took another deep breath and began again. He grasped the LAWS in both hands, he turned toward the bungalow, with the rear of the LAWS pointing backwards over his shoulder. He aimed at the front door, took a deep breath, muttered *Au revoir, Quentin,* and pressed the trigger. The blast out of the rear of the LAWS burst against the tree and rebounded, throwing him forward, the tube dropping away. Frantically he grasped for something to hold onto as he felt himself falling. His right hand grabbed something and he closed it violently bringing his left hand to grab under his right. There was a jerk and he felt himself swinging. Bam, he hit the trunk of the tree and rebounded but he didn't let go of what he knew was the rope. The swinging stopped, his ears rang and he felt dizzy. He shook his head and tried to orient himself. Through blurred eyes (actually just his right) he saw flames and smoke. Closing his eyes he squeezed them tight and then opened them. Yes, flames and smoke. Lights on the wall were illuminating the twenty feet outside the wall but he was still in the dark. He heard yelling, and saw bobbing flashlights moving toward the flames that marked the inferno that was burning the Bastons lifeless bodies. It was then with the brightness of the flames that he realized that he had lost his night vision goggles. *What an ass*, he started but then reminded himself, *time to go.*

As the thought was processed, another realization came to him. He was already moving down. His left hand, always suspect since the poisoning because of his broken left arm which was probably affected by the poison like his right leg, had taken this opportunity to quit. The only thing keeping him on the rope and from free falling was his right hand. His feet hit a branch and he crumpled, fell forward, jerked and kept going down. Faster and faster. The ground came suddenly and quite hard. His right leg hit awkwardly and pain shot upwards enveloping his brain.

He was lying on the ground on his back, something hard poking him in his spine and something was burning. He felt the heat and knew that his back was on fire. He sensed it was his backpack and he struggled out of the straps. *Move, Move*, a voice inside him called. He rolled over and rose to his hands and knees. His right leg hurt like the devil and felt useless. Gathering his left leg under him, he pushed himself to his feet and stood. Looking around he saw lights to his left so he turned to his right where there was darkness. He stepped that way, without thinking, and used his right leg to take the step. As his weight shifted to that leg he felt the ground under his foot rolling and pain shot through his body once again. He fell head first into the tree that had been his protector but now seemed to be his tormentor. He rolled away from the tree and flung his arms out to stop his fall. His right arm felt something round and he grasped at it as his left palm hit the ground hard and the arm collapsed. He rolled several times, finally ending on his back after he hit another tree.

He lay there for a moment as one voice inside him yelled, *Move, Move, you idiot* and another voice countered with *I can't move. I'm hurt.* But then a third voice said, *Injured or not, they won't give a shit and they are coming to get you and they have guns, lots of guns.*

Opening his eyes, he raised his right arm up and looked to see what he was holding – the LAWS tube. Cursing now but keeping it under his breath, he rolled over and got to his feet leaving the tube on the ground, turned his back to the lights and set off into the jungle. He didn't run at first – couldn't run – walked slowly, one foot after the other always testing that right leg and holding his left arm across his stomach. Soon his head cleared and his night vision improved and suddenly he was thankful that it was a virtually cloudless night. He stopped and looked back and saw only darkness. He listened but all he could hear were sounds of the forest fauna. Nothing human at all. *OUI (YES)*, he thought briefly exuberant before thinking, *your pursuers will not be making any noise. They will be listening for you.*

He set forth once more moving slowly and then faster and faster, his right arm out in front of him, warning him of impending collisions with trees. After some time, he stopped and listened again. Just jungle noises. He looked around seeing only trees and vines. *Où diable je suis* (Where the hell am I?) He realized he was lost. But, he had his smart phone – if it wasn't broken. And for the first time that night, things started to go right. The smart phone worked. He initiated the GPS app and in a few seconds he had a screen. He found the GOTO button and pressed it and received an answering blinking question mark. He entered, "j" and the screen responded with "Jeep." He pressed that and a dotted line appeared on the screen. He turned in the direction of that line and set out, moving as fast as he could. Thirty minutes later he saw his jeep. Five minutes later he was on the road headed away from destruction and death – *not his own*, he thought thankfully.

***

Instead of going back to the dive he had been staying in during his surveillance, he went to a ritzy hotel resort he had booked and stayed in when he first arrived. He had explained to the hotel that he had some traveling to do but didn't want to risk losing his room.

On his way, he had pulled off the main road and drove to a third place he had rented, this a garage where he had stored his Lexus rental car. There he had changed out of his camo gear and dressed in something more appropriate for the hotel – beige Dockers and a white polo shirt, over which he wore a black guide shirt. He was glad he had that because of his injuries. He also used some easily applied makeup so that his appearance would conform to his passport. This was the same persona he had used in St. Maarten, at least arriving and leaving. He practiced his Anglo accent while he stuffed all his camo gear and other detritus including the adult diaper into a burn barrel outside the garage, doused it liberally with charcoal starter and set it burning. He had waited until the flames had been reduced to burning embers before he left. He didn't want a blaze to attract attention. He had rented the garage for a month but felt that it would be longer than that before the owner came to see what was being stored there. He had purchased the off-road vehicle from a used car lot. Let the garage owner worry about ownership. His body ached all over and he longed to lie down and take a rest, but he knew that he couldn't. He needed to put as many miles behind him as he could but he had to do so stealthily.

When he arrived at the hotel he told the attendants not to park the Lexus because he would be checking out and leaving. In his room, where he had only spent a couple of nights, was a small carry-on suitcase with minimal clothing and a laptop in a carry case. He then checked out explaining that family emergency necessitated him leaving. It was an eight-hour drive to La Fortuna. Actually only six, but he had to give himself extra time. Leaving his rental car in airport parking, he boarded a regional aircraft to fly to Drake with a stopover in San Jośe. There he went to a locker and removed a small package containing new identity papers. The others went into a pocket in the carry-on to be destroyed when he arrived in his first destination – Panama City. In a bathroom stall in Tocumen International Airport just 15 miles from Panama City, Panama, he changed his appearance to match his new persona – an Italian playboy (naturally) and he was happy that for this one he could use an eye patch over his left eye. "It happened in my childhood. We were fencing with twigs and my brother poked me in the eye." From there he traveled to Cartagena, Colombia, where he spent a few days recovering, seeking revenge, and plotting.

Part IV
Damage Control

Chapter 33

I kept in touch with happenings on St. Nantes by reading *Le Journal de Saint Nantes*, the St. Nantes weekly newspaper, on-line. They have done this just like other newspapers to improve readership. In this case, the publisher hoped that visitors to the island would want to learn more about it beforehand and be enamored enough to want to stay in touch. It was thus that I learned about Huard Jubert's disappearance.

ISLAND ATTORNEY MISSING

Three days ago, the fishing boat belonging to St. Nantes Prosecuting Attorney Huard Jubert was found abandoned forty miles from St. Nantes. The boat named *Je suis la Mer (I am the Sea)* did not have any petrol. There also was no radio aboard. The island gendarmerie has theorized that Huard and his live-in girlfriend Francine Dubois had gone out on the boat in the evening. Neighbors reported hearing the boat go out about eight o'clock. What they were doing is unknown but the couple spent many weekend hours at sea. It has been discovered that Huard Jubert bought a

diamond ring that he had sized and had
picked it up that day.

The report was disturbing because Huard Jubert
had prosecuted the case against Elise and Howard. Prosecuted, that is, in the French sense. He prepared the
case, compiled the evidence, subpoenaed witnesses, and
did all the other preparation. He made opening and closing remarks, but the questioning of the witnesses was
one sided. That is, to say that the presiding judge Michel
Villar asked the questions. Both prosecuting and defense
attorneys could submit questions in writing to the judge.
However, if he did not feel they were germane he could
choose not to ask them. Huard Jubert had done his work
well and prepared an excellent case. Any lapse – and I
could not recall any – was the fault of Michel Villar.
That thought bothered me as I moved through the online pages and I could not pull up the reason until I was
paging quickly through the want ads. Something unusual
caught my eye and I flipped back a page.

In the real estate section was a picture of the St.
Nantes waterfront. The picture was extremely similar to
the one I had taken. What set my heart to pounding were
the two lines under the picture:

Three went out. One came back.
We know what happened.

I had sent a picture like that to Keith Mitchell
and it had sent him over the edge. The wording of the
first two lines was different: "Four went out. Three came
back." And I knew what had happened to Huard Jubert
and Francine Dubois. For some insane reason, Michel

Villar had taken the couple out to sea and dumped them overboard as I had been dumped. However, I was certain that they were either dead when they were dumped or were killed in the water. Michel Villar would not have taken a chance they would get back to shore. I knew their bodies would never be found. I could notify the gendarmerie and some day in the future I might, but right now I couldn't take the chance. And, of course it was that picture I had sent Keith Mitchell that was the one flaw in the prosecution's case. But then Huard Jubert hadn't known about the picture.

I now knew that Michel Villar's vendetta was wider than I had realized. And I knew that there was one additional probable target that I had not thought would be involved: Chyrise Callahan, Howard's attorney. I would have to warn her but I didn't know how. I logged into the email account that Beecher McFalls and I had set up and checked the drafts folder. There was an email waiting me. The content made my blood run cold.

> Last night shortly after the Bastons had returned to their lodgings, a LAWS was fired and destroyed the building. A search found that someone had been spy-ing on the compound from a tree. It was from that tree that the rocket was fired. There is evidence that the person who fired the LAWS had not checked for clearance behind and the concussion knocked him or her out of the tree. There was a backpack containing surveillance implements on the ground as well as night goggles. All efforts to find the in-

truder have failed. I am sorry to be the
bearer of this bad news. I am satisfied
that the group I hired did their best. They
protect some very important people at
different times. I do not know how the
Bastons' location was found. The agreement that I have with these people is that
I get minimal information. I don't even
know where they were.

I was shell-shocked and wept uncontrollably.
Quentin, Celesse, Pierre, Marie, Pay-Koo. Damn,
Michel Villar to hell! And that was where he was going.
I was going to make certain of that. The only question
was: Where in the hell was he now?

I had been in Caracas for a week and had gotten
nowhere. His condo had been sold and the money put
into a trust and nobody would give me access to it. In
fact, nobody knew who had access to it after the money
had been put there by his lawyer. None of the neighbors
knew much about him – at least in the neighborhood he
was a secretive person. I found a tennis club he had
joined, and they remembered him. "He was a formidable
tennis player. I liked to play with him but wish I had
won more." "I wish he was my partner in mixed dou-
bles, we would have been unbeatable," one lady said.
"He was quite a hunk," another lady said and looked
dreamily like she would have liked to have been bedded
by him but hadn't been.

The newspaper was of no help. No one could
remember who brought the obituary in. I found the mor-
tuary where the body had been taken. There had been no
autopsy because a doctor had pronounced him dead by

heart attack, nothing suspicious. The funeral home where his body had been taken told me that it had been cremated – that information brought back visions of the night I had cremated "his body" on St. Nantes and I shuddered. The ashes had been placed into an ossuary, a common place within the funeral home. It was just a big box with what looked like dust in it. No scattering at sea this time. And so Maurice Vitor just disappeared. I admired Michel's choice of his last name. It was from a medieval personal name from the Latin *Victor* meaning "conqueror", an agent derivative of *vincere* "to win." Of course, when choosing an alias, many people keep the same initials and this was what had helped Pieter Devenpeck in locating him.

But I was at a loss. I knew beyond a doubt that he was alive in the process of carrying out a campaign of vengeance, not caring what innocent people got killed. He had to be stopped, but I had no way to even begin. All I could do was to try to warn anyone who might be on his list. I had warned everyone who was close to me but even that hadn't helped. I had one last hope in Venezuela – a man who had been recommended to me by Beecher McFalls who knew him only by reputation: Juan Carlos.

Chapter 34

The entrance to the ranchero was as impressive as the one to The Ponderosa, or at least as impressive as I remember it. Ben, Hoss, Little Joe, and Adam riding under a gateway of wooden posts and a curved board over the top emblazoned with "Ponderosa." This gateway was flanked by two stone columns and stonewalls extending at least a quarter mile in either direction. From there chain link fence took over. *Strange*, I first thought, *barbed wire was the traditional ranch fencing. Must be different down here in Venezuela.* Spanning the space above the entrance was a sheet of curved black steel with the name of the ranch cut out: Casa Zumbado. Spanning the space between the two stone columns was a heavy wrought iron gate. Again strange for a cattle ranch, but I knew this was anything but a cattle ranch.

I pulled up in front of the gate and looked to see if there was any kind of a monitoring system. There wasn't one visible, but that didn't mean anything. So I sat there. In about five minutes, I saw a cloud of dust from the straight road that stretched from the other side of the gate. Soon a jeep pulled up with four men, all dressed in camo and wearing fatigue hats. The two in the backseat were armed with AK-47s or something similar. Should have paid more attention in Beecher's class, but then it doesn't matter whether you are killed from a bullet fired from an AK-47 or an AR-15 – you're still dead.

When the jeep stopped, the driver got out and stood beside it with a hand on the pistol in his holster. The two men in back jumped down and moved to either side halfway behind the stone columns, their weapons aimed at me. The passenger waited until they were set and then he got out and walked up to the wrought iron gate and stood there. His uniform was meticulously clean and pressed. I opened the door of my SUV and got out and started for the gate.

"Where you are is fine, señor."

"How do you know I speak English?" I asked.

"What else would a man speak who stops at the gate of Casa Zumbado without an appointment?"

He had me there.

I wanted to say, "If he'd been in the phone book I would have called," but I didn't.

"I want to see Juan Carlos."

"Many peoples want to see Juan Carlos, but he don't want to see dem."

"Beecher McFalls sent me."

The man stood there for a minute and then said, "What is his number?"

I gave it to him and he stood there for another minute. Then he motioned to the driver who unlocked the gate and motioned me to come in.

"What about my car?" I asked.

"You dink dat anyone one would steal dat from Casa Zumbado?" he indicated the car with some disdain.

He was right. Here or elsewhere it was a piece of crap.

I got into the back of the jeep with one of the armed men, the other remaining on sentry duty. I knew that he wasn't watching the car, but for people who may have accompanied me. The other man got in front and I could see that he had an ear bud, which explained why he hadn't done anything when I gave him Beecher's name and then phone number. Whoever was monitoring him must have made the call.

As we drove toward the distant house, I began to see signs that this wasn't your typical cattle ranch. In fact, I began to wonder if there were cattle at all. A hundred feet from the gate on either side of the road there were pillboxes, the tops about three feet above the ground, covered with camouflage netting, and I knew why there wasn't a guard or monitoring system at the gate. As we approached the house I saw at least five other buildings behind it, several looking like barns and two more like barracks. In fact, there were two groups of camo-dressed men drilling in the area behind the house. It really wasn't a house, more of a mansion, just short of a palace.

I was escorted in the main door that was opened by a black man also dressed in camo fatigues. He was about my size but in much better shape. He motioned me inside and then indicated that I should assume the position against the wall. I did and was hand frisked and wanded before he led me down a hallway to the back of the mansion and into a room with a wall of glass looking out onto the drill field. The cavernous room held only one major piece of furniture – a huge ebony desk facing the window. Behind it in a black leather chair sat an equally impressively sized man (tall and muscular, not fat) dressed in camo fatigues straight from the laundry. In front of the desk was a simple wooden chair and I was directed to sit on it with a gesture by my guide, who then disappeared from the room.

The man sitting behind the desk was smoking a cigar and watching the activity in the drill field, looking past me like I wasn't there. It was several minutes before he bothered to acknowledge my presence. He did this by knocking the ashes off the cigar into a huge crystal ash-tray on the desk and then setting the cigar in it. Then he looked at me, saying nothing. This went on for a minute or two before I summoned the courage to speak.

"I am looking for a man. A man I thought I killed."

Juan Carlos looked at me, waiting. Waiting.

Chapter 35

"His name is Michel Villar. He was a man of power – life and death power. The legal kind. He was the best in his country. Actually a Caribbean island but his reputation was far reaching. He was respected throughout the Caribbean and France as far as I know. He had problems – women. They weren't the problem but his dalliance with them was. Destroyed his marriage. But it was more than women. It was money.

"He became a middle man in a money launder-ing scheme with a European group. I won't say more than that because I respect their anonymity. He skimmed, not much but some. Then he made a mistake. He didn't think so at the time, but as it turned out it nearly got him killed."

That brought a raised eyebrow from Juan Carlos.

"No, not me, not yet. A defense lawyer in an im-portant case took exception to the way the case was handled. Not his handling and not the prosecution but by the judge. He ran the case. Asked the questions. Con-trolled it. That is the way of the French Court system. The lawyer didn't like it and hired a hit man. That's when the judge came to me. He wanted me to help him die – appear to die."

Again an eyebrow rose, this time asking the question, *Why you?*

"Because I had done it. Faked my death – rather survived an attempt on my life but then made it appear as though I were dead. So we came up with a plan. An automobile accident putting him in the hospital where the hit man would make his move. We knew he liked to put drugs in IVs. But the judge was scared. He didn't want to die."

Juan Carlos shrugged as though to say, *Who does?*

"Didn't want to take the chance so he tried to bribe the hit man (he had used him before) and it back-fired. The hit man went to the lawyer who upped the ante big time. So the judge almost died and then, after I had saved his ass, went after the man who had tried to kill him. Someone sent a crooked cop to try to scare me, but it didn't work. As it turned out, the cop was naïve – no, just plain stupid. He took a simple ploy and pushed a dummy button that wasn't – boom. I didn't know then who had sent him and so I helped the judge kill the hit man (well, he died of a heart attack) and the lawyer. Then by sheer accident, I learned about the judge. He had made up a French cartel for which he was fronting, but I learned it didn't exist. It was another … again, I respect their anonymity. He also was the one who sent the cop to kill me.

"I felt that he would continue to come after me – for my money. I was the man who laundered the money. Actually more than laundered, I invested it and made a mint for them – and for myself. That is what he wanted. So I felt I had no choice. I found the judge hiding here – in Caracas. I poisoned him. A special poison – a new fancy poison, which paralyzes and then stops the heart. The problem was that I left before his heart stopped. In the short time between paralysis and cardiac arrest, something happened. Either the drug didn't work or someone saved him somehow. I don't know the details. I can't find out the details. Everything was covered up."

Juan Carlos sensed I was finished.

"I know of this man. When he was here he called himself Maurice Vitor. After you – I am guessing that you are the one – failed to kill him, he took the name Henri Godot."

I nodded thinking that was a name that completely characterized Michel Villar and explained it to Juan Carlos.

"He probably took that name after *Waiting for Godot* by Samuel Beckett. Godot never appears in the play. The play is simply what happens as two people wait for him to appear. Most people think that Godot symbolizes God. I think this man believes himself to be God. Maybe even more so after surviving my attempt to kill him."

Juan Carlos listened to this explanation and then we both sat silently for a moment before he picked up his cigar. After taking a deep drag and blowing a cloud of smoke toward the ceiling where ventilation fans sucked it out, he said, "I don't know who he is really, but you have told me more than I knew. I appreciate that. Beyond that I cannot help you. At least not at this time."

He thought for a minute. Then shrugged.

"I had a request by someone for help. A body was needed. A male body. I could help so I provided a body. You see, you cannot publish an obituario without proof that the person was dead. In this case, a body was needed. And of course a certificado de defunción (death certificate). Beyond that….”

Juan Carlos shrugged.

“He has vanished. I know because I have looked. You see, I also have a score to settle with this man. He gave my niece a lethal overdose.”

He motioned to his bodyguard who had appeared from nowhere and I knew that my session was over, so I stood.

“However, there are two things.”

“Yes,” I said expectantly.

“Give Dilan your cell phone number. If I learn anything, I will call.”

I nodded.

“If you find that hijo de puta (son of a bitch) before I do, tell him ‘Juan Carlos sends his regards’ and then kill him.”

I followed Dilan to the front door giving him my number before he turned me over to the jeep squad. Again it was a silent ride back to the gate. I got out and the guard who had remained opened the gate and I passed through and got into my car. When I looked, the jeep, with the man from the gate in the back seat, was on its way back to the compound– I mean, what else would you call it after what I had seen? It stopped around a hundred feet from the gate and the two men in the back got out, one on either side, walked over to a pillbox and then seemingly disappeared into the ground. Shortly two other men came up out of the ground, one from each pillbox, got in the jeep and it disappeared in the distance.

I hadn’t learned much except that Michel Villar had survived, possibly saved by Juan Carlos’s niece who was then rewarded with a deadly overdose. I also learned by innuendo that Michel Villar had disappeared into thin air. I had a feeling that if Juan Carlos couldn't find him, nobody could. But I sure as hell was not going to quit looking.

Chapter 36

It was late afternoon and the narrow back street of Cartagena was empty. That was understandable because for much of the populace it was hora de la siesta (siesta time). But even so the street was unusually empty. In fact, the only human, if one might consider this creature to be so, was the beggar sitting near the entry to an alley a block from the Corzo de Cantina. He had been there about a week. No one knew where he came from – no one asked because no one cared. He was unkempt and smelled but that wasn't the worst – he was legless or at least below the knees. A filthy scraggly black beard covered the lower part of his face. Under a battered straw hat, a bandana covered his left eye. He was on what appeared to be a heavy wooden cart with big rubber caster-swivel wheels raising the platform about four inches off the ground. He propelled the cart with his fists pushing on the ground. His hands were encased in leather gloves, reinforced where the knuckles would hit the pavement and the tips of the fingers cut off at the second knuckle. He was there from early morning until late evening, a battered cup sitting on the pavement in front of him. The cup collected a pittance of coins, but the people who passed, mostly those who lived in the neighborhood, were generous with food – be it a crust of bread or a half-eaten sandwich, none of which remained in sight for very long. At night, when the shadows deepened, he disappeared into the alley and no one knew where he went because no one cared. The people in the neighborhood called him La Criatura (The Creature).

Being siesta time, it was strange that another man appeared from the alley next to the cantina. He was dressed in dirty ragged clothes, but not nearly as ragged and dirty as The Creature's. Despite his shabby looks, in his right hand he carried a smartphone upon which his eyes were glued until he came out of the alley onto the street. Then he raised his head so he could see. His hair, at least what could be seen sticking out from under the straw hat, was dark and dirty. His eyes were dark though difficult to see in contrast to his dark skin, skin darkened by the sun indicating that he lived and worked outdoors. Looking back at the smartphone, he turned to his right and proceeded about ten steps until he reached the door of the cantina. There he stopped and turned to face the cantina's door, which was closed at this time of day – the bartender apparently needed his siesta too. The man looked at the door and back at his smartphone. Then he shrugged, opened the door and disappeared into the gloom inside, the door shutting behind him.

The street was quiet again until ten minutes later when a dark sedan came slowly up the street. It had come first about half an hour before and stopped in front of the cantina's door. Three men had gotten out: The Beast, The Doctor and a small nerdy-looking Latino man. The Beast had gone into the cantina and obviously checked the place for intruders because he reappeared and nodded to The Doctor and The Nerd who had gone in then. This time the sedan stopped opposite The Creature and The Driver, dressed in a chauffeur's livery, had gotten out, walked across the street to where The Creature was apparently asleep, and dropped some coins into the cup. "Gracias," muttered The Creature although never looking up. He knew from the previous drive-by that the windows of the sedan were darkly tinted and nothing could be seen inside. The Driver got back into the sedan and it proceeded up the street and stopped in front of the cantina. The Driver got out and hurried around to the cantina's door and knocked. The Beast opened the door, stepped out and visually swept the neighborhood. He nodded and the driver opened the passenger side rear door and held it while a person got out. Considering that the person was dressed in a baggy white blousy shirt and equally blousy pants, hair cut short and eyes concealed by large sunglasses, anyone not standing up close and personal would have had a difficult time guessing the person's sex. Not stopping to look around, the person stepped to the cantina's door and entered followed by The Beast and the door was closed once again. The Driver closed the sedan's door and then got back in the sedan behind the wheel.

As though on cue, The Creature seemed to come alive and propelled his cart across the street and down the alley next to the cantina. The Driver, who had settled back for a brief siesta, failed to notice. In less than two minutes, The Creature reappeared, stopped briefly behind the sedan, bent over and attached something under the car. Then he moved his cart around to the driver's window and rapped on it with his metal cup. In the sedan, The Driver became alert, grabbing for his pistol and then relaxing when he saw who it was. He pressed the button lowering the window to tell him, "Ya no más" when he saw that the metal cup had been replaced by the barrel of a silenced Beretta. He never heard the pffft announcing the bullet that killed him being fired. Then The Creature went along the wall between the cantina's door and the alley and left three small devices attached to short wires protruding from the wall. Moving faster than before, The Creature sped back to his alley, entering just inside and spinning his cart around. He picked up a small black box from between his legs, extended an antenna and pushed a switch. A light turned red and then green. The Creature looked at the cantina, pointed the antenna at it, said "Adios, Doña Giovanni," and pressed the button.

The bomb he had placed under the sedan's gas tank erupted tossing the sedan's rear several feet in the air, igniting the gas that added to the explosion and cremating The Driver's corpse. The charges placed in the alley wall of the cantina and the wall between the alley and the door exploded spraying stone shrapnel into the cantina's main room. The four people who were in there waiting for the new recruit to emerge from the toilet were killed instantly. Had the shrapnel not killed them, the collapse of roof would have finished them.

Chapter 37

Across the street, The Creature had vanished. As soon as the explosions had erupted, he had whirled his cart around and sped down the alley, across the next street and to the end of the next alley. There he had stopped and released the strap that held him on the cart. Groaning as he had every day when he extricated himself from his cramped position, Michel Villar pushed himself up revealing that he did in fact have lower legs concealed in a shallow cavity in the cart. He stretched and did several toe touches while the blood started fuller circulation and then jogged in place for a minute. Feeling both that he could walk and the urgency to leave the area, he quickly took off The Creature's clothes and put them in a plastic bag retrieved from the cavity in his plastic cart. Then he donned the clothes he had been sitting on. Turning the cart over, he folded the wheels into cart and then folded the cart in half making it look more like a suitcase. Picking up the cart and plastic bag, he exited the alley heading to the left away from the cantina's location, cursing the fact that his bad leg didn't let him move faster. Two blocks away and down another alley, he found his car in the garage he had rented over the phone. Opening the trunk, he put the plastic bag and cart into it. Using a wet washcloth taken from a zip lock bag, he removed the grime from his face and hands. Then he got into the car and backed out of the garage. After getting out and closing the garage door, he drove back to his hotel where he would relish in a much-needed shower and a good night's sleep, the first in a week. Tomorrow he would drive out of the city and find somewhere to dispose of the clothes and the cart – hopefully to burn them.

***

While in the camp Michel Villar had learned that Don Giovanni was in fact Doña Giovanni and was the woman who brought him his food and had consensually "raped" him. This discovery happened the evening after the encounter. He had heard music and singing and had left the tent, surprised that the guard wasn't there. The music was coming from the mess hall and he joined several men standing on the outside looking in. The woman who brought his food was standing on a table singing in accompaniment to music coming from a couple of speakers. Michel knew the music – it was Elvira's aria "In quali eccessi ... Mi tradì quell'alma ingrata" from Mozart's *Don Giovanni*, originally composed for the soprano Caterina Cavalier. It was for the Vienna premiere of *Don Giovanni* in 1788. He was surprised to hear the young woman sing – she had a gorgeous voice – but more surprised at the rapture and enthusiastic applause by the men when she finished the aria. There were cries of "Ole! Ole!," "Bravi Doña Giovanni" and "Encore" but she simply bowed, was helped down from the table and disappeared, accompanied by The Beast.

Michel hadn't seen The Beast around camp, but then the only time he had seen the young woman was when she came into his tent. He was surprised that he was being served (and serviced) by the camp's número uno.

It was on one of his walks through the camp on the way to his morning's lesson when he over-heard a couple of men talking about their recruiting. "Sí, también tuve que sacar toda mi ropa (Yes, I also had to take all my clothes off)" and "Sí, era el Curzo de Cantina (Yes, it was the Cantina Curzo)." That had given him the idea for taking out the "Doña." He had mentally constructed the cart and found a fabricator in Cartagena who would make it for him. Sadly, that man's shop had been burned and his charred corpse had been found in the shop's debris one evening shortly after Michel had acquired his cart. With the cart in his possession, Michel had started his daytime vigil and his nighttime explosive planting. Armed with the most powerful battery-powered drill he could obtain and the best masonry bits available, in the middle of the night he would enter the alley next to the Corzo de Cantina and drill holes deep into the walls. Then he put his explosive into the holes, with an igniter and a wire leading outside. Then the hole was sealed with a mortar colored to match the dirty wall as much as possible and he would rub dirt from the alley's floor to help disguise it. The defect was the wire that had to protrude about a quarter inch so that he could attach the radio receiver – this was done when he entered the alley after Doña Giovanni had entered the Cantina that afternoon. The trying part was planting the explosives in the wall facing the street, but he saved those for last and had gotten quite efficient with the process. He had finished the night before the Doña had arrived.

***

In the paper the next day, Michel read about the explosion and the eyewitness account by the man who was in the cantina's toilet at the time. He feigned innocence saying that he had been using the facility out of need and had no idea who the dead people were or what they were doing there. However, the police knew who they were or at least suspected as much. They never asked him how he could not see the two spotlights in the corner and not wonder what their purpose was. They did say that the charges placed in the walls had sent the force of the explosion directly into the room and the man had been saved by the closed door of the toilet.

Chapter 38

I was depressed. Ten days in Venezuela and I was no closer to Michel Villar than when I had arrived. So I decided to try to put events into perspective by making a list of people he might be after, starting with those who had already felt his vindictiveness and why. Those targets that had been hit, I sadly struck through and added those killed as a result. `

Target	Reason	Collateral Dead
~~Zàkpa~~	Stuart Andrews	The Petersons and crew (4)
~~Andrews Investment Management~~	Stuart Andrews	Alan and staff (13)
~~Huard Jubert~~	Knowledge of MV	Fiancée (2)
~~Quentin Baston~~	Stuart Andrews	Family (5)

At this point I stopped to contemplate the havoc Michel Villars had caused. No, strike that. **What havoc I had caused!** Better to have died at sea. There are several names then that should be added: Elise Andrews (my no good wife); Howard Blake (her brother, my equally no good brother-in-law); Keith Mitchell (Howard's friend who had helped in the attempt to kill me); Fredek Gavrilovich Kondrashin (DBA/AKA The Facilitator); and Phil Dombrey (Elise's lawyer and the man who hired The Facilitator to kill Michel Villar.) That was a total of twenty-nine. All because Elise had tried to kill me (or have me killed) for a measly twenty million dollars. A pittance in today's money but for one person – a fortune. Maybe I could lay the blame on her. Yes, for the first three who died in this scenario (herself, her brother, her brother's friend), then two who died as ... Christ, I forgot. There are all those "Circle of Brothers" mercenaries who attacked the house led by Jacque St. George (Mr. Pork Pie Hat). I have no idea how many there were, but I killed them with the help of Tres and Beecher McFalls. Oh, yes, I forgot Guillaume Martineau, Michel Villar's best friend and tennis partner who tried to extort money from me by kidnapping Pay-Koo. True, he had hired people to kidnap me and learn where my money was hidden and how to access it, of that I am certain. I had managed to thwart and kill him with the help of Beecher McFalls. I am certain that Michel Villar would be after him, but of all the people I was concerned about, he was the least of my worries.

I couldn't dwell on what had happened before but had to get on to the living and try to protect them from Michel Villar's bitter vengeance.

Target	Reason	Collateral Damage
Joaquin Gagalac	Stuart Andrews	Wife and two children
Pieter Devenpeck	Former employer of Michel Villar and of Stuart Andrews through Michel Villar and provider of documents to both.	Family (?)
Chyrise Callahan	Lawyer to Howard Blake	

For an hour I sat and stared at the list. Three names were all that I could hope to save. I know that Joaquin and his wife had taken the children and gone to ground somewhere, most likely to a place chosen by his wife who was much more knowledgeable about things like that. I couldn't see Michel Villar venturing into so alien a place as the Philippines himself. Much more likely to hire someone. As far as that went, there was no evidence that any of these tragedies were directly perpetrated by Michel Villar, except perhaps for Huard Jubert. But I knew that he had his hand in them all. After looking at the list for a while, I couldn't think of any reason that Michel Villar would want or need to eliminate Chyrise Callahan and removed her name from the list. That left me with Pieter Devenpeck and therefore I decided to go there. The best and fastest connection I could get took me through Miami International.

***

After landing and going through passport control, baggage claim (although I had nothing to claim), and customs I went through security and started through the concourse to my gate to Amsterdam. Halfway there I stopped dead in my tracks. Since I had crossed Chyrise Callahan off my list, something had been nagging at me and I couldn't wrap my brain around it. But as such things happen, suddenly it came back: "I tried to pick her up after the execution," Michel Villar had said. "She was civil in her turndown, one of the nicest I ever had. I don't think she was in on it."

Michel Villar hated to be turned down by any woman. Immediately I went to a service desk and checked on flights to Los Angeles. The fastest was from the Hollywood International Airport in Fort Lauderdale, and I could make it if I hurried. I paid for the ticket and then headed back through the airport, walking fast and dodging around and through throngs of passengers hastening to gates. In my haste I wasn't being diligent in my looking, I guess, because I bumped into a lady and she dropped the handle of her wheeled carry-on and it made a racket when it fell. I apologized and picked it up and hurried onward. It was strange – I could sense something was wrong. Almost the kind of feeling that one gets when he or she knows that someone is trailing him or her. At one point I almost stopped and turned around but told myself it was silly and pushed onward out past security and followed the signs to ground transportation where I got a taxi and settled back for the half hour drive.

* * *

Michel Villar had been sitting in the waiting area for his plane to Dallas looking at some email when a noise jarred him from his contemplation. He looked around and saw a woman in the middle of a crowded hallway, people moving around her as though she was a boulder in a stream. Someone was stooped down in front of her and then the man stood up and offered her the handle of a wheeled carry-on bag. A fairly tall, middle-aged black man. But he wasn't middle-aged at all. He was in his mid-forties. Stuart Andrews! So close that if Michel Villar had a gun, he would have – could have – been a dead man. As Stuart started to move on, Michel Villar closed his laptop, shoved it quickly into its bag and stood, putting the computer bag strap over his shoulder and grabbed his duffel carry-on from the seat next to him. Threading his way out of the rows of seats between people's feet and carry-ons, Michel Villar reached the passageway and started after Stuart who by this time had a good lead. It was time that most people were headed to and not from planes, so both he and Stuart were like salmon swimming upstream and he could not gain any ground. Finally he saw that Stuart was leaving the departure venue and in order to follow him, Michel Villar would also. That would mean having to either miss his plane or reenter through security. What was Stuart doing in Miami? Possibly paying last respects to his former place of business but he would have done that weeks ago, wouldn't he?

Hearing the first boarding call for his plane, Michel Villar turned around and headed back. He would keep with his plan to fly to Dallas, rent a car and drive to Los Angeles, picking up armament somewhere on the way, but no place close to Los Angeles.

Part V
Fighting Back

Chapter 39

The water from the sudden rain still dripped off leaves, landing in small puddles or streamlets soon to end their brief existence in the rain forest. Joaquin stopped and took off the lightweight camouflaged poncho, quickly folding it and sticking it in the small bag attached to his belt. It was welcome when the rain started because walking through a hot humid jungle in wet clothes is uncomfortable, but wearing a poncho over dry clothes is even more so. As he performed this act, he looked around trying to ascertain if he indeed was alone. He was less than an hour from the small hut that he and Jovelyn had constructed in the clearing on the side of the mountain. When they had received the warning from Josef that somehow Michel Villar was still alive and on the hunt, they had gathered their two children and meager supplies and fled from their home outside Bacolod. Jovelyn had picked the site because she had camped there while on a military survival exercise. She had been on her own and doubted that anyone knew about it since it was over a half day's walk on jungle paths from the nearest habitation. It was from that village that Joaquin was returning with supplies, something that he did twice a week. He also had used the lone computer in the village to check email for any further word from Josef but there had been none. That email check was a big reason for the bi-weekly supply trek.

Shifting the heavy pack into a more comfortable position, Joaquin started again on the path that was angling away from his ultimate destination. Hearing an unexpected noise, he seemed to melt into the foliage on the side of the trail opposite that from which the sound had come. His eyes searched the greenery, his nose and ears alert to any deviation in the usual jungle smells and noises. He wished that Jovelyn were here as she was much better in the jungle than he was, but of necessity she was staying back providing mother's milk for their youngest child. It had been their decision when they had started the family to have their two close together so they could be playmates, and their parents could get through the diaper age as quickly as possible. Both had been girls and although Joaquin had wanted a boy, he was happy that both were healthy. His finger tightened on the trigger of the Beretta as the noise caused by a movement of leaves and the falling of water from them came again, louder and obviously closer. Silently he prayed that it was not someone tracking him and, as though his prayer had been answered, an adult Baboy Ramo (Wild Pig) emerged from the foliage on the other side of the path followed by four small piglets. Just as quickly as she had appeared, the Baboy Ramo and her brood disappeared into the greenery just feet from where Joaquin remained motionless, his senses still alert for any changes in the normal rainforest sounds. He remained silent, hidden and vigilant for almost half an hour before he resumed his trek.

It took Joaquin another two hours to get home by backtracking and checking for any sign of a tail. He was ultra-cautious as he neared the clearing, checking several different points where telltale traps had been set.

None had been triggered. Satisfied that all was well, he still paused at the edge of the small clearing and gave the call of the maya bird. When Jovelyn answered, he shouldered his pack, looked around once more, and then trudged to the hut and disappeared within.

No sooner had he entered the hut than the foliage of a big tree slightly back from the small clearing's edge parted and the end of an RPG launcher appeared. The camouflaged face of The Sniper showed teeth as he smiled, and took aim on the hut's window that was only covered with flimsy curtains. It had been a month-long hunt for him and it was now at its end. A lucrative contract had brought him to the Philippines where he had found the Gagalac house vacant. Posing as an old friend of the family, curious neighbors gave him his initial clues and from then on it was grunt work. Once he had located the small village where Joaquin got his supplies, it was two weeks of tailing him before he located the clearing.

When Joaquin had left earlier that day, he had followed him to be certain that he was gone. Although Joaquin was good at covering his trail and watching for followers, he thoughtlessly didn't use these skills when he had left the clearing. That was partially what had enabled the sniper to finally locate the clearing only hours after Joaquin had left. His orders had been specific: They are all to die together. Therefore after being certain that Joaquin had indeed left, he waited until the middle of the night when all was quiet within the hut to climb to his chosen perch. He had waited patiently the rest of the night and all the day until Joaquin had returned. The birdcalls were a cute touch – he had heard them frequently in the forest. But now the waiting was over.

With his weapon sighted, he squeezed the trigger and the RPG leapt forward parting the flimsy curtains and detonating, blowing the small hut to pieces and starting it burning. Dropping the empty launch tube, The Sniper picked up his M16 and fired magazine after magazine into the burning hut. There was no answering fire.

Chapter 40

Satisfied that his job was completed, The Sniper secured the rifle and pressed a speed dial number on his satellite phone.

There was a short wait.

"Speak."

"They are burning in hell."

"Are you certain?"

"I'll stake my life on it," The Sniper said as he watched the flames consume the remains of the simple hut.

"I will transfer the money."

"Roger that," replied The Sniper and prepared to break the connection.

"However," his employer continued. "If they aren't dead, you will be."

The Sniper chuckled to himself. *Sure,* he thought, *if this bloke was good enough to kill me, he should have done this job himself.*

"Look, mate," The Sniper said. "I have my reputation to keep up. If I fucked up, what good would that be?"

He realized he was talking into a dead phone. Putting the phone away, he removed his safety belt and stowed it in his pack. Attaching his rifle to the pack, The Sniper took a rope from where he had it secured, tied it to the pack and then lowered pack and rifle to the ground. Then The Sniper dropped the rest of the rope over the other side of the limb and grasping both pieces, slid down. Once on terra firma, he released one rope end and pulled the rope from the tree until it lay semi-coiled on the ground at his feet. Bending over to pick up the rope to begin to coil it for transportation, the sound of a weapon being cocked behind him made The Sniper freeze. Slowly raising his arms into the air, fingers widely spread, he straightened himself. Then slowly, expecting a bullet to crash into his body at any moment, he turned around and, in the dim light of the setting sun, found himself staring into the face of death.

Had he been born in the Philippines, The Sniper's name would have been Juan Battista. But born on a sheep farm in Australia's outback he had been named Jon Bataan. His parents had come to Australia a year before his conception looking for a better life and had chosen the name honoring his grandfather who had died during the Bataan Death March in World War II. Actually this was uncertain, but he had been a Japanese prisoner and never was heard from again, and so his family figured he was part of that fateful tragedy. They had found a new life in Australia, but it was hard work. They started as ranch hands on a sheep ranch to learn the business and then, having come with a nest egg, bought their own small ranch and struggled to survive. The Sniper's first memory was that of lying under an ewe trying to squirt milk from her teat into his mouth. That effort had been largely unsuccessful mainly because the ewe showed no interest in being milked and had wandered off, her young trailing plaintively behind.

When he completed high school, he joined the army and entered their Tactical Assault Group, a counterterrorism Special Forces branch. He retired when he was able and started freelancing and that is how he had come to the notice of Michel Villar. Villar had known that Joaquin and Jovelyn would go into hiding, and he suspected it would be in the jungles of the Philippines. He was in poor physical shape and lacked the requisite knowledge to search the jungles. So hiring someone was a no brainer. His mistake, as it had turned out, was in hiring Jon Bataan who, though a skilled counterterrorist, had no jungle training. That hadn't bothered Michel Villar because Jon Bataan had basically lied about his jungle ability. That lie was what had him looking into the business end of a Glock held by a determined looking mother.

"How...?" Jon stammered.

"You aren't Filipino, are you?" Jovelyn asked.

"Yes." Then Jon added, "By heritage."

"But you don't know the jungle, do you?"

"Yes..."

"But not good enough. You don't know your birds."

"What?" Jon was at a loss.

"The maya birds alerted me to your presence."

"The birds?"

"Yes, they have several different calls. One of them is the danger call, which is what alerted me yesterday morning after Joaquin left. They had quieted down and then became disturbed when you came. When Joaquin came back today, he gave the standard call and I answered with the conflict call. He knew there was a problem."

"But I destroyed the hut as soon as he entered."

"But you didn't know about the tunnel," came a voice from behind him.

Jon's instinct was to turn to face the voice of Joaquin, but the barrel of the Glock stopped that.

"What tunnel?"

"The tunnel the Japanese dug," Jovelyn explained.

"Japanese?"

"Yes, they dug tunnels for their forces."

"But out here?"

"Apparently when the U.S. forces came back in 1944, a couple of them, three as far as we can determine, fled into this jungle. They made a fortification and dug an escape tunnel – which also served as living quarters – from the pillbox into the jungle. We built our hut around the pillbox. The hut was more for show – we actually live in a room below. When Joaquin arrived in the hut, he dropped into the tunnel and closed the trap door. I was already at the other end, about twelve feet behind where I am now and came up when the explosion and your gunfire covered any noise I made."

Jon shook his head and muttered, "Pure luck."

"What was pure luck?" Jovelyn asked.

"You finding the pillbox."

"You mean when we built the hut?" Joaquin asked.

"Of course," Jon retorted.

"Not at all," Joaquin answered. "Jovelyn discovered it when she was dropped here on military survival training."

It was at this inappropriate moment that from the jungle behind Jovelyn, the muffled cry of one of the young girls came up from the tunnel through the trapdoor opening. And for that briefest of moments, her concentration was diverted and her eyes and head turned ever so slightly. Alert for just such a distraction, Jon's hand darted for the pistol at his side, but he wasn't fast enough. Behind him Joaquin's attention had not skewed and two bullets from his Beretta found their target in Jon's back and he pitched forward onto the jungle floor. Jovelyn stepped forward, rolled him over with her foot, pointed her Glock at his head and said, "When you see him in hell, tell Michel Villar you screwed up big time," and double-tapped him. Then she turned and hurried to the tunnel's entrance and her crying child.

***

Later, when Joaquin joined her after dragging The Sniper's body to the burning hut and rolling it into the flames, she looked up from breastfeeding her youngest and said, "We can't stay here any longer."

"I agree," Joaquin said as he started to pack their meager belongings in preparation for a move, "and we can't go home yet."

"Then it's plan B."

Chapter 41

When I got to Los Angeles, I resumed my persona of William Wilcox, the man in his early sixties who had flown from Ft. Lauderdale to Atlanta and then vanished, being replaced by Robert Walker who flew to Los Angeles and then disappeared in a one of LAX's multitudinous restrooms. I knew that I had a day or two to kill because Chyrise Callahan was completing a trial, although her assistant didn't expect the jury deliberations to take longer than one day.

I did go online and checked the draft file in a g-mail account Tres and I had established. There was a message from her.

We are both fine. The baby is growing like a weed. We are safe and get around the neighborhood as needed with no one giving us the slightest notice. The news here is sparse especially with my minimal language abilities. Keep in contact and be safe.

To anyone else who managed to get into this account, the only indication of where she might be was her mention of language abilities, and to those who knew her that meant she was not in either an English or French speaking country. But that was not what that sentence meant. It was simply an indication of which one of many mailboxes we had, I should use to reply. I deleted the message and logged off. When she logged on again the empty draft folder would tell her I had a reply waiting, but in another account.

My reply to her was equally terse.

> Here in the sun, all is well. Have to bide my time to rent the car I want. Problem is that my insurance was canceled. When rental goes through, shall head south.

Innocent enough but it told her that I had to wait to see Chyrise, there had been no further sign of Michel Villar, and I would be joining her after I had seen Chyrise. Little did I know how wrong that was.

***

In actuality it was three days before I got to see Chyrise because the trial had run long and she had another meeting so I had to reschedule for late the third day. It was after five o'clock when I got to see her.

"Mr. Wilcox," she said as she emerged from her office holding her hand out. I rose and shook it. She looked tired. I knew it was from the ravages of the trial, but I also had learned by listening to her secretary and paralegal that her schedule was full. "Please come into my office."

I took a seat opposite hers and looked around. It was not the typical well-to-do lawyer's office – the only wall adornment being her law degree. But then I knew that she was anything but well-to-do. She had risen from the projects and struggled through college. Her LSAT scores got her into a private law school in Michigan. After a superlative One-L year, she had transferred to Florida State. Upon graduation she had taken a job with the State of Florida for the experience and because her law school loans would be paid off if she worked a requisite number of years. That obligation completed, she had gone home and opened an office not far from the projects. Most of the cases she had handled were pro bono. Her big break came when she defended an indigent white man accused of raping three black women. She won the case when she offered proof that the real rapist was a black man. That notoriety brought my no-good brother-in-law Howard seeking her counsel in his trial for "killing" me. Since then her practice had prospered enabling her to hire a secretary and a paralegal.

"Now what can I do for you? Your message was simply that it was important. Did you say a matter of life or death?" She settled back in her chair prepared to listen.

"Yes, I must admit that maybe I overstepped a bit with that statement, but it may not be far from the truth."

"So, I judge the person we are talking about – the one in this life or death situation – is not you?"

I smiled. "That is correct."

I paused after my statement more for effect than gathering thoughts. She waited patiently. I sighed and said, "The person whose life may be hanging in the balance ... is you."

That brought her straight vertical.

"Me!" she laughed. "Who would want to kill me?"

I watched her face for a reaction as I said, "Michel Villar."

The reaction was not what I expected. Rather than be shocked, scared or disbelieving, she laughed.

"Ridiculous. Are you paired with the woman who was in here yesterday?"

"Woman? What woman?" I was mystified.

"Hispanic, I think. She had a slight accent – not much but some. She was asking questions about the trial."

"You mean the trial in which you defended Howard Blake?" I was mystified. I had no idea what was going on. When we were searching for the person who had hired The Facilitator to kill Michel Villar, we were looking at the lawyers in that case. Huard Jubert was dismissed easily leaving Chyrise and Phil Dombrey, my wife's lawyer. In order to ascertain Chyrise's involvement, we had sent Jovelyn posing as a writer interested in the story about the trial and my disappearance.

"Yes, but she said it was only one of many murder trials in the Caribbean that had non-fortuitous aftermaths."

"You mean that fact that Michel Villar died in a suspicious accident?"

"Yes."

"Well, I..."

"But that's not all," she continued. "There was another man today who came in to see me unannounced. I was in the trial, but he talked to my secretary saying he needed to see me about that trial."

"What did he want?" I leaned forward anxiously, dreading the answer.

"He wouldn't say, but he insisted that he would wait."

"Did he?"

Chyrise nodded. "For about an hour. Then he left saying he would come back."

"So what happened?"

"When?"

"While he waited."

Chyrise appeared nonplused. "I don't know. What do you...?"

She was interrupted by her secretary bursting into her office carrying a laptop.

"Something terrible has happened downtown." She set the laptop down on the desk and I moved around behind Chyrise to see it.

Chapter 42

Traffic in the Los Angeles area is always heavy, but rush hour is unbelievable – Interstates slow to a crawl and streets downtown are bumper to bumper. In all this gridlock some people have found profit – the homeless have found a way to make some money, easy or not. They get buckets of water, usually rancid, matching rags and throw water onto windshields of cars and begin cleaning with the rags, more times as not making them worse. Thus it was with Captain Juliet Mills, a recent promotion still bringing a chill whenever she looked at her shield or put on her dress blues, which wasn't often enough in her opinion. Now today, here she was on her way home, sitting in her cruiser at a deadlocked standstill. She watched with a smile on her face as a one-armed homeless man with a bucket in his right hand limped down the row of idling automobiles and prepared to start cleaning the windows of the vehicle in front of hers. Putting his bucket on the ground, he pulled a wet rag out with his good right hand to start washing the window. The rag was one of the worst she had seen and she pitied the job it would do on the window. The driver must have sensed that also because he had his arm out the window holding a bill in it, wildly waving it at the man from the time he approached his car. Ignoring the bill, the vagrant started to wash the window and the arm disappeared and then reappeared holding what was more than one bill. Dropping the filthy rag into the bucket, the vagrant limped to the window, leaned against the door with his back to Juliet, and bent over, seemingly to speak to the driver. Then, after a short moment, the man bent down, picked up his bucket and limped back toward Juliet's cruiser.

She sighed and opened her purse and pulled out a ten-dollar bill and held it out the window. The homeless man didn't even start to wash her window, but upon reaching her door put his bucket down, leaned against the frame facing the front of the cruiser, bent over so she could see his face and whispered, "Je t'aime, mon cher. (I love you, my dear.)" Juliet's fake smile vanished and a look of disbelief appeared on her face as her eyes strained to focus on the man's features. Her keen and trained eyesight recognized the man's grubby appearance as makeup except for the gray cast of his left eye (which, in truth, was virtually blind). Her eyes widened in recognition.

"But…" she stammered, "you're dead!"

A trademark sardonic grin preceded, "No, my dear Julie, I am very much alive. You, on the other hand, are not."

During this short dialog, Juliet Mills noticed a gun appearing from the man's left side – a small gun with a silencer. The gun was pointed straight at her and that is the last thing that she saw in this life.

Other people saw the one-armed homeless man pick up his bucket and limp toward the next car in line just as the deadlock broke up and the cars to the right started moving, but the cars in this lane didn't. Reaching the car behind Juliet Mills' cruiser, the one-armed homeless man said, "Sorry, my dear," to the female driver who had a twenty–dollar bill in her hand. "C'est la vie," was the last thing she heard before the bullet entered her left eye and ended her life. Then the one-armed man limped quickly across the street, dodged a car in the inner lane, and threw his bucket of putrid water at the window of a car in the outside lane whose driver blew the horn at him from sheer frustration. The bucket hit the window, but being plastic did no damage except to spew its contents all over the window.

* * *

On the laptop's screen, Chyrise and I saw a man standing somewhere with police cars, lights flashing, in the background. A banner on the bottom of the screen said "KABC ACTION 7 BREAKING NEWS." On the upper left of the screen was the channel's logo assuring that it was an ABC affiliate. Chyrise's secretary hit the play button.

> "Two civilians and one female police officer have been shot to death apparently by a homeless vagrant. During one of LA's afternoon all too frequent traffic deadlocks, a one-armed man, who appeared to be washing car windows for donations, apparently took exception to the amounts being offered and killed three drivers. As traffic started to move, the man then moved across the opposing lanes, dodging the first car in the inner lane and throwing his bucket at the oncoming car in the outer lane. The police are withholding names of the civilian victims but have released the name of the female police officer: Captain Juliet Mills was a twenty-two year veteran of the Los Angeles Police Department.
>
> Witnesses descriptions are vague, but everyone the police talked to who had any knowledge of the

incident agree that the man had a grubby face, dirty tattered clothes, and one-arm (his right).

The LAPD urges anyone with information about this crime to call the LAPD at …

* * *

As I watched and listened in shocked disbelief, I was flooded with memories of Juliet Mills. First, she had been Michel's lover while he was in law school and she was an undergraduate at the University of Virginia. That put her on his personal list. Second, she was also the officer in charge of the investigation of Keith Mitchell's suicide where she or one of her investigators – I would place my bet on her – found a picture that I had sent Keith. A picture that may have been a key point in his unraveling. The picture was of the harbor in Genivee, St. Nantes, from which Keith, my no-good brother-in-law Howard, and I had set forth on that ill-fated fishing charter aboard Quentin Baston's Mahi Mahi. Because of that charter and Quentin's appearance as the primary witnesses against Howard and my wife, Quentin and his family were dead. The picture alone might not have made the impact, but the two sentences on the back certainly did:

Four went out, three came back
We know what happened

I reaffirmed my vow to see Michel Villar in hell. I also thought that it had been his plan all along to remove those who posed a threat to him personally: Huard Jubert, Juliet Mills for certain. Perhaps Guillaume Martineau if he had still been alive.

Chapter 43

Chyrise turned and looked at me in shocked disbelief, "She was a witness at the trial."

"Yes, and Michel Villar's lover at one point. Do you believe me now?"

"Yes. What do we do?"

I turned to the secretary. "There was a man here to see Chyrise when she was in court today. He waited then left."

"Yes, this morning."

"What did he look like?"

"Shorter than you, white, about the same age."

"Hair?"

"No, his head was shaved."

"Facial hair?"

"Yes, a beard. It was strange, he was fairly well dressed and the beard, a bit unkempt. Didn't go with the look."

"Eyes?"

"Sunglasses all the time."

What else? "How long was he here?"

"An hour, give or take."

"What did he do?"

"Just sat there reading one of our magazines."

"The whole time?"

"Yes ... no. I went to the restroom. Just for a minute." She looked at Chyrise for reassurance. "When I came back he was standing by George's desk."

"George?"

"That's me," said a voice to my right. I looked and saw a thirtyish man impeccably dressed in suit and tie, standing in the doorway. Chyrise's paralegal.

"Was anything disturbed on your desk?"

George thought. "Yes ... well, not on my desk. My chair was slightly pulled out. I'm anal retentive on that. I always push it all the way in when I leave, even if just for a minute."

"What about you?" I asked the secretary.

"Maybe ... but I don't know."

I turned to Chyrise. "I may be wrong but I think he's planted some explosives. Remotely detonated. He did it in Miami. We need to get out of here."

George headed for the door.

"NO," I shouted. "Not through the front." Turning to Chyrise, "There has to be another way out."

"Yes, there is hallway between their two desks. A door at the end opens onto an alley."

"Okay, everyone out that door."

The secretary reached for her laptop.

"Leave it," I said, "Leave everything. Just get out."

I followed the three of them as we went out into the main room, around the secretary's desk and down the hallway. A sign over the door read "Emergency Exit Only" and the door had a push bar. George pushed on it opening the door and we all went out. The three were all standing there.

"Move," I said pointing to the right and they did. Not fast but not slow. I had taken no more than ten steps when there was a loud explosion and I was flung forward by the blast. Ears ringing but otherwise unhurt, I picked myself up and looked back. The rear of Chyrise's office complex was lying in the alley, smoke and flames pouring out. I turned around and saw George getting to his feet. The secretary, never did get her name, was on her hands and knees screaming. Chyrise was just getting to her feet, a look of horror on her face.

"My God, we could have been killed!"

"Yes, but it may not be over. I don't think they are in danger," pointing at George and the secretary, "but you still could be. I advise you to disappear. Here," I gave her a card. "That is a gmail address and password. Check it every day. When all is safe, I will send you an email. Otherwise, don't use it."

Then I turned and headed down the alley away from them.

"Where are you going?" Chyrise cried.

"I can't stay here. You are safer without me."

Once past the debris from the blast, I ran to the other end of the alley and turned right. I waved down an empty taxi as soon as I could and got away from the area. Fortunately I had a rental car waiting for me at the airport. Once there I drove away from Los Angeles as fast as I could and didn't stop until I reached Phoenix. There I spent the night and then flew back to Los Angeles to catch the overnight to

Amsterdam knowing that I would most likely be a day behind Michel Villar.

I read about it online the next day. Chyrise and her staff said that a man they didn't know had come in and started to talk and then had yelled, "Get out. There's a bomb! Get out." The man had raced down the hallway and they had followed: "A bit like sheep," Chyrise had said; "Cattle in a stampede," the secretary said; "Lemmings," was George's opinion. No sooner had they gotten out than the explosion occurred. When they picked themselves up, the man was gone. "A guardian angel," the secretary said. "If it had been a woman, I'd call her fairy godmother," Chyrise was quoted. "Poof, like a David Copperfield disappearing act," George had said. As far as descriptions, all they could agree on was that the man was black: light-skinned; more like Chyrise; the ace of spades. *When I give her the all clear*, I thought, *I will compliment her and her staff. I just hope she listens and goes underground. Deep underground because Michel will be livid.*

***

And Michel was so mad he wanted to scream, but he couldn't. He was in a waiting area in the Los Angeles Airport awaiting a flight to Amsterdam going after Pieter Devenpeck, the last name on his list before "Stuart Andrews." He knew he had missed Chyrise, at least for now, and he knew that Stuart had saved her. He didn't know how, but he was convinced he had. He had walked by the office making certain that Chyrise was there and had seen her in her office talking to someone. That paralegal George had been at his desk and the secretary was walking into Chyrise's office carrying something – a file he had thought. It had only taken a couple of minutes for him to be far enough away to be safe and not draw attention to himself when he pressed the button. How had Stuart done it? He knew he was involved, but he didn't know how. In recompense for that intrusion, he would take extra pleasure in ending Stuart's life. And he started dreaming up the ways.

Chapter 44

It was about two years ago, give or take a month or two on either side, that Beecher McFalls and I pulled Pieter Devenpeck aside to have a conversation about Michel Villar. To be honest, that is not entirely correct. We didn't "pull" Pieter Devenpeck aside – we grabbed him by the arms, held a gun against his side, and led him several blocks away to a small house I had rented. Oh, well, make it "we kidnapped Pieter Devenpeck". And the talk wasn't about Michel Villar, at least not at the start. It was about a group called "Circle of Brothers". In French, the language in which it was first revealed, it was "Cercle des Frères." But then by freak accident, while Tres and I were having a drink in an outdoor cafe in Philipsburg, St. Maarten, we discovered that the members of the group, at least those who had tried to kill us by invading The House at the End of the Road (which ultimately resulted in its destruction), were Dutch. In that language the group is "Cirkel van Broers". It was then that pieces fell into place and I decided that the head of the group had to be Pieter Devenpeck. After the conversation with him during which, among other things, he identified Michel Villar's picture, he adamantly denied knowledge of the group and told us that naming a group was stupid because all it did was bring it attention. I made the decision to go forward with Pieter Devenpeck on my own and Beecher McFalls went back to St. Martin. When Pieter Devenpeck saw me after being released from his questioning confinement, his comment was, "I thought it was you. One dead man chasing another." It was then we formed a partnership to search out and kill Michel Villar. Actually he did most of the searching and I did the killing, or at least I tried.

As we talked, trying to come to an agreement, which was not difficult, Pieter Devenpeck said, "I think it is important that you understand two things. First, how Michal Villar came to be in my employ; and second, how you came to be in my employ."

"I think that I understand the second one."

"Part of it but not all. I'll get to that. As a young boy, Michal Villar was somewhat of a loner because he was a studious type. Got the best grades in his class and had a little bit of arrogance – more likely a lot more than he had when I first encountered him. I guess you would rate him a nerd or possibly a dweeb, if I understand the English parlance correctly. As a result of that persona, the guys didn't like him and the girls couldn't tolerate him. 'Too bookish. Not manly enough.' Those were his words. So he didn't date, probably couldn't get a date, and naturally, when he graduated from school on St. Nantes and was ready to go to Harvard where he had a good scholarship, he had 'zero conquests on the sexual side of his ledger'. Again his words, because at the time I encountered him, he was headed for the Harvard business school."

"He wasn't pre-law?" I was surprised because when I came to know him, he was the preeminent jurist on St. Nantes and in most of the Caribbean.

"No, that came later. The summer after graduation from high school but before he started at Harvard, he left St. Nantes and went to Europe to broaden his horizons. The term 'broad' there was intentional because his plan was to figure out how to get laid. Once that happened, his plan became to get laid as many times as he could, but I am jumping ahead. It was natural, with this aim in mind, that he would come to the Netherlands where prostitution is legal and medically supervised. He found the Red Light District near downtown."

"West of Damrak Harbor."

"Yes, you have availed yourself ...?"

"Never had the need to pay for sex." That was being truthful, not bragging.

Pieter Devenpeck nodded his approval.

"Well, Michal Villar did. At least at first. He found the area mid-afternoon of his first day and checked out the merchandise. Daytime offerings pale by comparison to those at night and at this point, having to pay for it, he wasn't about to lose his virginity to just any whore. She would have to be young and good looking. And definitely not fat. So he continued searching and later that same day, in the middle of the night, he found the one he wanted. There is always the bargaining – so many of you Americans would say dickering just to be cute – and the girl, whose work name was 'Britt' after the movie star Britt Eklund from *The Man with the Golden Gun*, agreed to generous terms. This was mainly because she was intrigued that someone would come so far to lose his virginity with her. She later told me that she was surprised, even the first time, with his tenderness and seemingly innate knowledge of the sexual act. He did confide in me that he had watched a lot of porn and read a lot of material. This was one driven young man. Once that initial encounter was completed, he started making the rounds to see how similar and how different various women could be, but he kept coming back to Britt."

"How did you become involved...?" I injected, but he indicated that I should wait.

"One night, after about two weeks, when they had finished their tryst, he discovered that his wallet was missing. As careful as he had been, he had fallen victim to one of our many light-fingered types. Britt understood and was willing to let him return to his room to get more money. However, he had to be accompanied by one of the bouncers – I guess that would be the proper term for someone who kept order in the quarters. It just so happened that I was there that night and agreed to accompany him back to his room, which at that time wasn't very far. Even that young, he made a habit of changing rooms every couple of days." At this point, Pieter Devenpeck laughed.

"When we reached his room, he put his hand into his pocket for the key and he didn't have it. Honestly, I don't know why he hadn't checked, and I thought it was a ploy, that he didn't have the money and was trying to rip us off. Britt had explained that he was a regular, but I knew nothing about him. We went to the desk of the small hotel and the night manager didn't know him, but agreed he was registered so he accompanied us to the room and opened the door. Not surprisingly the pickpocket had been there before us. The room was ransacked and all Michel's valuable belongings were gone. The key and its fob were nondescript, so all I could figure was that Michel Villar had been a target for some time. Oh, I guess at this point I should say that he had a remarkable facility with languages. He had been in the Netherlands only two weeks and was fluent enough to carry on a conversation with me. He knew French, of course, and English. The outcome of this was that he had lost everything. His money, of course, and most importantly, his passport. Now what was he to do?"

Chapter 45

"We returned to the District and, in consultation with some colleagues, we reached an agreement. He would become a 'watcher', looking not only for troublemakers, but people using the crowd to make a living as they had with him. This necessitated him taking a crash course in light-fingeredness and he was a quick and skillful learner. I agreed to be his supervisor. He was good at his job, and I have no doubt that while he kept others from helping themselves, he didn't deny benefiting himself.

"It was during this time, and because of his job, that he took up fitness. He tried working in the gym but found it boring."

"No kidding, I've never been a fan of treadmills and other machines although they are useful." On St. Nantes my treadmill had been in front of the slider looking out at the Caribbean.

Pieter Devenpeck nodded in agreement. "As you know, my physical abilities are somewhat limited nowadays and at best I do a fast stroll."

We both laughed.

"Anyway this is when he took up tennis and discovered that he was quite good at it. He would spend several hours a day either taking lessons or practicing. By the time he left to go to Harvard, he was quite good and made the team his second year."

"Okay, so in order to get to Harvard, he had to have a passport provided by...," and I indicated Pieter who laughed.

"You are correct, he needed a passport, but it didn't come from me. He got it."

"Really," I said. "I would have thought it would be cheaper through you."

"Oh," laughed Pieter Devenpeck. "He didn't pay for it. He didn't need to. It was his."

"How in the world...?"

"Admittedly he had a little help from me. Since he was to be one of us and we protect our own, I sent word out to be on the watch for anyone trying to sell or use a French Passport from St. Nantes. It took several weeks and by the time the passport surfaced, Michel was physically fit and nimble fingered. I forgot to mention, he had also been taking lessons from one of my friends on the use of a knife because he felt in need of some kind of protection. We learned that there was a pickpocket offering a French passport for sale. We knew who he was and where he lived, so Michel Villar and I went to scope him out.

"We saw him leave his room, actually the front door of the building, and Michel Villar immediately recognized him. We trailed him and watched him hit several marks. He was good, very good. We discussed several ways of dealing with him, but in the end, I left Michel Villar alone to deal with the problem. I don't know exactly what happened, but the man's body was found floating in a canal the next morning.

Michel Villar had his passport and, just as suddenly, a lot more money. He didn't say so, he didn't flaunt it, but I knew."

"How did you know he had killed the pick-pocket?" I asked. "Was it just a sense?"

"Oh, he never said. But he had his passport back. And," Pieter Devenpeck had grinned broadly at what he was about to say, "the body had no fingers on his right hand."

"No fingers? A trophy?"

"No, I think a warning to his friends."

"Did they ever find the fingers?"

"No problem there. They were in his back pocket with his wallet, which was untouched. At least it had all the standard things one would have in a wallet except money."

"So, Michel was vengeful."

"Just as he is now. I got the feeling that over that summer, Michel Villar grew up and changed in many ways; some for the good and some for the bad. I imagine the next time his parents saw him, they didn't recognize the man their son had become."

Pieter Devenpeck was quiet for a minute and I sensed the end of the story.

"So about me?" I said interrogatively.

"Oh, not yet," Pieter Devenpeck said. "I was just gathering my thoughts. Michel Villar came back every summer to work, to grow, to add more con-quests to his sexual ledger. However, except for Britt, he no longer went with prostitutes. He picked up lo-cal girls, used them for his purposes and then discarded them. Some for the better and some for the worse."

I must have grimaced or raised an eyebrow or something, because he countered with, "Oh, no. He didn't hurt them. I don't think he ever hurt a woman, in fact, he defended them. There was one incident his last summer. That was between his junior and senior years at Harvard. When he had gotten back from the States, he came to see me. 'I've decided to enter the law,' he told me, adding that because of that he would not be returning. At that I was shocked. There had been no mention of law at all. It had always been business. The previous summer, he had talked about getting an MBA. I was all for that because I had visions of him joining our business and keeping the books, in fact that was his main job for that summer. But I am digressing. Age, I guess.

"He wasn't on duty that night, I think he had set up a rendezvous with Britt, but it was earlier than the time set for that. The B team was on duty and just about to go off. There was one gal who probably should have been on the C team but wasn't. The customer in question was not one of her standards. He was a stranger. Big man, muscular, some fat but not much." He paused and looked at me. "Not that it matters, at least I don't think it does, but he was black. Very black. How do you Americans say, 'Black as...' "

"... the ace of spades," I replied.

"Yes, that's it. Anyway, he started punching Aya, that was the gal's name. She screamed and Michel Villar was near and came in. The guy was on top of her, his knees on her arms and he was pummeling her viciously. The rooms were spartan – a bed, a dresser, a sink, toilet. No weapons and the man would have killed Michel Villar except for the club that was in the hall, hidden but all our men knew where it was.

"By the time someone else arrived, the black man's head was a bloody mess. They had to pull Michel away and forcefully remove the club from his hands. Then he was, how do you say? Spirited away before the police arrived. Nobody outside remembered seeing anything. There weren't too many left. When the noise started, they scattered."

"What about the girl?"

"She lived but never worked again. She didn't need to. Michel Villar saw to her basic support. I was surprised he had the money then, but he did and it never stopped coming. Well, it did when he 'died' but that was to be expected."

Chapter 46

"There did come a time when I needed Michel and it happened to coincide with his appointment to the bench on St. Nantes. I had kept track of his career, as I do with most of my clients." When he said this he looked at me, and I knew exactly what he meant. "I knew that he was doing well. As a lawyer, he had been relentless as the advocate for his clients, no matter how heinous their offences or how obvious, at least to me, of their guilt. I knew that when he wore the robes of a judge, he would be fair but punitive.

"My business interests had grown and increased and my money was in need of sheltering or, if you wish, laundering. I was in need of someone to do that and so I sought out Michel. At that time, I was able to do it via the Internet and so I decided to send him a picture and a phone number. I had no doubt that the combination would alert him to the fact that I was the one behind the picture."

"What picture was that?" I was definitely curious.

"It was a picture of the pickpocket's five fingers." He must have noticed the look of astonishment on my face and, in fact, I was curious as to how he had obtained the picture. All he said was, "I have my ways." Of course, I thought, probably several members of Amsterdam's finest were in his back pocket.

" 'How?' Pieter Devenpeck continued, "was the question he asked when I answered the phone. 'Michel, my friend,' I responded, 'you think I am without means? I may be a poor Dutch man, but I am not stupid.' 'What do you want, Pieter?' was his response, and I knew that he wasn't happy. 'I want to make you some money,' I said. His silence told me he was interested. So we met at a place of his choice and at my time." He grinned at me. "Omaha Beach in Normandy."

"We walked and talked and reached an agreement. He was to find and oversee, with the help of my computer experts, a person who would manage my assets." He grinned at me. "Yes, I had you all picked out. From the time I got you that first passport in the name of Jośef Viljoen, I thought that you might be useful to me. So, of course, you were one of the ones I tracked. I knew that you would take the job."

"You knew?"

"Yes, I am a fairly good judge of people. Why else in the world would you want a fake passport? You couldn't be totally on the up and up and need a fake passport, now could you?"

"But that was just weeks after I was here."

"Yes, we worked fast. I knew, through some sources, that you were already hiding money in offshore accounts."

"Even before I came to you?"

"Yes, I have friends everywhere."

My immediate thought was my offshore bank-er at that time. The man I trusted with everything. I had thought that if my information wasn't safe with him then it wasn't safe anywhere.

"I didn't care where you were getting your money. I just knew that it couldn't have been legiti-mate. You were skimming something somewhere. Faking sales, who knows what and I didn't care. I knew that you might do the same with me, but I was willing to take that chance. There was just something about you that made me feel secure."

"So, I don't understand. Michel Villar just ac-cepted your recommendation because I never met him. I received a phone call."

"You never met with him? Really? I am im-pressed. He is a man with multiple resources."

"You are implying – really, saying – that I met with him before he called me?"

"Yes, if I remember correctly, he used the name Michael Kincaid. He was a Scot; independently wealthy was the story I believe he used. He wanted someone in the States to handle his money. He talked with you a couple of hours. This was before your business expanded. I think you had just three assis-tants. Your partner had left and you were alone. Struggling but about to hit it big."

I thought back, running the name "Michael Kincaid" through my brain's database. It would have made sense at that time, at least from what I under-stood, for Michel to use a similar first name so as not to become confused. But he was good at accents, for the most part, and had played his part well when convincing Agatha Spenser to rent us her town house as part of our plan to get at Fredek Gavrilovich Kondrashin (aka The Facilitator). I remembered Michael Kincaid as a wimpy Scot and that was a bit of a surprise, but we did talk for several hours. At the end of that time, he told me that he had others to interview and would get back to me. I never heard from him and wiped him off my list and almost out of my memory.

"I remember," I said. "He was a bit of a wimp. Guess a hang-over from his youth."

Pieter Devenpeck sadly agreed, "Yes, but then who knew?" He shrugged and held his hands out, open palms up – you would have thought he was Jewish. He must have sensed my thoughts, because he looked at me and smiled. With that out of the way, we got down to business. Over the course of the next several hours, Pieter Devenpeck and I, former and future business partners, became friends. And now I was on my way to try to save him.

Chapter 47

Everyone who had noticed, and there weren't too many, knew watches could almost be set by the time of day that Pieter Devenpeck went for his morning walk. It might be a short one or a long one depending on the weather, his destination, or friends he encountered who wanted to talk. He was in no hurry because he was retired. If asked why he never appeared to rush, he would say, "If there is a hole in a dike, don't call me. I'm retired." And then he would quickly add, "I wouldn't know what to do anyway" or "Point me in the direction of high ground," the latter not very abundant in the Netherlands.

This morning was no different. The door to his apartment building opened precisely at 9:01 a.m. and he emerged, carrying his cane, more a walking staff with a blue glass ball on the top. He used it as an aid getting down the steps and then, when he walked, it was just there for show more or less. Today he appeared to be hurting because he didn't walk fast and his head was down, perhaps because he was looking where he was walking as though he was uncertain of his steps. The people he encountered seemed to realize that something was amiss because they stepped out of his path and didn't bother him. And so he walked almost as in a fog to the bridge across the canal at the left of his house where he paused, looked around as though ascertaining where he was, and then turned around as though to retrace his steps.

One person watched his progress with great interest, but watched from afar. But not too far. Michel Villar's viewpoint was from an attic window diagonally across the street and canal from Pieter Devenpeck's apartment building door. His view was unobstructed and he had watched his quarry's progress through the telescopic sight of his Armalite AR-50. This is not a weapon he would have chosen if he had a choice, but he hadn't. The Armalite AR-50 weighed 34 pounds and was long: 59 inches with the buttstock, 49 inches without. That had made transporting it difficult. When he had found a dealer in the Netherlands, he discovered that his options were few and very expensive. Having no time to shop around and not wanting to cause too much notice, he had paid what the seller wanted. However, because of this "injustice", his list had another name appended to it to be taken care of sometime in the future.

He had left the attic window closed until his quarry had appeared and only then had he opened it. He had a clear shot, but had never had a clear look at the man's face, and he wanted positive ID before taking the shot. He would have preferred to get a LAWS or RPG and take out the entire apartment building, but had been unable to acquire either. He knew that he would only get one chance. When the man stopped at the bridge, and looked around, Michel had an almost straight on view of him. Through the scope of the rifle he could see that the man was **not** Pieter

Devenpeck. The disguise was good but not good enough to fool Michel. It was a trap and he had walked into it. Immediately his search pattern changed, from the street to the opposing rooftops and upper windows.

The man Pieter Devenpeck had found willing to take this death walk was Bram Vandenheuvel, his first cousin on his mother's side. They had been raised together because Bram's parents had died in World War II. As boys they had been inseparable, but as adults had gone different paths although they had remained close. Bram had remained in their boyhood hometown of Haarlem where he had taken a job in a grocery and within twenty years he had owned it and two others. His personal life had not been as success-ful. His wife was unable to conceive and at age forty had died of a pulmonary embolism. Five years ago, Bram had developed lung cancer and, although it had gone into remission, six months ago it had reap-peared with a vengeance, and he was given less than a year to live. When Pieter Devenpeck had ap-proached him with the suggestion, he had jumped at it. "If he's a good shot, I'll never know what hit me. That's better than letting this cancer get me." So, in truth, it was his own pain and physical weakness that caused his uncertain manner of walking and those people who knew Pieter Devenpeck recognized him as a stranger and ignored him.

***

I had watched Bram's progress from an attic window a doorway to the left of Pieter Devenpeck's own and, had I wished so, I could have continued to watch his progress. However, I was on the lookout for Michel Villar through the lens of my Brno ZKK-600 sniper scope. I had been searching all the buildings across the canal because we were certain that would be Michel's choice. Although the man who had sold Michel the rifle had promised not to tell anyone and been paid handsomely for it, he had been a long time friend of Pieter Devenpeck and had alerted him of the purchase.

I had been searching for over an hour before Bram had begun his walk, and had seen nothing through my closed window, opening it only when he had appeared. In my searching there had been nothing to raise my suspicion – just people going about their daily routines. The only "interesting" thing was a young woman getting dressed, visible through a second floor window. She seemed oblivious to the fact that she was visible – but then, maybe she wanted to be seen by somebody, but I was not the one and quickly moved on. I did go back and check after deciding that such a scene could be set to allay suspicion with a domestic scene. On second view, the woman was gone. Almost at the far end of my purview I could see another man doing the same thing I was, but from a second floor window. Had I not known in advance that is was Stijn, Pieter Devenpeck's son-in-law, I would have been worried. He was armed with a much older weapon – World War II vintage. The rifle had belonged to his father and he had eschewed a more modern weapon because this was one with which he was familiar. There were only the two of us serving as spotters. First, because we didn't want to draw any more attention than necessary, and, second, because no other of Pieter Devenpeck's men was comfortable enough with a rifle to help. Not that I was comfortable, but at least I had some experience. Admittedly only on a gun range, but that was better than nothing.

Then as Bram had neared the bridge where he was going to pause and turn around as agreed, I had spotted the open attic window just across from the bridge. I couldn't be certain who the shooter was, but I was positive that someone in that attic was tracking Bram's progress with a rifle. I tried to calm myself and quickly ran through everything that Beecher McFalls had tried to teach me about making such a shot. I relaxed and sighted in. What the! The rifle was no longer pointing at Bram, but was traversing the area to my left and within seconds would spot my location. And that's the reason that my shot missed. That and the fact, as previously attested, I was a poor shot but was the best that we could find. I wished that Tres were here. She would not have missed.

***

Michel Villar had spotted the open attic window on the other side of the canal fairly quickly and had just sighted in his rifle on it when a bullet zipped by his ear and embedded itself in the wall behind him. He loosed a shot and then looked to see where his original target was, but apparently he had taken cover on the bridge. He thought briefly about taking another shot at Stuart – if indeed that was whom the shooter was – when a second bullet shattered the attic window's glass. That was way too close for comfort. He dropped the rifle and fled, down the three sets of stairs with the echo of a third shot behind him. He was out the back door away from the canal where he had a bicycle stashed and in a minute was a block away and moving fast.

***

Just after I had fired my first shot and was loading a second, a bullet impacted the window frame and I was pelted with wooden splinters. Instinctively I ducked and then, with the realization that I had missed, I quickly sighted in the window and fired a second and then a third shot although there was no answering fire. I knew that I hadn't hit him, but he had missed and I was certain he wouldn't try again. At the sound of the first shot, two of Pieter Devenpeck's men had raced out of his front door and toward the building where Michel Villar had been hiding. Everyone in the area had taken cover when the first shot was fired and they had reached the target building quickly, but Michel had vanished. Bram had indeed taken refuge on the floor of the stone bridge. Given time to reflect, he was glad that he was alive and would live a few more months, cared for in a hospice fully covered by Pieter Devenpeck.

Chapter 48

Istanbul, Turkey, is unique in the "capital" cities of the world. It is not the capital of Turkey, that honor belongs to Ankara, Turkey's second largest city – Istanbul is the largest. Actually, Istanbul is the second largest city in the Middle East and third largest in the world for people living within its city limits. But that is not what makes Istanbul unique. Its original name was Byzantium when founded in 657 B.C. It became Constantinople in 330 A.D. and served as capital city of four empires: the Roman Empire, the Byzantine Empire (before and after the Latin Empire), the Latin Empire (when the area was "liberated" by the crusaders), and the Ottoman Empire. When the Turkish Republic was established in 1923, the city became known by its current name. That alone is enough to make it unique, at least in my opinion, because I do not know of another city that can make that claim. But again, not the uniqueness that I mentioned. It is the fact that it is the only major city that belongs to two continents: Europe and Asia. If there are others that share this distinction, it is certainly the largest such. The continents are separated by the Bosporus Strait or Golden Horn, as it is known there. The Bosporus connects the Sea of Marmara and the Black Sea. The one-third of Istanbul's population who live in Asia are connected to the Old City or

European part by seven bridges and numerous ferries.

I had been in the city for three days enjoying
the wonders that it had to offer. My favorite spot was
the Spice Market, the second largest covered shopping complex in the city, the Grand Bazaar being the
first. Admittedly the Grand Bazaar had more to offer,
but the spices were wonderful. Both were crowded
and were good places to get lost or lose a tail. I didn't
know if I had a tail, but I used it to try to shake anyone who might have been following me. Unfortunate-
ly, I wasn't as adept at losing a tail as I should have
been. I probably picked up the tail when I made a
mistake. I undoubtedly made many mistakes, but this
one was certainly the one where I had picked up my
shadow. In one of many underpasses enabling pedestrians to cross under the busy streets of the city were
a series of shops. There may be other such places, but
I had been drawn to this one. I believe it was near the
Atatürk Bridge. The shops in which I was interested
in sold weapons and I most desired a pistol because,
with all the airline security and carrying only hand
luggage, I hadn't been able to bring a pistol with me.
It was strange walking through an area with food ki-
osks and other stores and then seeing one selling
guns. I hadn't checked out the gun laws, but did have
a work permit (fake as was all my identification) and
had hoped that I would be able to buy a small (easily
concealable) handgun. The clerk, in very passable
English (summoned by the first who was English illiterate) explained to me that it was possible to buy a
shotgun, a weapon with a smooth bore, but that

weapons with rifled bores were much more difficult to obtain. Based on previous experience, he didn't believe I would qualify. There was nothing to do except shrug and move on. The kiosk had been busy with people from all walks of life and apparently from all countries based on the variety of dress. I had hoped that someone might follow me and say, "Excuse me, sir, but I might be able to help with your problem." That didn't happen.

It was two days later, mid-afternoon that I realized the mistake I had made. I still don't know what I could have done to avoid it other than not trying to purchase a pistol, but at the time I felt that I needed one. And, as it turned out, I was correct. Michel Villar was still loose having fled after the attempted assassination of Pieter Devenpeck and I didn't want to run into him weaponless. Of course, in this country, it was possible that he would also be weaponless. It was mid-afternoon and I was crossing the Golden Horn on one of the pedestrian ferries. I was standing at the rail contemplating my next move when I sensed someone next to me. Out of the corner of my eye, I saw that, at least by appearance, the person was an Arab, dressed in the traditional white thawb and black and white keffiyeh but wearing reflective sunglasses. He had a well-trimmed mustache and goatee.

"If you have been fortunate enough to acquire a handgun, I would advise you not to reach for it. I am armed and will shoot if you make any attempts."

The voice sent chills up and down my spine. Michel Villar.

Chapter 49

"You've led me a good chase, Stuart," Michel Villar said. "Lost me a couple of times in the Spice Market. Wonderful place, isn't it? I think I like the Grand Bazaar better, but that's a personal preference."

"Okay, okay, you've got me. So shoot and get it over with," I said standing with both hands on the rail.

"Don't be silly. I don't want to do it any place where I might be arrested, for heaven sakes. Besides you have a lot of information that I need."

"What?"

"Well, for starters, where that wife of yours and your brat are hiding."

"You are as crazy as I think you are if you expect me to tell you that."

"Well, if you don't, I can find her within a couple of days."

At that I turned suddenly to face him and saw that bulge of the pistol in the cloth of his thawb. I also noticed the determination and a hint of desperation written on his face.

"How?" I asked.

"Well, that may have been your second mistake, Stuart. In the past three days you have walked down Savaş each day, one block in particular. I am certain that if I would habituate that street I would spot Tres quickly, no matter how she dressed and without or with your offspring."

I had tried to be careful, but he was right. I had made that mistake too. I was being careful to be certain that no one was watching her, and that no one was following me, but I had screwed up big time. I was afraid that it would be the death of the three of us.

"You have gotten sloppy, not only with letting me tail you but in trying to get my money."

"What money?" I asked. "I haven't tried to get your money. If I wanted it I would have it."

"You didn't remove money from ..." and he named an account.

"I didn't even know about it."

"Did you try to get in any of my accounts?" Michel Villar persisted.

"As I said, if I had wanted to, I would have."

The ferry doesn't take long to cross the Golden Horn and as we neared the European side I was looking for an escape and Michel Villar was wondering if I was telling the truth about his finances. If I could get away, I might have a chance. I could call Tres and prepare – she might be able to flee before Michel Villar reached Savaş and located the apartment. Then I might be able to acquire a gun, even a shotgun and blow him to pieces.

"Don't even think about it, Stuart." It was as though he had read my thoughts. "I am very good with a handgun and you wouldn't stand a chance. Besides I have a man watching that block of Savaş and he has a very good description of Tres. A simple phone call and if he spots her, she is dead."

"You touch her..."

"And you'll do what? You're impotent, Stuart. Without Beecher McFalls, you are helpless. You haven't been able to stop me."

I stared at him and smiled.

"Oh, yes, Pieter Devenpeck. That was very ingenious. But I am not worried about him. I have a big file and if he opens his mouth, I give it to the authorities."

I had to chuckle.

"No, I am serious. And he knows it. I mailed a letter."

"That's not what I am laughing about."

"Then what?"

"You missed Chyrise!"

"So that was you!"

"I guess I am not as inept as you thought."

"Well, you missed on all the rest. You and your family are all that remain. Once you are out of the way, I will disappear."

"Then what, run from the law?"

"I'm dead. There is no body to chase."

"That's not what the papers my lawyer has says."

It was Michel Villar's turn to laugh just as the ferry touched Europe, and people started moving toward the lowering ramp.

"Just wait, Stuart. We'll let the crowd thin before we move."

I watched the people moving by anxious to get about their business in the old part of the city.

"And I don't believe you about the papers."

I looked him straight in the face.

"Well, you should. When I realized what was happening, I started writing. I have detailed everything starting with my attempted drowning through the attempt on Pieter Devenpeck. I mailed that before I left Amsterdam."

Michel laughed – actually he cackled. "You're writing a book about all this?"

"Yes. And the last chapter is a doozy."

"I'll bet. 'Michel Villar died in a blast of gun fire as Tres and I emptied our automatics into his body'?"

"No – my lawyer announces a twenty million dollar reward for your body brought to my lawyer's office."

"And you expect someone to take this contract?"

"I know two people who will."

"Two? Let's see," and I could see the grin on his face change to serious concern.

I held up a fist in front of his face.

"One, Pieter Devenpeck or at least people in his organization."

Michel Villar nodded slowly.

"Two, Beecher McFalls. And he is a relentless bloodhound. They may even work in unison. They've cooperated pretty well thus far in this search."

Michel Villar swept his eyes around the thinning crowd, looking for stragglers – any of my watchers he might not have caught. At that point, I knew that my "ploy" had him worried.

"You'll have to dig deep and become a hermit. Hope you have enough money left." I said starting to move toward the gangway. He stepped behind me, and I could feel the muzzle of his gun in my back.

"Just don't do anything stupid, Stuart. No heroics. I know the way to Savaş so don't try to lead me astray."

***

It was a twenty-five minute walk. I was in no hurry, and he knew he couldn't force me. I thought about just stopping and trying to wrest the pistol from his grip. I would most likely get shot. I would either wind up dead or in the grasp of the Turkish police. Then all would be out. They would run checks, fingerprints, DNA and somehow I would turn up. Then it would probably be all over for me. If I were dead, Tres and our child would follow in short order. I didn't believe he had a man watching for Tres. That was his bluff. He wouldn't want a loose string to lead to him. It would be too many dead people to ignore. Not that three aren't too many, but four certainly would be, especially if one of them was a resident.

I did stop once. "I'll give you enough money to live comfortably the rest of your life," I said.

"I'll get that anyway, and face it, Stuart. Neither of us is going to let the other live. You already tried to kill me. I'll be certain you're dead with a bullet or two in the head." The gun's muzzle prodded me in the back. "Now get going. Tres is waiting."

Chapter 50

Ten minutes later, I was standing at the door of the apartment Tres had rented. She didn't know I was coming. I couldn't call because she didn't have a phone. I was to contact her by email to let her know I was coming. I had planned on doing that today and show up tomorrow. I didn't know what her reaction would be. I didn't know whether or not she was armed. She could blast me through the door if she was armed. Because of the trouble I had trying to get a weapon, I doubted that she had. She had never said. I felt the pistol's muzzle in my side. Michel Villar was standing to the left of the door to be out of sight when it opened.

I knocked and waited. I knocked again – two raps, a pause, one rap, a pause, and two raps.

"Ce qui?" came from inside the door.

"It's Daws," I said.

I was surprised when the door swung open. Not because it swung open, but because as it did, Michel Villar shoved me forward, and I stumbled into Tres's waiting arms, and we fell to the floor. I saw the look of surprise on her face as we fell and then the look of horror when she must have seen Michel Villar. I felt something grab my shirt and pull me off Tres.

"Get up," Michel Villar hissed. "Don't make a sound."

We both obeyed and he hustled us into the back room, which was the bedroom.

"Sit on the bed," he commanded and we moved toward it together. "Not side by side. One at the head and one at the foot."

As we sat, his eyes were moving around the room, assessing. Near the bed was the bassinet in which our child was asleep. He stepped to it and looked down.

"Aww," said he. "But all jungle monkeys look the same."

I thought that Tres was going to attack him at that comment and he must have sensed something because he quickly pointed the pistol at our child.

"Just sit still, Tres." She relaxed and he continued looking at the room.

"Stuart, get that wooden chair. Slide it to the foot of the bed and sit in it, hands behind you." As I performed this task he reached inside his thawb and produced a handful of zip ties that he tossed on the bed.

"Tres, fasten his arms behind him and his legs to the chair's legs."

She complied and returned to the bed. Michel Villar moved to the chair and checked, giving each one an extra pull to check tightness. Then he moved to the doorway and gave the living area a quick look.

"There's another chair out here. Come and get it," he said motioning to Tres. She did as asked and thus in short order we were both seated on wooden chairs with our hands zip tied behind us and our legs fastened to the chair legs in the same manner.

Suddenly our child began to cry, and Michel Villar pivoted toward it, pistol pointed.

"Shut the kid up," he snarled.

"A little difficult to do from here," Tres snapped.

Producing a knife, Michel Villar moved behind Tres and put a long zip tie around her right arm and the chair's leg. As he pulled on it he cut the zip tie holding her hands together. The left arm became free and the right pulled against the chair leg. He was certainly prepared. Then he moved to the bassinet, picked up our child who he then handed to Tres who cradled it in her left arm. Sensing security, the whimpering stopped.

"What do you want?" Tres asked looking up at him, hatred extremely visible on her face.

"I want you dead. The kid first," Michel Villar sneered. "I want to see you both in tears before you die. Then, Stuart, you can watch Tres die. Finally you … you who were first … you will be the last to die."

Reflexively, Tres held the child to her bosom.

"You bastard," she said, "killing a small innocent child."

"Innocent?" Michel Villar screamed. "It's as guilty as you are."

All I could do was to stare at him. Tres was fighting for the life of our child. I was too stunned to react. She was fighting with a mother's instinct to save the life of her own blood.

"How did you reason that?"

"Sins of the parents are passed on to their children. At least that's the belief of..."

"You can't seriously believe that. Are you as stupid as the Chinese and Koreans?"

"Believe it or not, the child dies," his answer punctuated with one of Michel Villar's trademark sardonic grins.

"NO," Tres screamed clutching the child closer if that was at all possible.

"YES," Michel Villar screamed in response. "If you don't put the child down, then you'll have to die with it." He laughed maniacally. "Two with one bullet."

"Try three," Tres said.

"My, my, Stuart." Michel Villar's gaze shifted briefly to me, his Sig never moving from its target of our child's head. "You've been a busy boy. But then you blacks always are sexually active."

I said nothing. I was too stunned at the revelation that Tres had another child in her womb. But then, there was nothing I could say. He was clearly mad. Mad as a hatter. Months of chasing us down. Months of being foiled at every turn with the objects of his vendetta eluding his grasp. Possibly some of the madness was a side effect of that drug I had used to try to kill him. It had affected him in other ways – the blindness in his eye. There in that thought was a small ray of hope.

"Before you kill us, answer me one thing, Michel."

Michel Villar laughed. "One thing? Gladly. It won't matter with the time you have left on this ... what did I say in that obit? 'Mortal coil'?"

"Who saved you?"

"What?" he answered, apparently uncertain of the context of the question.

"Who saved you from that drug when I left you for dead?"

"That would be me," a voice said from behind Michel Villar, who was obviously startled and started to turn, the Sig moving away from its target.

Before he could move very much, a plume of red burst from the front of his right shoulder and there was, simultaneously two soft pffts – two shots fired from a silenced muzzle. I turned toward Tres as much as I could. She sat crouched over our child protectively. I could see no red from her back but couldn't tell about her front. There was a sound and I saw and heard Michel's Sig hit the floor.

I looked up at him. His face was a mixture of pain, fury, and surprise. His left hand moved to his right shoulder and came away bloody as he completed his turn. I followed his movement to see who had spoken. Who had fired that saving shot?

Part VI
The Searcher

Chapter 51

ONE YEAR BEFORE.

She had realized that something was wrong through the haze of the drugs that he had given her. She knew what it was and also knew that it was deadly if she didn't do something fast. She felt the rubber tube around the arm and found the syringe still embedded in her vein. Ripping it out, she tried to stand but couldn't. So she rolled off the bed landing on her hands and knees and crawled into the bathroom. Next to the shower was a linen closet. She reached up and grabbed the handle. She felt like an eighty-year-old woman with no strength and it took a great effort to even get up on her knees. She felt her consciousness ebbing and knew that she didn't have the time or the strength to get to her feet. Slowly she inched her way into the shower, her left hand holding the knob on the linen closet door. Her right hand sought for the faucet knobs in the shower. Finding one as her strength waned and her consciousness fled, she turned it and prayed it was the correct one. She slipped to the floor into the full force of the water.

It had been some time before she regained consciousness. The first thing she realized was that she was cold, freezing cold and at that she smiled. The cold had restricted her blood vessels slowing the flow of both blood and narcotic through her system and as the cold spread, it had slowed her heart rate. She was still alive but she wasn't out of the woods yet. Still, with the narcotic effect greatly decreased, she was able to move more easily. She still couldn't get up, but she could crawl. And crawl she did back into the bedroom to her nightstand where her cell phone lay. It had been a long-standing practice of hers, even before she met him, to keep the phone by her bed in case someone tried to break in. Finally reaching the nightstand, she had gotten the phone and dialed 171[3].

"Overdose," she stammered and her address.

The next thing she remembered was being in an ambulance, an IV in her arm, oxygen mask on her face, and a female voice "Vas a estar bien. (You are going to be okay)." Later she woke up in a hospital room. She was weak but alive. She anticipated spending several days in the hospital and then thought about the threat of rehab.

"Look," she had said insistently. "Do you see any tracks?" Baring her arms at the authority. "Look at my feet. There are no tracks."

"Yes, there are signs," was the response.

"That was ages ago. Years ago. I went through rehab. I've been clean for four years."

"But ..."

"It wasn't me. It was ... a friend. I know that a friend wouldn't do that. It was a loco friend. A crazy person."

The argument had gone on for a long time, but in the end she had won. She had been released from the

---

[3] Venezuela's version of 911 at that time.

hospital. Returning home the first thing that she had done was to check her bank account. It was untouched. But still she moved the money to another account. One that he … that bastard Henri Godot, at least that was his current name – or was it? … knew nothing about. Then she logged into one of his accounts – one that he didn't think she knew about and could access. She had skillfully moved part of the money – a million dollars – through several different accounts, time and time again until she felt it was safe. She knew fairly well that he was good with computers, but she was better. She had been learning after she quit nursing, but he didn't know that. The rest of the money in the account she had moved sloppily, easy for someone with his knowledge to trace and recover. He would probably think he had been hacked. To make it look more realistic she had "tried" to hack into several of his other accounts and been rebuffed. He would know that someone had tried and been unsuccessful. He would move the money and she would track it. And she would track him and know where he was. She would find him and she would kill him. And it wouldn't be easy – or painless – or quick. He would know that he was going to die at her hand and he would grovel. She knew he would grovel. But he would die. If she died in the attempt so be it. But that didn't matter. What mattered was vengeance. Bitter vengeance.

But she was going to need help. With current airline restrictions she couldn't carry a weapon with her. When she needed one she was going to have to get it wherever she was and that could be difficult. She would need a source in each country and some of them might be difficult. She had no idea where she was going to go.

But she had someone with connections. Time to see her godfather.

***

Even though she had called ahead and was expected, just like everyone else who came to see her godfather, she sat in her car in front of the gate to Casa Zumbado and watched the trail of dust rising behind the jeep as it approached the gate summoned by the guards in the pillboxes. Even Juan Carlos had to be conveyed to the house in the jeep when he had been abroad, his vehicle scrutinously examined before being driven to the compound. All other vehicles underwent the same meticulous inspection but remained outside the gate.

"Welcome, cariño (my dear)," Dilan said. He had been standing in the open doorway as she had alighted from the jeep. "It has been a long time." His face, which had been abeam, took on a look of concern. "You don't look well. Have you been ill?"

Putting her arms around him in a big hug, she said, "If having one foot and most of the other in the grave is being sick, I would say so."

Even though she had taken her shoes off before starting down the tiled hallway to her godfather's office, he met her at the door. "Cariño," he said in shocked disbelief when he saw her, "what has happened to you?" Without waiting for a reply, he took her arm and led her to a seat. Sitting down as Dilan entered the room with a tray bearing glasses of iced water and a bottle of brandy, he said, "Tell me what has happened," and so she did. When she got to the part of calling for an ambulance he said, "You should have called me. I could have made you disappear in case he comes looking." He looked at her. "We did it for him."

"I wasn't thinking clearly then except for saving my life," The Searcher responded.

Juan Carlos nodded in understanding.

"I am not going to hide," she continued. "Let him come and find me."

Then she finished the story by briefly telling of her hospital stay and how she had avoided rehab.

"I'll kill the hijo de puta (son of a bitch) myself," her godfather said.

"No," she said emphatically. "I am going to do that."

Juan Carlos stared at her and saw her resolve.

"Then we had better get started," he said and summoned Dilan, who had been waiting just outside the door.

"Get our newest recruit situated and set up her training to start tomorrow."

"Today," The Searcher said standing and following Dilan out the door of the room.

Juan Carlos looked after her and shook his head. "I would hate to be that hijo de puta when she catches him," and he knew that she would.

***

If there was any question among her fellow trainees about her ability or resolve that was quickly dispelled within the first week when she started besting them at the target range in both handguns and rifles, although the latter was by her godfather's insistence rather than hers.

"I am going to be looking that bastardo in the face when he dies. He is going to see the flames of infierno in my eyes before he sees the real flames that will burn him through eternity."

She was up a good hour before the others running and doing calisthenics. All her godfather could do was shake his head and smile.

Chapter 52

From the time she began her recovery and training, The Searcher was looking for her quarry. She knew that it wasn't going to be easy. Henri Godot – if that was his real name – had always been secretive, but she had been able to ferret out some of his secrets, especially that one bank account she had looted and would use to fund her vendetta. She had no picture of him, he eschewed cameras. Every day she would use her laptop to search the Internet for news stories, anything that might be something that Henri would do. She knew that he was after more than the man who had tried to kill him. She cursed herself for her blind loyalty to a man in whom she had put her trust and given her love. If she had let him die, she would most likely have had his condo that was much grander than hers and, of course, that one bank account. Maybe with time she could have gotten into the others. But, she kept reminding herself, that was in the past. She was living in the present and preparing for the future. Despite her lack of progress, she did not lose her resolve. Every day she grew stronger, fitter, smarter. Her training was honing her to be a complete assassin.

Finally her diligence paid off. First was the article about the missing yacht and the life ring that had been found. "R.I.P. Zàkpa" was an interesting epitaph, if that is what it was. But what was the relationship be-

tween Henri Godot and Josef Viljoen? The next article
was the one about the explosion destroying the Andrews
Investment Management Company. Whoever had carried it out had obviously done it in an act of revenge. A
Google search for "Stuart Andrews" had brought up the
articles about his "suicide" and then the arrest, extradi-
tion, and trial of his wife and brother-in-law. That
brought up the surprise appearance of Quentin Baston
who had perpetrated a fake death so that he could eventually give testimony about the killing of Stuart Andrews. She expanded her search and discovered that the
judge in the case, Michel Villar was dead as the result of
a car accident that had been reported as a "hit and run."
And then there was the explosion of the home belonging
to a "drug lord" following some kind of home invasion
by a force of ten or more men. Then, not long afterward,
the judge's bailiff Guillaume Martineau had gone missing. All very strange for a quiet Caribbean island. She
thought that perhaps she should check it out. And so she
landed on St. Nantes in the early afternoon of a typical
gorgeous St. Nantes day. She had addresses for two
people to whom she wanted to talk to get information
for a book about the trial and its seemingly shocking aftermaths. The people were Quentin Baston and Huard
Jubert. As she was interested in the judge, for whom she
could find no pictures, she went to the home of Huard
Jubert first.

   To her surprise, there were police there. Asking
the taxi driver to wait for her, she walked up to one of
the gendarmes.

   "Excuse me, is this the Jubert residence?"
   "Oui, mademoiselle, why do you ask?"
   "I interested in talking to Mr. Jubert."

"Just a moment, mademoiselle," and the man called another over.

"Sergeant Aubuchon, mademoiselle," the man said introducing himself. "You say you have interest in talking to Mr. Jubert?"

"Yes, I am a writer and wanted to get his opinion about trial of Elise Andrews and Howard Blake."

"Ah, yes, the trial of the century," Sergeant Aubuchon said with a smile. "At least here on St. Nantes. Did you have an appointment?"

"No, I just came hoping to see him and some other people involved."

"And do you have credentials?"

"Credentials, I don't … oh, you mean from a newspaper?"

Sergeant Aubuchon nodded.

"No, I'm freelance …" and noting the puzzled look on his face, added, "I work alone."

"I understand," Sergeant Aubuchon. "But sadly, Monsieur Jubert is not at home just now."

"I guessed that by the crowd," The Searcher said. "Is there a problem?"

"I am sorry," Sergeant Aubuchon said, "but I cannot say more. Now if you will excuse me." He turned and walked away into the house.

The Searcher walked over to the house next door where two women were standing.

"Excusez-moi," The Searcher said to the women. "Do you know what is happening?"

"Oui," the older of the two ladies said. "Zey are missing."

"Who?"

"Monsieur Jubert and Mademoiselle Dupont. Zey found his boat this morning with nobodies on et."

Another mysterious disappearance, The Searcher thought.

"Gracias," The Searcher said, the mistake intentional. "Oops, sorry. Merci."

She had the taxi driver take her to the Baston residence and wait again. She walked up to the front door and was about to knock when she heard, "Zey are not zere."

The Searcher turned and saw a frail looking old lady standing on the small porch of the house next door. She walked over.

"The Bastons?" she said indicating the house.

"Oui. Zey are not home."

"At work?"

"Non. Zey have gone." And the old lady waved her hand in the air.

"You mean they are on vacation?"

The old lady shrugged. "Gone. Zey are très populaire."

"What do you mean?"

"I told zat man yesterday zey were gone."

"A man was here yesterday to see them?"

"Oui. Homme étrange."

"What do you mean?"

"He was …" and she fumbled for words, "upset zey were gone."

"Tell me about the man."

"Étrange, très étrange," seemed to be the best the old lady could say.

Chapter 53

Back in the taxi, she asked the driver about the Bastons.

"He eez a fishermans. He is well known from the trial. I heard they were gone."

"What about Monsieur Jubert?"

"He is gone too, missing. His boat was found this morning. With no one in it."

"Do you know who found it?"

"Louis Marchan, a fisherman."

"Do you know where he is?"

"With his boat, I think."

"Take me there."

There were three boats tied up at the dock where the taxi driver let her off. She had his cell phone number and would call if she needed him. Two men were standing on the dock talking.

"Je vous dis, Patrick, il y a des choses étranges qui passe sur St. Nantes (I tell you, Patrick, there are strange things happening on St. Nantes,)" one of them was saying as The Searcher walked up.

"Excusez-moi," she said. "Do you speak English?"

"Of course," the one fisherman said.

"Do you know Louis Marchan?"

"I am Louis," said the other man.

"You found Huard Jubert's boat?"

"Oui," he paused as though looking for words, "...this morning. Il flottait sans personne dedans," and he looked at Patrick for help.

"He said there was no one in it."

"Any blood?"

"I am sorry," Patrick said. "The gendarmes, police, said that Louis cannot say anything. It is an ... enquête ... police business."

"I understand. Do you know about the Bastons?"

Of course, Patrick did and because that was not police business, he told The Searcher all about being lowered in a sling and how Quentin and his family had flown away in the helicopter.

That information led her to St. Marrten whose Princess Juliana International Airport was the nearest international port although she knew they could have flown out on a private airport just as well and there was L'Espérance Airport on the French side. Yes, she was told, there was one big helicopter on the island. A Russian made MI-8 owned by an American named Beecher McFalls who lived in St. Martin, the French side of the island. He was a rather secretive person she was told with a private compound where, it was rumored, mercenaries were trained.

And so it was that, wearing a blonde wig and a hopefully beguiling outfit she was making the rounds of bars in Grand Case near L'Espérance. Several days later she was sitting at a small table in a crowded bar nursing a glass of wine when she heard, "Excusez-moi, mademoiselle. Tu attends quelqu'un?"

She looked up and saw a good-looking young man dressed in some kind of uniform.

"I'm sorry," The Searcher responded. "Je non parle …"

"Je ne parle pas français," the young man corrected. "That's okay because I speak English," as he indicated the empty seat across from her. Sensing her approval he sat down as he continued, "German, Spanish, and French, of course. A little Dutch also, but not very much." He offered her his hand, "Guillaume Valentin."

"Rosetta Fernando," The Searcher said taking his hand in hers.

"Can I buy you another," Guillaume asked, "since I have imposed myself?"

"Yes, of course," The Searcher said in her best beguiling voice.

"Be right back," and Guillaume left. The Searcher watched him leave, simultaneously searching the bar for anything suspicious. She knew that it had been Henri Godot at the Bastons and that meant that he could be here as well, doing exactly what she was doing. Trying to find out where the Bastons had fled … and why. Guillaume was back in five minutes.

"And what brings a beautiful girl like you to my island?" Guillaume said as he put fresh drinks for them both down and the table and seated himself.

"Your island," The Search said, "I think the French government might have something to say about that."

Guillaume laughed, "And the Dutch too. A bit too presumptuous, but I feel like it is mine. I love it here."

"So do I," giggled The Searcher seductively. "I am a freelance writer. I am working for a large travel agency that wants me to do a brochure about the islands here in the Eastern Caribbean. This is my first stop."

"Oh, then I'll have to show you around. Well, if you're here in two days."

"You're leaving?"

"Yes, tomorrow morning."

"Oh," The Searcher said trying her best to sound sad. "What do you do?"

"I work for a charter airline. I am a steward on private flights."

"How exciting. Where are you going?"

"Tomorrow Miami. A family flew here two weeks ago and tomorrow they go home. We will over-night and then fly some businessmen back the next day. I'll be back in the early afternoon."

"I'll be waiting," The Searcher cooed. "Where else have you been recently?"

"A couple of days ago, we flew a family to Costa Rica. The kids were so cute."

"Oh, I love kids," The Stranger said. "How many?"

"Three, two boys and a girl. One of the boys a mere toddler."

"Oh, how exciting," The Searcher said as some-one bumped the table going by. She looked up and saw the back of a man standing there surveying the crowd as though looking for someone.

"Strangest thing. They didn't have any lug-gage."

She returned her attention to Guillaume.

"And they went all the way to Costa Rica?" The Searcher said. "Three kids and their parents and no lug-gage?"

"Yes, they arrived at the plane in a van. Don't know where they came from before that. They were picked up in a big off-road vehicle. I thought I saw guns but not certain."

"So, this one was to Costa Rica. Where else have you flown?" She was trying to appear interested but really wanted to leave and get to Costa Rica. The man standing by the table moved away.

"Well, I just got back from a short hop to Martinique."

"I hear it's very romantic," The Searcher said she extended her hand toward him, knocking his glass over and spilling its contents into his lap. She hoped it looked like an accident.

"Oh, I'm so sorry," The Searcher said.

Guillaume said, "That's all right, it's just beer. I'll go to the men's room and dry off a bit. Don't go away." And he was gone into the crowd and thirty seconds later so was she, leaving a note written on a paper napkin. "Had a call, have to run, see you in two days." Below this was the impression of her lips. It was a date she had no plans on keeping although Guillaume would wait several hours hoping she would turn up.

Chapter 54

The Searcher couldn't believe her luck. She had been in this little Costa Rican town no more than an hour and who should walk into the café where she was eating lunch but that asshole Henri Godot. He looked different but it was Godot, without a doubt. Of course, she was different also. No long hair, everything neatly trimmed short. No earrings, not even a stud. Her skin was darker, her figure leaner after all the training. She was wearing dark glasses and men's clothing. With her small breasts she would easily pass for a man given just a quick glance. The Searcher kept her head down reading her newspaper and looking at a map she had picked up in an attempt to get familiar with the area. Godot ordered something so he was going to be a while. She might as well relax for a bit, and so she did, but then had another thought. Maybe she should be outside in her car, just in case. She hadn't noticed whether he had driven up or walked. She would have to be ready no matter what.

Getting up, The Searcher paid her bill and left, crossing the street and walking down the other side to her car. Inside she wished she had stopped and seen that man about a gun. What was his name? Oh, yes, Pedro. Well, she would do that after she found out what Godot was doing.

She didn't have to wait long. Her quarry came out and got into a jeep type vehicle. He pulled out and drove right past her without even looking, but she had slumped down in her seat. Having started her SUV when he came out, she put it into gear and executed a U-turn. If he had been observant, he might have noticed her following him in a clean car, most cars were dirty showing that they had been used. Also she would be easy to spot as traffic wasn't that heavy. The Searcher had taken careful note of his car just in case she had to abandon her tail, but she didn't. Three turns and five minutes later he stopped in front of a shop of some kind. She turned into the street just before it and pulled to the side. From her backpack she took a bug to attach to his jeep in order to track him from afar.

Hurrying to the corner she saw him enter a store. She walked quickly down the street to his jeep. As she approached it, she faked a stumble and dropped her water bottle, deliberately propelling it under the jeep. Muttering under her breath, The Searcher got down on hands and knees to get the bottle while furtively attaching the transmitter to the jeep. Water bottle in hand, she rose and started to turn back the way she had come when she saw the name of the store he had gone into. It was the one she was supposed to visit to acquire information and armament. She smiled to herself. *Of course*, she thought, *how many gun dealers can a small town have?*

Back in her SUV, The Searcher activated the receiver and saw that she had a strong signal. She was certain that he was oblivious to her presence. It was twenty minutes until the blip that was Henri Godot's jeep started moving. Giving it a head start she started following him and ten minutes later the blip stopped moving at a small shopping center. She pulled in and parked where she could see his jeep. He was gone for twenty minutes and returned with several bags. Another ten-minute drive and he pulled into to a cheap motel, the kind she never thought that he would deign to use. That was before, The Searcher reminded herself. She didn't know this person and couldn't fathom what he was doing.

He gathered his purchases including a small black suitcase and went into one of the rooms. In a few minutes, he came out, got into the jeep and returned to the shopping area. There he went into one store and was out in a few minutes. Then to a nearby cantina where he remained for less than half an hour. Then it was back to the motel room where the curtains were pulled.

After half an hour she figured he might be settled in for a while so she returned to the first store where he had stopped.

The windows were dirty, the offerings inside were nondescript based upon the signage, but that didn't bother her. The inside of the shop was as dirty as the windows. Judging from the dust that seemed to be everywhere, the shop didn't do a lot of business. There was no light other than that filtering through the dirty windows. There was a tiny bell that had rung when she entered the store and after she had stood in the gloom for a few moments, a man came through a curtained door on one side. He was tall, three to four inches taller than she, and heavy but not obese. One look at him and she knew that she would not like to meet him alone on a street in broad daylight much less in an alley at night. Despite the fact that this was a small town, she decided to take a chance and stick to her cover.

"Are you Pedro?" she asked.

The man eyed her head to feet and back again.

"Do I look like Pedro?" was his sullen retort.

"If I knew what Pedro looked like I wouldn't be asking you, now would I?"

The man's expression didn't change. He seemed used to this.

"Who wants to see Pedro?"

His insolence angered her.

"Well, obviously I do."

The Searcher started for the curtained doorway but was blocked by his body. She put a hand out to push him away, but he pushed her back. That one hand pushing on his body let her know that he wasn't as tough as he looked.

"Who are you?" the man asked.

She reached into her left breast pocket and removed a piece of paper that she handed to him.

"Who I am is not important. Tell Pedro that I come from Juan Cortez of Caracas."

The man didn't even look at the paper.

"Wait here," he said and vanished through the curtain. The Searcher was tempted to follow him but without any armament to help her force the issue, she held her ground. The man returned after a few minutes.

"He will see you," he said and held the curtain open for her to pass through.

Chapter 55

The room into which she walked was totally different from the store that she had just exited – that had been brightly lit and clean. This room wasn't big, about half the size of the store and the only piece of furniture in it was an old desk, placed kitty-cornered in the rear left of the room. Behind the desk sat a big man, not tall, just fat. He had no hair on his head except for a handlebar mustache that he was stroking. The desk was immaculate, holding only a cell phone, a Sig Sauer with the muzzle pointed toward her, and a sheet of paper with obvious creases. She knew it was the letter from her patron. Pedro, if that is who was, had on a white short-sleeved shirt that had seen better days and hadn't seen a washing machine after a week of wear. With a little work, she could have given him his menu for the past five days. He sat there with his hands folded across his chest. She had taken all this in quickly as she had entered the space. As she stood there waiting, the man from the shop came through the curtain behind her. She could sense his presence, smelling his stench as he stood too close behind her.

"What about you want to see Pedro?" the man behind the desk asked.

"A pistol like the one you have there, ammunition."

"Is not a problem. You have money?"

"Yes, but there is more."

Pedro's left eyebrow raised. He sat there waiting.

"I need information."

"In the town square, there is a small kiosk with a blue sign with a white 'i' on it," Pedro said, lips curling into a sneer. "That is for information."

"They can't tell me what you can."

"Please, you make me sound so … intelligent." He waved his right hand and then placed it on the Sig's butt.

"What information does Pedro have that you want?"

"There was a man in here this afternoon."

"Si, there were several men and another señorita. I am guessing you are a señorita and not a señora?"

"Irrelevant. The man was about five ten, dark, not negro. He has a black beard. He was wearing sunglasses. Never took them off." Pedro's left eyebrow raised at this.

"There could have been such a man."

"What did you sell him?"

Pedro's right hand came up off the Sig, index finger raised, hand waggling.

"No, no, señorita. My business is between me and whoever buys or sells. Pedro he does not talk, how do you Yankees say, out of escuela?"

"My patron asks you to help me," she said, indicating the paper in front of him. "That should tell you that I am not a Yankee, as you say."

"Si, and I am. I am giving you a pistola and bullets – for a price, of course."

She nodded in agreement.

"But I need information about that man," and she indicated the letter.

"Si, your patron he mention that I should help you with things such as I can. But …"

"And you can tell me about this man."

Pedro was silent for a moment.

"This man, he is important to you. You and he were … amantes?"

"That is not important."

Again the finger waggled.

"To me it is important. If I am to betray a trust, let the kitty out of the sack, then I must also have some information."

She was hesitant but she could feel the pressure from Stinky Man behind her and knew that if she didn't cooperate, at least a little, she might not get out of the room alive.

"Yes, we were amantes."

"In Caracas?"

"Yes."

"And he … what, cheated on you?"

"No, he tried to kill me."

"Ah para. So now you want to kill him?"

She nodded, wanting to move away from the Stinky Man behind her. He could kill her in a second if she wasn't ready. She had practiced in situations such as this and knew that there was a fifty-fifty chance she could survive if it got ugly, but she didn't want it to go that way. Bloodshed would bring police or partners exacting revenge.

"So, if I tell you what you asked …"

"I will go and find him and kill him."

"With a pistola?" Pedro picked up the Sig and laughed.

Before he could move, she whirled, raising her right knee into Stinky Man's crotch and before he sank to the floor had his shirt tightly grasped in her left hand and a sharp stiletto stuck in throat. "No mover un músculo," she hissed at him as she looked back at Pedro who was so stunned at the rapidity of her movements that he hadn't moved a muscle. She looked at Pedro and noticed the sweat beading up on his forehead and his lip twitching. Nobody moved and the only sound was that groan from Stinky Man whose one thought at the moment was the intense pain from his testículos. She looked at the floor in front of Stinky Man where his Sig had landed when he had dropped it. Pedro followed her eyes.

"You think you can …" Pedro started.

"You know I can," she said. Pedro believed her and holding the Sig with two fingers he put it on the table. By the time he had done that, she had released the hold on Stinky Man's shirt, tossed the stiletto into her left hand and picked up Stinky Man's Sig, stepping away from him.

"A LAWS," Pedro said.

"You sold him a LAWS?" she asked incredulously.

"Si, si. He wanted it."

"You have more?"

"No, no," Pedro lied, but she let him. "Just the one."

"Why does he want it?"

"To kill somebody, I think." Pedro was now sweating profusely.

"Who?"

"I don't know, señorita. I swear. He came here a week ago. He too has a friend who said I should help him."

"Who?"

"That is not important, señorita. His name is mine to know. He is my … boss, my patrón. He said this man was his friend and I was to help him."

"How else did you help him?"

"Night vision goggles, some listening equipment, a pistol," Pedro indicated the Sig on the desk.

"Information?"

Pedro shrugged. "Si, but about places, not people."

"What places?"

"Places where people go to hide."

"Guarded compounds?"

He didn't seem to comprehend.

"Compuestos vigilados?"

"Si, si," Pedro nodded vigorously. "Compuestos vigilados."

"Push the pistol, the letter and your cell phone to the front of the desk." Pedro complied. "Don't you move, stinko," she snarled at the Stinky Man, who was struggling to rise. He glared at her and sank back to the floor, hands moving to his crotch in a comforting movement.

Stepping to the desk, she took the Sig, sticking it into her belt with her left hand – Pedro had no idea what had happened to the stiletto. It had vanished as quickly as it had appeared. That tonto de un cuerpo de guardia (fool of a body guard) was going to have a lot of explaining to do. She picked up the paper and folded it and stuck it into her left breast pocket. From the left front pocket of her pants, a smart phone appeared and she pressed a button. Someone obviously answered and she briefly told that person what had happened. She listened and then handled the phone to Pedro. The voice on the other end of the phone said (in Spanish), "This woman is my niece. She is family. If she does not call me every day, you will answer for it. Do you understand?"

"Si, si," Pedro said. He didn't have to ask who was on the phone. He knew.

***

Fifteen minutes later, she walked out of Pedro's shop carrying a small duffel bag with everything she needed. He hadn't wanted any money, but she had put two thousand dollars on the desk. Pedro hadn't moved from behind his desk, Stinky Man had gotten what she needed. At the curtained doorway she turned around and said to the Stinky Man, "Tomar un baño (take a bath)."

Chapter 56

After leaving Pedro's and checking to see that her quarry, whatever he was calling himself, hadn't moved, she went and bought supplies she might need for an extended vigil: bottled water, energy bars, and adult diapers included. Then she went back near his room and set up a watch. It grew dark and the hours passed. She felt safe getting out of her vehicle and walking around the neighborhood for exercise. The next day came and the early morning hours passed. She was beginning to wonder if he had somehow eluded her when her receiver vibrated. He was on the move.

Letting him have a safe lead, she followed with her parking lights on, trusting her GPS and tracking device. It was an hour later that the signal turned stationary about a mile up the road. She closed to within a quarter mile and found a place to pull off the road. Grabbing her backpack, she put on her night vision goggles, and checked her Sig before walking up the road to within a hundred feet of where he had apparently pulled off and took to the jungle. Moving as quickly as she could, but being as quiet as possible, she advanced toward his vehicle. She watched for movement and seeing none pulled out her thermal imaging goggles, replacing the night vision goggles with them. The only heat she saw was from the jeep's motor. Stowing the thermal goggles and replacing the night vision goggles, she approached his vehicle. It was locked and empty. He was on the move toward his target and she didn't know where it was. It was foolish to try to trail him through the jungle at night having only a vague idea where he was going.

Decision made, she ran back along the road to her SUV, tossed her equipment on the front seat, and then started in the direction she had been driving. In ten minutes she passed a road and could see lights not far off. Whatever his target was, this was it. Again she knew that he was on the same side of it that his jeep was and it would be suicidal to try to locate him by walking through the jungle. She would either encounter guards from the compound (she sensed that is what it was) or be ambushed by him. Continuing on up the road, she found a small trail off on the other side of the road and pulled in about twenty feet. The track was weed covered and she took that as an indication that it was infrequently used. Grabbing her gear and donning the night vision goggles, she eliminated any sign that a vehicle had entered the track before she crossed the road and entered the jungle, angling back toward the compound but getting further from the road as she went. After twenty minutes, she could see where the jungle had been cut back from a high wall topped with three rows of razor wire. She knew it would be monitored and if she had to cross the wall she would have to be careful. In her gear was a rope with grappling hook but that was useless if the wire was monitored. So she moved along the wall looking for a tree from which she would see over the wall and not be seen. The one she found wasn't perfect, but it would have to do. She didn't know this, but Michel Villar had scouted this side also and rejected the tree. Having a place to nest, she moved away from the wall and deeper into the jungle. She found a small but sturdy sapling she would use for a ladder and she cut it down using her combat knife and slicing at it like a quiet beaver. Using some of the lower limbs, she fastened them crosswise to the trunk using zip ties. With the ladder complete, she returned to her nest tree where she laid it on the ground where it would be invisible unless one was very close to it. Then she climbed the tree, tied herself facing the trunk on the side of the tree away from the wall, and covered herself with camouflage netting. This meant she had to peep around to see what was going on, but concealment was of utmost importance. She watched the night patrols and observed the same pattern as Michel Villar had and knew that she would be able to get into the compound, but it might mean silencing a guard. She wasn't certain when Henri Godot would attack but she would be as ready as she could. Thus prepared, she let herself doze off.

As with Michel Villar, laughter awakened her and she saw three children running up the center of the compound toward what she judged was the main building. Two of the children, a boy and a girl, were approximately ten years of age, and a smaller boy was two or three. Behind them walking hand-in-hand were their parents or so she judged. They were the Bastons, of that she was certain. They had come from the middle bungalow on her side. That was perfect, easier to get to without being seen by Henri. But where was he? She was certain that he would not attack during the day because that would make escape risky. So the attack had to come at night, probably after the family had settled in. That meant she would have to be ready when it got dark and get across the wall and warn them. No way that she could stop Henri because it was risky for her to climb down and leave during daylight and at night she wouldn't have time to get around. But where was he? She pulled a digital monocular out of her backpack and started looking. It didn't take long to spot the tree she felt he would use. It was almost directly across from hers. It took her over an hour of slow searching to spot him, and it was only a small movement that alerted her. He was on a branch hidden by much of the tree's foliage and was difficult to see if you didn't suspect someone was there.

Knowing where he was didn't make the task any easier, but it did give her a feeling of confidence. She would rather have been able to stop him, but since she couldn't, thwarting his plan by saving the Bastons was second best.

It was a long day through which she dozed for a great part. As the sun started to set she began to get ready. The Bastons went to dinner and she tied a nylon rope to the limb she had been straddling and lowered herself to the ground. She pulled a couple of items from her backpack sticking them into one of her pockets, and then put the backpack at the edge of the woods where it would be easy to retrieve. Night vision goggles in place and taking her "assault" ladder, she moved quickly to the wall, wedged the base firmly into the ground and tested it. To ensure that it wouldn't twist, she had tied a piece of branch at the very top on the other side of the sapling from the steps. This top "step" was thus against the wall. She quickly ascended the ladder until she was at the top, then from one of her pockets she pulled a wire with alligator clips on both ends, a pair of wire cutters, and waited for the guard. It was less than five minutes before he came by and she waited until he had gone be-tween two bungalows before she attached the alligator clips to the wire about an inch apart and cut the wire between them. Then she waited but nothing happened. Either the clips worked or the wire wasn't monitored. It was fortunate she was so small because she could slip under the middle wire, but if she had been much bigger she couldn't have. Getting a grip on the far side of the wall, she pulled herself under the wire and slipped over the wall. She fell to the ground, hitting and rolling, and raced for the back of the bungalow with time running out before the next guard came by. She tried the slider on the small patio and found it unlocked. The Bastons had either forgotten or were feeling very safe, but it saved her a minute or so having to pick the lock. She slipped inside and closed the door only moments before a guard walked back between two of the bungalows.

She found a place to hide out of the way so that the Bastons wouldn't see her immediately when they returned. Then she settled in to an interminable wait. Finally she heard the sounds of children laughing and the parents talking. Then the front door opened and the three kids rushed in followed by their mother. *Where was Quentin?* thought The Searcher briefly panicking. But then she realized that Henri would not shoot his missile without Quentin in the house so she waited.

"Enfourchez votre pyjama et entrer dans (Get your pajamas on and get into bed)," Celesse said to the older two as she carried Pay-Koo into his bedroom. There was laughter and giggling as the three children got ready for bed. She heard Celesse tell her youngest good night, and a door close. Then Celesse went into the room of the older two and tucked them in wishing them good night.

Chapter 57

Celesse closed the bedroom door and turned around. A figure dressed in black was standing five feet from her, an evil-looking weapon in her hand pointed at her. The person had a finger to its mouth. "If you want to live, don't make a sound," said The Searcher. The scream was ready to burst from Celesse's lips and she clamped both hands over her mouth and sank to her knees.

"Where's your husband?" The Searcher asked.

"Who … are … you?" Celesse asked, moving her hands from her mouth to be clenched between her breasts.

"A friend. Where is your husband? We don't have much time."

"What?"

"Where is your husband?"

"In the main house. He …"

"When will he be back?"

"Soon … in a minute," Celesse's mind was racing. "He'll be back with someone."

"No he won't," The Searcher said smiling, "but nice try."

"What do you want?"

"To keep you safe."

"But there are guards."

The Searcher sighed. "They aren't doing a very good job, are they? After all, I'm here."

Now Celesse was getting panicked. Her eyes kept darting to the front door, thinking of some way to warn Quentin.

"Why?" she finally asked.

"Why what?" responded The Searcher.

"Why do you want to kill us?"

"Kill you?" The Searcher had to laugh a little. "I'm trying to save your lives, not kill you. If I wanted to kill you, you'd be dead."

"But the gun?"

"Would you have listened if I didn't have the gun?"

Celesse shook her head.

"Correct. You would have screamed, brought the guard."

"Did you?"

"No, just a stun gun. "He'll be fine. Probably have a headache and a lot of explaining to do." The lie was just to convince her of her vulnerability, hoping she would be more willing to listen and comply. "But look, time is of the essence. As soon as your husband is back, I'm guessing you'll all be dead if you don't get out of here. Get your children."

"But ..."

At that opportune moment, the handle on the front door turned and The Searcher turned toward the front door as it opened and Quentin stepped inside.

"Mon cher ..." Quentin started and stopped when he saw Celesse on her knees and a person in black with a big pistol pointed at him.

"Close the door and get inside. Quickly," the person said in English.

Quentin thought about ducking back outside but he wasn't fast. He would take a bullet before he moved very far. Especially with that laser sight on the gun. So he did as he was ordered.

"What do you want?" Quentin said when he had closed the door.

"We don't have time for questions," The Searcher said, backing away so she could keep an eye on both of them. "Do you know Henri Godot?"

Celesse and Quentin looked at each other, then at The Searcher shaking their heads.

"What about Michel Villar?"

The look of panic on their faces gave her the answer.

"Well, he is out there," she indicated the front door with her Sig. "He has a LAWS and he is going to put it right through the front door in about thirty seconds. Get your kids and get out the back door."

Celesse was up and heading into little Quentin's room as Quentin dashed to the bedroom of his older children. He didn't take time to even try to wake them up but grabbed Marie who woke as he grabbed her. He put her arms around his neck and she grabbed his torso with her legs. "Hold on," he said. Then he picked up Pierre and slung him over his shoulder and headed out the door.

Pierre started struggling. "Chut (Be quiet)," Quentin said. "Nous avons du mal (We have trouble.)"

Celesse was disappearing through the rear slider as Quentin came out of the bedroom. The Searcher was standing by the door waving her hand. "Hurry, Hurry," The Searcher said.

Moving as quickly as he could, burdened with his children, Quentin was out the door and moving across the small patio and then onto the grass with The Searcher right behind him. They were no more than twenty feet from the house when it exploded. The concussion wave knocked Quentin to the ground, dropping Pierre but able to hold onto Marie tightly using his body to shield her from the blast. Small debris rained down on them and they lay on the ground, Pierre scooching up next to his father. After a minute when the debris stopping falling, Quentin stood up still clasping Marie.

"Celesse. Celesse. Où es-tu (Where are you?)."

"I'm here," she said in English so that The Searcher won't think she was planning anything. "We are okay. Dirty and bruised but okay. What about Marie and Pierre?"

"They're fine," Quentin said. "Dirty but fine."

It was at this point that Quentin realized that they both were shouting and his ears were ringing. There were other people shouting too. Far away, but getting closer. The area was suddenly illuminated with light, light darting around by flashlights being carried by people running. Two guards dressed in their dark blue uniforms came up, flashlights in one hand, some kind of gun in the other.

"Is everyone alright?" one of them asked.

"Yes, we're fine," Quentin said hugging Celesse, who had just arrived by his side.

"What happened," the guard asked.

"Someone fired some kind of missile at the house," Quentin said.

"Missile!" the guard exclaimed. "How would you know that?"

Quentin looked around for The Searcher but saw no one.

"Someone warned us," Quentin said.

"One of us?" the guard asked.

"No," Quentin said. "Someone from outside."

Immediately the guards turned into protective mode and moved them away to the main house. One of them used a radio to notify the rest of the guards and a manhunt was started. But nothing would be found because Michel Villar was long gone and The Searcher was over the fence and running away.

Chapter 58

The Searcher had been thrown into the air by the explosion but landed rolling and was up quickly, driven by the knowledge that the guards who would appear momentarily would not be at all friendly toward an invader. She took the rope off her shoulder, uncoiled it, whirled the grappling hook around a couple of times and released it. As it flew over the wire at the top of the wall, she was pulling the line in. As soon as the hook caught on the top wire, she was climbing the wall not caring about the alarm that was sounding in the main house. Reaching the top of the wall she pulled herself up using her hands and dove over the wall, landing in a tuck and rolling almost to the edge of the jungle. Once again she was thankful for her gymnastic training.

Grabbing the pack and donning her night vision goggles, she pulled a can of pepper spray from the pack and sprayed an area of ground in front of her. Then she stepped in it a couple of times to coat her shoes and took off running into the jungle away from the wall. *Let's see dogs track that*, she thought. After about an eighth of a mile she turned right, headed for the road and pulled out her iPhone. Using the GPS she set a course for her car and came to the road about a hundred feet away from the lane she had used. Seeing no lights, she darted across the road, almost certain that the people at the compound would be more concerned about the Bastons and any injuries and the burning bungalow than any intruders. The guards would come but not immediately. She used her thermal sensing glasses to scout the area around her SUV before she approached it.

She put all her gear into her knapsack and tossed it in the back. Using a container of wet naps, she took off her camouflage makeup. She took off her clothes and adult diaper, sealing the latter in a zip lock bag and cleaning herself with wet naps all of which went into another zip lock bag. Then she donned a dress and sandals she had purchased at the airport upon arrival. After brushing her hair and applying makeup, she backed the SUV out of the side road and headed back toward town. As she passed the compound she could see the light of the bungalow still burning and wondered what was happening. What she didn't see was the man with the camera and infrared flash who took her picture.

Only past the compound did she power up the tracking receiver and curse when there was no blip from Henri's jeep. She passed by the location, but didn't stop because she didn't know if there were people waiting – there weren't. She cursed her luck because she had found Henri only to lose him, but she took small satisfaction from the fact that she had foiled his attack. He probably would never know until she managed to catch him. As she neared the small town, the tracking receiver went active. She followed the blip, turning off the main road, until she was about a quarter of a mile away and then she turned off her lights. When she was a hundred yards away, she pulled to the side of the road. Taking her Sig and the thermal imaging glasses along with the tracker, she moved toward the source of the signal. It was a dilapidated garage outside of which was a burn barrel that was still hot as was the engine of the vehicle in the garage according to the thermal imagers.

It was easy to open the cheap padlock and inside the garage she found what she had expected – Henri's jeep. He had another car and by now was well on the way out of the country, but from which of the many airports she didn't know. She did know that the regional flights all went through the San Jośe airport, but she couldn't wait around to see if he arrived. By the time she got there he could be gone. She returned to her SUV and pulled up next to the garage and managed to get the smoldering embers in the burn barrel to ignite some wood she had gathered. She siphoned some gas from her SUV and soaked the clothes she had worn. She wrapped the adult diaper and wet naps in the clothes and then dumped them into the burn barrel where they quickly ignited. Let the locals worry about the fire.

Now she had one objective and that was to get out of Costa Rica. Mexico was her choice and there she would decide her next step.

The picture taken with the infrared flash camera would prove to be of no use in tracking her down.

Chapter 59

The Searcher's plan was to go to Los Angeles to talk to the only remaining lawyer in the Stuart Andrews' case because everything seemed to point to that case, but she didn't know why. What she did know was that Henri Godot (aka Michel Villar) had been the judge, Quentin Baston had been the key witness, Huard Jubert had been the prosecuting attorney, and the dead lawyer in Miami had been one of the defense attorneys. Like the latter, they were all dead – at least to Henri Godot. The only survivor, other than the witnesses and judges, was Chyrise Callahan and she was in Los Angeles, so that is where she was going and why she found herself in the Miami Airport. But again, coming from Central or South America, that was pretty standard.

She was sitting in a waiting area reading the local newspaper when a commotion in the corridor grabbed her attention. Instinctively she looked up while simultaneously grabbing the handles of her computer bag and carry-on, ready to flee if necessary. She couldn't see what caused the commotion because of the number of people in the corridor, but out of the corner of her eye she saw a man in a waiting area diagonally to her right get up and quickly enter the corridor moving to her left. *Henri Godot. That bastard!* Immediately she was up and following, although staying on the same side of the corridor as her waiting area. In just a couple of minutes, Henri stopped and stood looking down the corridor in the direction he was going. She followed his gaze but saw nothing other than passengers who had deplaned heading for baggage claim, a couple of college-aged men and an elderly woman in a gray and black outfit seemed to stand out, but nothing was special. An announcement came over the speakers for all passengers for Houston aboard Flight …. She didn't catch the number, but observed Henri turn and hurry back toward the area from which he had come. She crossed the corridor trailing behind him and watched as he went through the door into the jet way boarding a plane bound for Houston, Texas. She went to the desk to see if it was possible to get on the plane but it was full. However, there was space on a flight three hours later, but she would have to go out past security to the ticket desk.

She walked away disappointed but knowing that when she got to Houston, it would be extremely difficult to find Henri who would be traveling under an alias she wouldn't know. Best to keep to her plan, go to Los Angeles and interview Chyrise Callahan.

***

In Los Angeles, she found Chyrise's office, but learned that she was in a trial at the present time and might have some time at the end of today or tomorrow, depending on how long court ran. There was nothing to do but come back late in the day and hope that she could see the lawyer.

***

"By way of introduction," began The Searcher, "my name is Maria Angelica Fuentes, and I am a graduate student in history at The University of Miami..."

Chyrise, who has been absentmindedly browsing papers handed her by her secretary, suddenly raised her head and glared at The Searcher.

"What!" stammered The Searcher. "Did I say something wrong?"

Chyrise laughed. "No, of course not. It's just that I went to Florida State and we're big rivals."

The Searcher sat there looking nonplussed.

"I don't..." she began.

"Oh, not a sports fan I guess."

"Oh, sports. No, I mean, not here, back home..."

"Where's home?" Chyrise said trying to bring civility back into the conversation.

"Uh, Caracas," The Searcher responded not thinking clearly.

"Oh, then soccer is your sport?"

"Yes, but now I have no time for sports. I have to get my degree."

"I understand. Now, what is it that I can help you with? History, you said?"

"Yes, I am majoring in Caribbean history and am writing my dissertation on Caribbean court systems."

Chyrise held up her hand. "I don't know anything about Caribbean courts."

"But you defended Howard Blake in a trial on St. Nantes."

Chyrise put down the pencil she had been fiddling with and sat back.

"Not another."

"What do you mean?"

"There was a young woman here a year ago ... no, longer than that. Almost two years. She was also interested in that trial."

"That is just one of the trials in which I have an interest. But not the trial itself."

"Then what?"

"My particular topic is what happens in the aftermath of some trials. In particular, mysterious or unexplained deaths of the trials' lawyers."

"Well, this case certainly qualifies."

"Yes," The Searcher started pressing, "you are the only ... how do you say it ... major player left?"

Chyrise laughed. "Major? No ... there's Huard Jubert, the prosecuting attorney."

"He's disappeared," and The Searcher recounted the story.

"Oh, my gosh!" Chyrise was stunned. "It's like someone is out eliminating everyone. Remember I mentioned someone else here two years ago. She wanted to know about the trial. In particular, about Phil Dombrey, the other defense attorney. Then within two weeks, he was dead. Suicide."

"Yes, there was a letter indicating that he had molested and raped women."

"Yes, he..." Chyrise stopped. "So what is it you want to know? My time is short?"

"Is there anyone you can think of who might have wanted to kill you all?"

"All ... me?"

"Well, you are the only one left!"

Chyrise just stared at The Searcher.

"It began with the judge," The Searcher probed, trying to get more information.

Chyrise just stared at her.

"Then Phil Dombrey. And recently Huard Jubert."

" Coincidences."

"Really? What if ... one of them isn't really dead?"

Chyrise laughed. "Really? Michel Villar died in a hospital after an automobile accident. Phil Dombrey put a gun to his head."

"Huard Jubert is missing!"

"Yes, well ... there's no reason. And, I think, that's enough. I'm busy and tired. I said I would talk to you and I have. I don't think this is going anywhere. Please leave."

The Searcher had no option but to comply.

Chapter 60

Outside she paused to reflect upon the meeting. She was certain that Chyrise was clueless that Michel Villar was still alive. At least, if she was correct in her assumption. And, looking at the record of things, that made Chyrise a target. Michel Villar had gone to Houston. But from there ... who knew. He could have gone there to throw people off track. He could have gotten another plane, taken a train, bus, car ... She would have to put a watch on Chyrise for a few days.

Checking out the neighborhood, there was a bodega at the corner with a sign in the window "Querido ayuda" (Help Wanted). She found a secondhand store, bought some clothes more in keeping with the area, changed, applied for and got a job at the bodega. It was two days before Michel Villar showed up.

It was early in the afternoon and she noticed a well-dressed man walking down the street toward Chyrise's office. Well-dressed men stood out in this neighborhood making them easy to spot. She recognized him immediately from his walk – the limp was impossible to disguise. Also he was wearing dark glasses. That was not unusual but together with the limp – bingo. He entered the office and remained over an hour. Then he came out and walked the other way. She could have followed, but if she had, she would have lost her job and she knew he would be back because his target was not there. Because he had remained for an hour, she knew that whatever he was planning would take place there. It just wasn't the time.

There were people in and out of the office all day. Late in the afternoon he reappeared shortly after an elderly black man had entered. Michel Villar was not dressed the same as earlier, this time more in keeping with the area but again, the limp combined with the dark glasses was a dead giveaway. He was walking quickly as he approached the office and slowed as he passed and then picked up the pace again. He crossed to her side of the street just past the bodega and stopped on the opposite corner. From his pocket he took what appeared to be a cell phone and he looked at it as though he was dialing. Then he looked toward the office and pushed a button. The front of the office burst outward in a tremendous explosion of fire, smoke and glass, rattling the bodega's windows. Instinctively she had turned to look and then returned to look where he had been. "Had been" – he was gone. She left the store, as did the few customers and the owner, all of whom hurried toward the burning office. She turned in the other direction after the hurrying Michel Villar.

He was easy to tail. He did look back occasionally, but not as one seeking to see if he was being tailed. He was feeling pretty smug, she thought. Ten blocks away from the bodega, he entered a small hotel. She felt that he was staying there. Knowing his habits, he would shower, change clothes and then leave because his mission was accomplished. She didn't have time to go and get her stuff but she took advantage of the break and bought some different clothes in a nearby store. She wore what she had purchased, carrying her bodega clothes in a plastic tote from the store. Thirty minutes after her quarry had entered the hotel, he emerged and hailed a taxi. She did the same. Her taxi driver was Hispanic and she used their commonness to get him on her side. "That's my lover," she explained. "He said he was meeting a friend, but I think he is leaving me and our child. Please follow him and don't lose him." The simpatico taxi driver did as requested and when Michel got out at Los Angeles Airport's Tom Bradley International Terminal, she followed, giving her new compadre a good tip. In the terminal, Michel Villar used a ticket kiosk to get his boarding pass, easy to do with nothing to check. She managed to get close enough to see that he was going to Amsterdam. She didn't know why he was going but she was going to follow. She had no choice. She left the terminal and found a cab that would take her to her room. There she would arrange for the first flight to Amsterdam she could get and then she would look for that bastardo.

She couldn't get a flight until the next night, the same flight Michel Villar had been on the night before. She had a business class seat and had just settled herself in when the man sitting down across the aisle drew her attention. He was a tall black man with a goatee and short hair tinged with gray. He was wearing khaki pants, probably Dockers she thought, and a powder-blue shirt. He wasn't wearing glasses but she could almost picture him with them. She studied him for a moment and then turned away and closed her eyes and thought back through recent events, starting with the Miami International Airport. There was the disturbance when she had first noticed that bastardo. He had been following someone and had stopped short of the exit gates and was staring at that someone who had gone through. In her mind's eye she could see a tall black man pulling a small carry-on on the other side of the exit. The carry-on had a green ribbon on it and she realized that was what first caught her attention here – the man putting his carry-on in the luggage compartment above his seat. It had a green ribbon on it. Then she moved forward as though fast-forwarding though a DVD. There had been a black man who had gone into the lawyer's office just before Michel Villar had reappeared. At the time she had not taken special note because she was watching for Henri Godot. The black man had been in there when the explosion had occurred. It was the same man and here he was – alive. What had the news reports said? *A black man had warned them to get out and then he had disappeared. At least that is what they said.* Opening her eyes, she looked across the aisle. It was the same man. She knew rather than sensed that he was somehow linked to that bastardo and here they were – both of them going to Amsterdam where that bastardo was waiting. She knew that if she followed this stranger, she had a good chance of finding the bastardo. Better than nothing.

She turned to the book she had picked up: *Dutch for Dummies.* She wasn't a dummy by any stretch of the imagination and had a facility with languages. By the time the plane reached its destination, she would have a basic working knowledge of Dutch.

Chapter 61

After they landed at Schiphol, The Searcher made certain that she was close behind her quarry. She chose a different passport line, but was through just after him. He opted to take a train into the city, and she did also. From the airport she followed him into the city proper and down a narrow side street where he entered a small hotel. There was another just across the way and she chose it requesting and getting a room with a window on the street. Then she settled in to wait. She didn't have long when he came out and set out walking just below her view. She was out quickly and had followed him for about twenty minutes when he took a street along a canal. In a few minutes, he encountered a man he seemed to know. The man was shorter, elderly, and carrying a walking stick with a blue glass knob on top. After talking for a few minutes the two continued walking the way The Quarry had been going. After a short distance, they entered an apartment building. She walked past and got the number: 22 Herengracht.

She walked up the street, crossed a bridge to the other side and took a seat on a bench. She hadn't brought a book or anything and knew that it would look obvious if she just kept sitting here, but she wanted to know what was going on. She wasn't prepared to wait, especially out in the open like she was. She tried to observe the building to get a feel for what was going on without being too obvious. After fifteen minutes she got up and continued walking the way she had been going, passing 22 Herengracht but across the canal. There was a small side street just past and she turned right onto it. A short distance down there was a small grocery and she stopped and looked in the window although in reality she was looking back at the buildings across the canal. She could not see the doorway to 22 Herengracht but a movement in an attic window two doors away caught her eye.

She saw the window open and what appeared to be the barrel of a rifle moving side to side. She fought off the feeling to hide, telling herself no one was going to shoot. Then The Quarry stuck his head out the window and looked around while apparently talking to someone behind him. Then he disappeared and the window was closed. She wondered how he had gotten there without coming out on the street. Possibly there was a back alley or the buildings were connected in some manner. She bought an apple and returned to the canal moving in the direction of her previous walk going further away from number 22. There was another bench and she sat and ate the apple. She had just finished it when the door to number 22 opened and The Quarry appeared. As he went down the steps, the door closed behind him and he walked purposefully back the way he had come. She followed at a distance but knew where he was going – basically the same place she would like to go, but

first she needed some things to make her less con-
spicuous in the future. After seeing him enter his hotel, she went shopping.

***

She was up early the next day, and it was a
good thing. She had just gotten dressed when he left
his hotel and headed off as he had yesterday. She
grabbed her shopping bag and followed. Today he
didn't walk up Herengracht but the street behind and
entered a house there. She knew that it must be connected so she retraced her route and walked up the
opposite side of the canal and took a seat on a bench.
She had a newspaper she could barely read and some
food. After about an hour she left, walking out of
sight. She stepped into a dark doorway and when she
reappeared it was as an old woman who shuffled
back to Herengracht and down to the same bench
where she proceeded to feed the few pigeons who
were around.

At nine o'clock the door to number 22 opened
and a man came out. To the casual observer it was
the same man as yesterday, but she sensed something was different. Not only was he walking with
greater difficulty, but also he didn't seem like the
same person. She got up and proceeded to follow him
although on the opposite side of the canal and trailing. When he reached the bridge, he stopped and
looked around. Suddenly there was a shot and everyone panicked. Some dropped in place and others ran.
She looked up at the building where she had seen
The Quarry yesterday and saw a rifle barrel protrud-

ing from the window. Then in rapid succession there were three more shots, one from her side of the canal. It had come from a building just the other side of the narrow street. She ran down the street to the small alley in back of the building and saw a figure on a bicycle peddling away. She knew it was Henri Godot but she had no weapon and no chance to use one if she had. Having failed in his attempt, Henri Godot would not wait around but would leave Amsterdam immediately. She also knew that The Quarry would leave also and proceed to his next stop and she would be there also. On the plane he had gotten up to use the facilities and stupidly had left his papers in his little cubicle. Within the darkened cabin no one noticed that she had taken a moment to peruse them and see that he had another ticket from Amsterdam to Istanbul. She would be there waiting for him and this time she would be armed.

Part VII
The Fat Lady

Chapter 62

In the doorway behind Michel Villar, feet spread, arms in front holding another Sig with a laser sight, stood a woman. She was dressed all in black from her shiny boots to the do-rag on her head. She was Latino from the color of her skin. She was about five foot two, not much more than 110 pounds. From what I could see, she was very muscular – her arms showed that – and her chest was virtually flat. There was no makeup on her face that I could tell, but then the face was contorted with an anger for which I had seen no match.

"You," Michel stammered. "But …"

"But nothing, you hijo de puta. I saved your life, nursed you back to health. 4And what did you do? You tried to kill me."

Michel took a step toward her.

"Don't move, idiota," she snarled but he did, taking another step.

The aim of the pistol shifted downward and there was another pfft and red erupted from Michel's left knee and he collapsed to the floor screaming.

"You bitch. You fucking bitch."

"Shut up or you'll get another and this time in your good leg. I told you not to move. You don't listen very well, but then you are an arrogant asshole."

She kept the gun on him but starting talking to us.

"Are you okay?" she asked me.

"Other than being tied up, yes."

"I am also," Tres said and I breathed a sigh of relief. "The child is fine."

"I don't know who you are except that you are not friends of Señor Grande Idiota. Still I can't take a chance, so for now you stay where you are. If you move …"

"We won't," we both said simultaneously.

"Good, because … what did you call him?" indicating Michel Villar with her Sig.

"Michel Villar. He …"

"Is an asshole. I thought that I had identified him correctly. No more information. I don't need no more."

She turned her gaze to Michel.

"Now, Michel. May I call you that?"

Michel Villar glared at her.

"Of course I can. I can call you whatever I want and you had better not object. I still have eight shots left and … I forgot … Another clip.

"So, Michel. Do you want to live?"

He glared at her.

"Do you want to live?" she asked again, her voice demanding.

"Yes," came the response thrown out venomously.

"Then you have to help me."

He glared at her and said nothing.

"Will you help me?" she asked.

Still he said nothing.

She stepped toward him, the Sig pointing at his right knee.

"Will you help me?" she hissed.

"Yes, yes," came his response.

"Good. I need some information."

Michel Villar looked at her saying nothing.

"I need some numbers."

"Numbers," he muttered.

"Account numbers ... and passwords."

Michel Villar shook his head vehemently. And she shot him in his right knee. Michel Villar screamed.

"SHUT UP," she screamed.

He continued to moan. She stepped forward and put her boot on his right hand and pointed her Sig at his elbow, the red dot very steady.

"Your elbow is next. If you notice, I am a good shot. I haven't hit any major arteries or veins yet. My nurse's training, you know. Of course you do. That's why you picked me. So that I could save your miserable life. I was so stupid."

She paused a moment looking down at him.

"I'm not stupid any more, asshole. Give me a bank and account number."

Michel Villar muttered something. She pulled an iPhone out and turned it on.

"Good signal. Now give me a bank and an account number."

Michel Villar repeated the information and she entered it into her iPhone.

"Now the password."

Michel Villar looked at her.

She kicked him in his right knee and he screamed.

"The password or you'll be doing everything with your left hand for the rest of your life."

He gave her the password.

She entered it.

"It doesn't like it, Mr. One Arm," and pointed the Sig at his right elbow.

"Kill them," he nodded in our direction, "and I'll give you everything."

"Them?" she motioned with the iPhone, the Sig never wavering. "Why?"

"They tried to kill me in Caracas."

"Good for them, asshole. Just because they failed – because of me – doesn't mean I should kill them. It just makes us more simpatico."

Then he turned to look at us. "But I got my payback. I got rid of all they held precious. Their yacht, their business, their friends..."

"Friends?" I said. "Like who?"

"For starters, that Filipino and his family."

"You mean Joaquin Gagalac?"

Michel Villar laughed almost manically. "Yes, he and his whore wife and their kids."

It was my turn to laugh. "Jon Bataan failed."

Michel Villar's smile turned to a scowl. "But he said..."

"He was wrong. Joaquin shot him and burned his body in the empty hut he had destroyed. The four of them are safe at sea on a fishing boat."

The scowl then turned to a large grin. "But those Bastons are gone. I blew them into a million pieces. Even that darling Pay-Koo." He started to laugh.

"No you didn't," The Searcher said and both Michel Villar and I looked at her in astonishment. "I was there. Tracked you to Pedro's gun shop and then out to the compound. I got them all out the back before you fired."

I breathed a huge sigh of relief as Michel Villar let out a howl of rage.

The Searcher looked at her iPhone. "But back to business, idiota. That last password didn't work." And to punctuate that, she kicked his right knee.

Michel Villar screamed a password and she entered it.

"Good. Now the next one.

This procedure was repeated five more times. Michel Villar was defeated and gave her what she wanted without protest.

"Now the next one."

"There aren't any more."

"You really don't want to live, do you, idiota."

"Can't I keep any money?"

"You can keep your life."

Michel Villar provided the information.

"Good, you do good," she said looking at me as if for approval.

"Done good," I said. "The term is 'done good' "

"Thank you. You done good, idiota." And kicked him in his right knee and he screamed.

She backed away from Michel Villar and put the iPhone into her pocket.

"Adios," she said to us.

"Not 'Hasta le vista?' " I said.

"I don't think we ever want to see each other again."

"What about cutting us loose?"

"Can't take that chance. You're enemies of asshole there but I don't think we're friends. Tell you what, though," she said, reaching into a pocket and pulling out a small box cutter which she dropped to the floor. "You get over here and you can cut each other free."

"And me," Michel Villar said pleadingly.

"I don't give a fuck about you," she said and walked out the door.

Michel Villar screamed after her, "I'll get you … you bitch. You'll pay for this."

She stepped back into the doorway.

"No, I won't." Raising the Sig she fired a shot. Michel Villar's head snapped and gray matter spewed; luckily neither of us was in the line of fire. "I'll do you one more favor," she said to us. "I give you an hour to get free and clean up what you can. Then amigos will arrive to remove the trash," indicating the corpse of Michel Villar. "They will also be certain there are no witnesses." Then she was gone.

Epilogue

There was silence in the little apartment. Michel's screams had not brought anyone. Very possibly they knew it was better just to leave well enough alone.

"We need to get that knife and get out of here," I said to Tres. We both knew what the woman had meant by "no witnesses."

"I can get it," she replied and started hopping her chair toward the box cutter, clutching our child tightly in her left arm and not looking at the husk that had hosted the life of Michel Villar. When she reached the box cutter, she positioned the chair and then carefully balanced our child on her lap and leaned over, stretching her right arm down but discovering that it was too short to reach the floor. Straightening up, she once again secured our child and then repositioned the chair.

"Here goes nothing," she said and began to rock the chair sideways until it finally teetered enough that she fell over on her right side. Our child let out a scream but she quickly hushed it. Then she laid the baby on the floor and reached to secure the box cutter. Quickly she cut the cable ties holding her legs and right arm. Then she got up, picked up the baby and walked to the front door of the apartment and locked it. She returned and laid the baby in the bassinet before coming over and cutting my cable ties. I stood and took her into my arms in a long embrace.

  "Were you serious?" I asked her.

  "About what," she said, looking up into my face.

  "Another child?"

  "Yes. It must have been that farewell tryst."

  "Why didn't you tell me?"

  "You had enough to worry about, didn't you?"

  We decided that the best thing we could do was to quickly sanitize the apartment the best we could and leave both it and Istanbul. It took us the better part of the hour but during that time nobody knocked on the door and when we left there appeared to be no curious by-standers. Sitting a block away with a couple of men in it was a dirty and battered pickup. We knew what its purpose was and walked the other way.

  We didn't get home for a week, taking care to cover our tracks as much as possible. We flew out of Istanbul, but from our first destination it was more conventional public transportation.

  I must admit that I have no clue how Michel Villar trailed me from Amsterdam to Istanbul and, in fact, how long he had been trailing me. Maybe it was luck! I have no idea. I also have no idea how that woman whom I have dubbed "The Searcher" got to Istanbul in the nick of time. I have pieced together what information I had gotten from Juan Carlos and the Bastons. Oh, that reminds me.

  When we were safely out of Turkey, I placed a call to Beecher McFalls and told him what The Searcher had said. He was dumbfounded to say the least.

  "You say they're not dead?"

"Not unless that woman was lying to me and I cannot see why she was. She knew too much."

"Okay, let me make a call."

In less than fifteen minutes he called back. "I'm sorry but it turns out that letting us know they were alive was against company policy. They had screwed up once and didn't want it happening again. They moved the Bastons to the main house and kept them inside for a week while they improved their security. Then they permitted them to move into one of the bungalows and resume their 'normalcy.' They will put them on a plane today and I will get them home."

Next I sent an email to one of the mail drops Joaquin and I agreed to use. It was a week before he responded. The family had taken refuge on a fishing trawler belonging to a distant cousin and were at sea several weeks at a time explaining the delay.

I had not been worried for I had great faith in them both. The youngsters had weathered the trawler well and Joaquin hoped they would want to go fishing when they were older.

With that done, I called Chyrise Callahan and told her that she was free to go back.

"Thanks," she said. "They've about finished rebuilding my office and I am going nuts up here in the mountains. Oh, please tell whomsoever donated a considerable sum that I really appreciate it."

I smiled as I hung up the phone. One more call to make.

* * *

One month after that last call, a taxi pulled up at the end of a long road on St. Nantes. The taxi driver turned around and asked his passengers, "Are you certain this is the right place."

"Yes," was the answer.

The driver hurried to open the passenger door, and a middle-aged man got out. Not a big man but not a small man. He was carrying a walking stick with the blue glass knob on top in one hand and a roll of paper in the other. After looking around as though getting the lay of the land, he helped a woman out. She was about his age but, at least for her size, not as heavy. She took his arm and they walked to the edge of the property where a "For Sale" sign had been pounded into the ground. Well weathered, it had obviously been there a while.

They stood there silently a while before she spoke, "It's beautiful, Pieter. Just like he said. We can happily live out our lives here." And she squeezed his arm.

"Yes," Pieter Devenpeck agreed as he pulled the "For Sale" sign out of the ground and let it fall. "We start today."

* * *

I realize that by writing this lengthy memoir I put myself at great risk with law enforcement groups and possibly others. But I feel that I must make my story known so that people who lost their loved ones in Michel Villar's vendetta will know why they died, although it most probably will not mollify them.

I erred greatly by not making certain that Michel Villar was dead in Caracas. But I now know that if I had stayed around that woman, whoever she was, would have arrived at the house, and I would have been forced to kill her. At least that certainly would have been an option. I don't know if I could have.

Looking back I know that the only people that I killed personally by pulling a trigger or pushing a button were trying to kill me. Those were the "Circle of Brothers" – men who were invading our house. I think that any jury would find me innocent of murder – I look on it as self-defense. I had used my phone to take a picture and that showed there was no doubt that Michel Villar was indeed no longer alive. Now everyone who was in danger is safely back home: Chyrise in L.A. continuing her work with the poor and disadvantaged and the Bastons returning home to St. Nantes where Quentin was extremely happy to get fishing again. Joaquin and Jovelyn were back in their home with their two children and resuming their lives. Beecher McFalls, never really in danger, goes on with his life. We have all had enough adventure to fill a lifetime.

If anyone feels the need to come after me for whatever reason, I will give them this warning: I won't go easily.

Meet our Author

Douglas Ewan Cameron

Douglas Ewan Cameron is a retired professor of Mathematics from The University of Akron, Akron Ohio. He grew up in Oak Ridge, Tennessee, attended Miami University (Oxford Ohio) and The University of Akron and received his Ph.D. from Virginia Polytechnic Institute and State University (Blacksburg, Virginia). Upon retirement, he and his wife Nancy spend their summers on the shore of Hubbard Lake in the part of Michigan's lower peninsula known as "Up North" and winters in Copley, Ohio. Douglas loves to fish and spends many summer days out on the lake fishing for walleye and smallmouth bass. Retirement has also afforded him and his wife time to travel and they have visited all seven continents. When not traveling or fishing he has been able to return to his writing, something that he was not able to do while working. The stories he writes are those that have occurred to him while either fishing or traveling.

Other books by Douglas Ewan Cameron

Muddy Waters
Payback is a Bitch
Payback is Bitter Vengeance
Payback is time to Again
The Body in the Perch Pond
The Body Under Ice
The Witches of Hibbard Corners

*****

And a preview of
The Body Beneath the Bridge

*****

From where the Eavesdropper stood in the dark hallway, just the left side of Sheriff Nathanial Jefferson could be seen. What was he doing in the kitchen? He had walked out of the Lake Room without a word. Upon noticing this, the Eavesdropper had followed, more curious than anything else.

"My boys are in jail. Two of them for a long time cause of me. The other only because he was the big brother and trying to help them and me. It's all my fault."

Ah, it was Butch, Briel, whomever, he was talking to, thought the Eavesdropper. *Perhaps the sheriff was curious as to why people called him Butch rather than Briel. That was easy. Everybody thinks Dame Edna is having problems with lucidity whether it's senile dementia or early onset Alzheimer's and wants her to feel more comfortable.*

"She's right, Dame Edna. She may be senile, but she was right. That rat Frenchman did come on that plane like she said, and my boys weren't here. It was the first day of deer season, and they was in the woods. Each got a deer that day. Best day ever. Anyways, I helps him to the guesthouse. Mr. Edmund wouldn't let him stay in the house for some reason."

No, it wasn't Mr. Edmund. It is Dame Edna who calls the shots in this house.

"We were there, and that French guy says to me that he needs to see Mr. Rolli. I asked him why, and he says there is a debt to settle. He was mad. He says that Mr. Rolli ratted him out to the cops in Montreal. A bank job or something; I don't remember it all. He was going to even things up. He had this pistol in his bag. He showed it to me. Checks it, and then puts it on the bed. Says we'll go after he uses the loo. Funny that. A Frenchie calling it a loo likes them English do."

What's Butch doing?

"I like Mr. Rolli. He always been good to me. He was a good friend of Dame Edna. They grew up together. I knows that if that Frenchie would kill Mr. Rolli, that it would break Dame Edna's heart, and she just lost her husband. Her son's not around much, so she's pretty lonely – she counts on Mr. Rolli to be company. I can tell they like each other. Not like lovers but like brother and sister. So, I know that I can't let that Frenchie do anything to Mr. Rolli. I takes the gun and stand over by the bathroom door. When he comes out I steps behind him, but he hears me and turns around. He sees the gun and reaches for it, so I shoot him, and he falls back against the bed. Then he starts up, so I puts a bullet in his head."

What? He's confessing to killing LeBeuf. Needed killing, that's a fact. But why confess? He didn't do it. But it did happen somewhat that way.

"Nobody heard the shots I guess cause I go back to the house, and tell Mr. Edmund that the French guy was taking a nap. Says he real tired and would eat in his room that night. I took him a tray like he was going to eat and flushed it all down the toilet. I wrapped him up in the bedclothes that already be spoilt and called my boys. I told them to deep-six him and the gun. But Burke didn't – kept the gun for some fool reason. Biggest mistake that boy of mine made was with that crate. He wasn't thinking. Tired after being in the woods all day, I reckon. He sees the depth as 50 feet like I told him and puts the motor in idle, but that old boat just kept moving and by the time they were ready to dump it, they'd passed up the slope. That's how it got found."

Can't save his boys from the crime of dumping the body, but he's throwing in another decoy as to who called him.

"Then that deputy comes and starts asking questions about that Frenchie, and I know there was going to be trouble. Dame Edna was real upset, and she calls Rolli and tells him about the deputy, so I knows I had to do something. So I calls and tells the boys to sideline that deputy who was causing trouble."

Now he's confessing to another crime he didn't commit. He didn't call the boys.

"Burt and Burl are good boys but not too swift. I should have waited and talked to Burke, but it might have been too late. They took the gun – the Frenchie's gun – and shot that deputy. Nows they's in trouble, and it's my fault. I ruined their lives just like I ruined mine.

'Sides that, me and Dame Edna got the same problem. Getting too old."

Suddenly the sheriff's form disappeared, and there was a gunshot.

"Shit," the sheriff said, followed by silence.

Mon Dieu, Butch shot himself. Why? The Eavesdropper started forward, but stopped when he heard the sheriff talking again.

"Barbara Ann, send some backup including Walker and Roberts to the Fitzgerald house. Also a squad, although that's a formality. Call Wallace Hibbs, and tell him that there'll be a removal."

Having heard all that needed to be heard, the Eavesdropper silently stole back down the dark hallway. *I cannot let Butch take the blame for those crimes. It wouldn't be fair to the boys no matter what they've done. It would kill Edna, too. She thinks the world of Butch. I need to do something to sideline this. Maybe another confession. Or two. I just don't understand why he killed himself.*